PERILOUS LADY

CROOKED PARADISE #2

EVA CHANCE
& HARLOW KING

Perilous Lady

Book 2 in the Crooked Paradise series

First Digital Edition, 2020

Copyright © 2021 Eva Chance & Harlow King

Cover design: Jodielocks Designs

Ebook ISBN: 978-1-990338-04-5

Paperback ISBN: 978-1-990338-10-6

Mercy

As unpleasant rides went, being tied up and tossed into the back of a van by masked gangsters wasn't the worst I'd ever experienced, but it definitely made my top five. And it was rising in the ranks with every passing second.

Colt leaned forward on the bench that lined one side of the van's cargo compartment and pressed his gun into the soft spot under my chin. The cold metal bit into my throat, prodding harder with the sway of the roaring vehicle. The bandana tied across my mouth left the taste of stale sweat on my tongue. Ugh. I swallowed thickly, not daring to move.

My ex-fiancé cocked the gun and waited for my reaction. When I remained motionless, a sick smile stretched across the face I'd once thought of as handsome.

"That's a good girl," he said, leaning back in his seat.

The gun stayed trained on me. "Any sudden movements, and I'll blow your brains right across the back of my van. We don't want things to get too messy now, do we?"

I searched for his weak spots. The best I could imagine was startling him enough that I could get the gun, which wasn't likely to happen with the rope lashed around my wrists behind my back. Also the three Steel Knights who sat next to him posed a slight problem.

I did take some satisfaction from watching the man whose nose I'd broken dab his balled mask against the blood streaking from his nostrils. His face was already swelling and purpling. Served him right.

It appeared that Colt didn't plan to kill me, at least not right away. A tiny bit of the tension coiled inside me faded. As surreptitiously as I could, I pulled against my restraints and found that they offered a little give. Good. I might be able to work with that.

As if reading my mind, Colt gestured to his men. "Check the ropes—and her pockets. I don't want any surprises."

One of the guys, a beefy-looking menace, dropped to my side. Before I could react, he yanked my hands farther behind me, making me wince. The man bared his teeth gleefully at my evident discomfort. Taking a second thick nylon rope, he double wrapped it around my wrists, tying it as tightly as he could.

When he was done, I could barely move my hands. He added another rope around my ankles for good measure.

The guy moved on to patting me down. His hands lingered on my chest, and he looked up and grinned at me. His eyes dared me to get his slimy fingers off me, knowing I couldn't do anything to stop him.

If Colt noticed, apparently he no longer cared how his men touched me. Disgust soured my mouth. In my head, I was already making up ways I would kill this douchebag slowly and torturously.

To my relief, he didn't reach right inside my pockets. I didn't want to know what he'd have done with my childhood bracelet if he'd noticed it. But the chain was too delicate to be noticeable through the fabric of my sweats, and he wasn't looking for something delicate anyway.

"No phone, no weapons," he reported to Colt. My fingers curled behind me, remembering my phone slipping from my grasp as I'd tried to fight off these pricks. No chance of tech wizard Gideon using that to track my location.

I was on my own here. If they would even have tried to come after me. Colt had suggested the Nobles had *wanted* me grabbed.

"Traveling light, are you?" Colt chuckled and wagged the gun at me. "How the mighty have fallen. I finally have you weak and pliant, ready to be crushed like the pest you are. But first there are some things I need to know, both for myself and my benefactors."

He'd claimed that the Nobles had made a deal with him. I found that hard to believe. Even the most powerful gang in Paradise Bend wasn't above backstabbing, but Wylder Noble had seemed totally genuine when he'd welcomed me into their ranks, and as heir apparent, his word was gold when it came to his men.

Colt was just screwing with me, trying to shake me up so I'd spill something.

"Let's start with this," Colt said. "The Nobles and I are very interested in hearing everything you can tell me about your father's plans for the Bend and any other gangs he might have been associating with."

Was he still hung up on this idea that my father had betrayed *him*? I'd already told him he was delusional. I resisted the urge to roll my eyes. Those delusions had gotten everyone in my family and the upper levels of the Claws murdered at this man's orders.

Colt took the bandana out of my mouth so that I could reply. I glowered at him, unable to hold my tongue completely. "I must be pretty formidable for you to show up personally and get your hands dirty. Couldn't trust your men to catch me on their own?"

Colt slapped me hard across the cheek with his gun. Pain radiated through my cheekbone. I was going to have a hell of a bruise there, and blood was trickling through my mouth where I'd bitten my tongue.

"I'm not playing games," Colt said darkly. "This will be over a lot faster and less painfully if you cough up what you know now."

I grimaced at him. I'd allowed him to corner me again, but I wouldn't let him break me. The memory of Grandma bleeding out on the restaurant floor, of her last gurgling breaths, swam up through my mind, and my stomach lurched. No, I wasn't giving this asshole anything.

"In your dreams," I spat at him. "If you're going to

kill me, just go ahead and get it over with, because I'm not telling you anything."

Colt glared back at me. "That's not how this is going to work. Make no mistake, I will not go easy on you."

"Just a week ago, you were offering me your hand. You wanted me on your side," I reminded him.

Colt's jaw ticked. "And you shot me down. It was the biggest mistake of your life."

"No, the biggest mistake was ever *considering* tying my life to yours."

Crack. He slapped me across my face again, the force of it whipping my head to the side. My ears rang, and a fresh trickle of blood dribbled down the side of my lip. I licked it before turning to him. "Is that the best you've got?"

Colt shot off the bench and grabbed my hair at the roots, pulling it back. I winced but tried not to show the pain on my face, instead turning my chin up to look at him. At this man who'd slaughtered my entire family in cold blood without blinking twice.

"You're going to tell me everything you know, bitch," he said, his dark eyes twin orbs of fury. "If you won't talk to me, I have a man waiting for us who's *very* good at digging answers out of people. By the time he's done with you, you'll be begging for a chat with me."

I gritted my teeth. My voice came out strained but steady. "Don't you know that information you get through torture is notoriously inaccurate? I might say a lot of things just so I can get the pain to stop, but what's the guarantee that I'm not lying? I could make up all kinds of ridiculous things. Then you'd look awfully ridiculous in front of your new master."

Colt looked at me as if he wanted to strangle me right then and there, but a flash of doubt crossed his face. He shoved me away, releasing my hair. "Gag her again. We'll let Billy deal with her."

As the gropey guy shoved the gross bandana back into my mouth, my ex-fiancé sat back down on the bench. I didn't like the look of concentration that'd come over his face as he stared at some distant point beyond the van wall. He played with his thumbs, paying no attention to me, as if I wasn't even in the van anymore. As if he had bigger things to worry about.

Doubt began to trickle into me. It'd been my mention of disappointing his "master" that had thrown him off. I'd thought that story was all a ploy, but maybe Colt really was answering to someone else, at least as far as this kidnapping went.

I'd dismissed Wylder as the one who had put Colt up to this, but what if I'd misjudged him? Even if it'd seemed like I could believe his promise to help me, I'd been incredibly wrong before... about the man right in front of me.

And I had to consider Wylder's father too, didn't I? Ezra Noble had just gotten home this morning. I hadn't even met the man yet, so it was hard to picture him hating me so much he'd throw me to the sharks, but Ezra hadn't established himself as the most powerful criminal in the county by playing nice. Who knew what might go on in his head?

If the leader of the Nobles really did want me gone, I was so screwed.

I shook off those doubts, trying to refocus on the here and now. Nothing mattered unless I could get away from these assholes. I'd figure out the rest later.

Colt barked at the driver to put on some music. A moment later, the screech of thrash metal reverberated through the enclosed space. My ex returned his attention to me, tapping his gun against his knee, but he didn't speak again.

The windows were tinted, so I couldn't make out more than a blur from outside. I assumed they were taking me out of Paradise City into the Bend, where Colt's power was based.

My mind whirled, trying to think of an escape plan. It seemed almost impossible right now. I'd have to see where they took me first.

The van finally pulled off the road with a rattle of gravel against the undercarriage. The door opened to reveal a yard of cracked concrete and stubby weeds—and a few more of Colt's men. Two of them dragged me out.

Several feet away stood a squat one-story building with peeling paint. The yard was so large that all the neighboring buildings stood at a distance—and from their grungy state, who knew if they were even occupied? Colt had picked this place to ensure there were no witnesses. I had no idea where in the Bend we even were.

One of the men shoved at my shoulder. "Keep moving."

They escorted me into the building. Pieces of trash and scraps of metal littered the floor. It didn't look like a place Colt did much work out of. I'd guess he didn't plan on keeping me here for too long.

Most likely, he planned on me being dead when we left.

The men marched me into a room at the back of the building and pushed me into the lone wooden chair in the middle of the space. The windows around me were so coated with dirt that barely any sunlight penetrated them, most of the room's illumination coming from the flickering bulb above me.

At Colt's gesture, his men untied my arms just long enough to bind them to the arms of the chair. "Good," he said. "I want her hands where I can see them."

I couldn't help taking a little satisfaction at his wariness of me. He'd already underestimated me once. Maybe he would again, and then I'd get my opening.

Colt's phone rang. When he saw the caller ID, he winced. Interesting. This mysterious boss of his?

He answered, and I caught the faint crackle of sound from the other end, but I couldn't make out a single word. "I'm working on it," Colt said. "We'll get everything we need."

When he'd hung up, he turned to me as if deciding what he wanted to do with me. I tested my arms, moving them slightly to check their mobility. Colt's men had secured my bonds so tightly that my flesh was going numb.

Colt's eyes roved over me for a second before he looked away. "She's ready for you, Billy."

One of the men who'd met us here stepped forward, leering at me so avidly my skin crawled. Then a jolt of recognition raced through me, turning my gut even colder.

I'd seen that face before—he was one of the guys who'd been acting as a server at the rehearsal dinner. One of the men who'd gunned down my family.

He took out a knife and turned it slowly in his hand. Anger and horror churned together inside me.

Colt gave him a sadistic smile. "You know what we want from her. Let me know when she decides to speak. I've got other business to attend to."

"With pleasure, boss," the man said.

Colt stalked out of the room with his other men trailing behind him. The door shut with an ominous thud and a click of the lock.

Billy walked around me, grinning and twirling his knife. "You and me are going to have *lots* of fun, darling."

Gideon

I FROWNED AT THE COFFEE I'D JUST TAKEN OUT OF the grinder. The texture wasn't quite right. Instead of pouring the grounds into my machine, which would be a waste of its complicated mechanics, I dumped them into the garbage and reached for the bag of dark roasted beans to start over.

I'd like to think I was a simple man with a simple but fixed routine. The trouble was that if something didn't go right with that routine, it left me irritated and restless for the rest of the day. And the truth was, my current irritation had less to do with my coffee and more with the data I'd been checking.

As I turned back to my desk, my frown deepened. I'd been going over the payments various Nobles members had collected on behalf of the gang and the funds that'd been moving through our various business operations as we laundered them. The numbers in the columns wouldn't make any sense to an outsider. There was an alphanumeric code written next to each column that specified the activity and source.

Concrete figures normally appealed to me, but as usual, this list was having the opposite effect. I probably shouldn't have bothered looking it over, since it wasn't technically my job, but for Wylder's sake, I figured someone from his inner circle should be keeping an eye on things. Definitely no one else in the Nobles approached the situation with quite the same precision I did. A lot of this information was hearsay or estimates long after the fact, and the numbers never added up as neatly as I'd prefer.

Somebody knocked on the door. "Come in," I said, even though I wasn't in the best mood for company.

Rowan stepped inside. "Hey, I got that information you wanted on the Prowlers."

I only grunted in response.

"That's what I get after you've been hounding me for a week about it?" Rowan scanned my desk and must have noted the lack of steaming mug. "Ah, let me guess. You're in caffeine withdrawal."

"Something I'll fix in a moment," I muttered, spinning my chair toward my coffee setup. The grinder's current output was at least satisfactory. I added it and started the machine running. The thrum and the trickle of liquid into the waiting mug smoothed out my nerves just a tad. "So, you found out what that commotion last week was about?"

Rowan sat down on one of the chairs by the chess table. "I finally tracked down someone who was on the scene and managed to get him chatting. He said the skirmish was between two groups of dealers within the Prowlers. One of them apparently got their hands on a hot new drug, something called Glory—the others wanted in on the action, and they had... trouble reaching an agreement."

I rolled my eyes. Just like the small-time gangs to end up fighting themselves rather than getting shit done. But that information wasn't entirely unremarkable. "We've heard a few murmurs about a new drug, haven't we? Any idea what's so special about it?"

"Not yet. It doesn't seem to have spread very widely in the Bend yet, although from what I'm hearing on the street, demand is increasing quickly. There haven't been any freak deaths so far, at least. But it sounds like potent stuff."

A note of concern had come into his voice. Rowan had always been a bit softer than I liked. It bothered him that people might be snorting or shooting up stuff that might send them reeling in a dangerous way.

As far as I was concerned, anyone who took the risk knew what they were getting into. They had the freedom to be idiots if they wanted to.

I was just glad Ezra had never been all that interested in the drug trade. We ran some low-level recreational stuff like weed, but nothing that'd really fuck anyone up. Too much hassle if one batch turned out to be bad and suddenly you had the DEA sniffing around.

"Well, keep your ears peeled for any new developments," I said. "Always good to know what's going around."

As we'd talked, I'd continued to scroll through the payment records. My fingers paused over the mouse. I peered closer. "That's odd."

Rowan leaned toward me. "What?"

"Let me just..." I clicked through to the previous month, and a few more before, checking the same code. A prickle of apprehension ran down my spine. "Everything's up to date."

"And that's a problem?"

I shot Rowan a quick glower and motioned to the computer screen. "Various operations belonging to the Steel Knights pay us a tithe like every other gang in the county. Normally there are at least a few things outstanding because payments get passed on in bits and pieces or delayed while they work something out on their end. Every other organization has a few loose ends."

Rowan knit his brow. "But not the Steel Knights?"

"Not as of a few months ago. All of a sudden, they made sure to pay off all their debts. And they've paid on time—even a little early—since then." I flicked my tongue over my lip ring and reached to collect my coffee mug from the machine.

"Is that something we should be worried about?" Rowan asked.

"I'd say so." I took a sip, letting the darkly bitter liquid flood my mouth, and raised my eyebrows at him. "When do we send people in to collect more forcefully?"

Understanding dawned in his eyes. "When they get too far or too much behind. They were doing everything they could to make sure we wouldn't go nosing around in their operations."

"Exactly. No other reason for them to get so conscientious all of a sudden. They knew they were up to something we wouldn't like." I'd dismissed Mercy's original warnings about the Steel Knights' plans to overthrow the Nobles because the idea had sounded ridiculous, but there'd been evidence right here all along. And clearly it was something Colt had been planning for a while.

Before I could dwell any more on that, the door to my study burst open. Wylder marched in with Kaige at his heels.

"Ever heard of knocking?" I said mildly. Wylder's family owned this entire mansion—technically he had the right to barge in wherever he wanted.

Kaige shoved past Wylder. "Have you seen Mercy?"

His obvious agitation unnerved me more than I liked, which made me irritated all over again. "I haven't seen her since yesterday night. What's the emergency?"

"She went for a run with me," Kaige said. "We were supposed to take three laps through the path around the backyards and then meet up at the front steps. I'd pulled ahead of her by the third time around, so I got there first, but she just... never turned up."

"I assume you checked the path and obvious places like her room in case she took a detour to get back to the house a different way."

"Of course," Kaige snapped. "She isn't anywhere, and it's been nearly an hour."

The obvious conclusion hit me, bringing an unexpected twinge of disappointment with it. I wasn't sure I liked that reaction either. "She took off, then. Decided to get her revenge on her own terms."

"Why the hell would she do that?" Wylder said. He kept his voice even, but the tension running through it brought me to sharper attention. *He* was worried. "I gave her my word just this morning that she's one of us now, that we're going to crush Colt. It wouldn't make any sense for her to leave the second she got what she's been pushing so hard for."

Rowan shifted in his chair. "Maybe she decided she can't take you at your word after the ways we've jerked her around." His tone was casual, but his shoulders had stiffened. I got the impression he wasn't okay with the idea that Mercy was gone even though he'd given every indication that he never wanted her here in the first place.

Kaige shook his head. "I don't think so. It's not just what Wylder said. I found this in front of the neighbor's house. I'm sure it's hers." He smacked a phone on my desk.

"Maybe you should have led with that?" I said dryly, and picked up the phone. It was the same brand of burner as the phone I'd seen on her. Opening it, I tapped through to the recent messages. Yes, there were the urgent texts she'd sent all of us last night trying to warn us about Gia—and an unsent one to Kaige that cut off in mid-sentence as if she'd been interrupted. *Maybe hurry your ass...*

I couldn't think of many things that could have caused Mercy to drop her phone in the middle of a text and not pick it up again, and none of the ones I could think of were good.

Kaige paced to my aquarium and back again. "Check the surveillance footage. Maybe that'll show us something."

"It doesn't cover the neighbor's lawn," I said.

"Just check it!"

Wylder clapped a hand to Kaige's shoulder. "We'll figure it out. Give the man room to work." He nodded to me. "It can't hurt to take a look. We might see something useful."

The words should have sounded like a suggestion, but there was an obvious command to them. I could feel the tension in the room pulling taut like a bow. All four of us—in our different ways—were disturbed by Mercy's absence. I supposed I'd gotten used to having her around, and now our dynamic had been thrown off just slightly again. It was nothing more than that.

I pulled up the feed for the camera that gave a view of the yard and sidewalk in front of the house. "So this was about an hour ago? How long was she out of your sight while you were running?"

"I guess... about ten minutes? After I'd come around the side of the house at the end of the street, I stopped for a few minutes figuring I'd let her catch up enough to give her a fighting chance. When she didn't come around the bend, I assumed she'd pulled some kind of fast one on me. But then I couldn't find her anywhere."

Playing back the footage at ten times the speed, I studied the screen. Kaige and Mercy set off running. Several minutes later, they reappeared neck and neck.

After another several minutes, they reappeared with Kaige several paces in the lead.

Just a few minutes after that, Mercy came jogging into view from the wrong angle, as if she was coming from the house rather than from the street. I slowed the recording down.

Kaige blinked, and a laugh sputtered out of him. "She *did* pull a fast one. I should have seen that coming. She must have made it over the fence with those parkour moves of hers and cut through the yard."

"That doesn't explain why she vanished afterward," Wylder muttered, stepping right up behind my chair and peering at the screen intently.

Mercy waited in front of the house for a minute, bouncing restlessly on her feet. Then she jogged out of frame toward the neighbor's. I was just reaching for the mouse to start zipping through the footage again when a white van whizzed past at breakneck speed.

Kaige froze. "What the fuck was that?"

"I don't know," I said, but I couldn't shake the apprehension that was creeping into my gut. Why would a regular delivery van be tearing away from here like a bat out of hell?

Nothing else showed in the footage except Kaige loping into sight a little later. I dismissed the window and stood up, grabbing my tablet. "I think we need to take a look at the actual scene. Show me exactly where you found her phone."

Kaige hustled along the hall and down the stairs as if Mercy's life might depend on how quickly we made it outside. I didn't like the knowledge that it very well might. As we stepped out into the warm summer sunshine, I couldn't help picturing her prancing out with a smirk to laugh at us for worrying about her. I might even have been hoping for it.

It didn't happen. Kaige strode to a spot about halfway along the neighbor's lawn and pointed to the edge of the sidewalk. "I found it right here." His hand dropped to his side, where it flexed and clenched as if just waiting for something—or someone—to punch.

The sidewalk and the neatly mown grass offered nothing. Wylder had already stalked over to the road. A breath hissed in through his teeth.

"It looks like the van took off from here in a hurry."

I joined him. Faint skid marks showed against the asphalt a couple of feet from the curb. There was no way to confirm what vehicle had made them, but the location was awfully suspicious. And—

My gaze caught on a few dark specks that gleamed wetly against the pavement right by the gutter. I knelt down and touched one. It stained my fingertip red.

My heart lurched despite my best attempt at self-control. "You fought back," I murmured.

Abruptly, I could see her in the back of my mind, striking out at her attackers with the fierceness she wore so well. Even through my concern, my cock stirred. As if this was a good time for *those* sorts of feelings. I straightened up, shaking off my imaginings, but the vise in my chest remained tight.

"What's that?" Wylder asked, coming up behind me to peer at my fingers, more urgency seeping into his tone. When I looked up at him, his eyes were stormy. He definitely wasn't unaffected by the situation either.

How had this woman managed to get so far under all our skins in a matter of days?

But that didn't matter. Right then, all I could think was that we had to get her back.

"There's blood on the pavement," I said. "The van must have sped over, and someone jumped out to grab her. In the struggle, at least one person drew blood." After seeing Mercy grapple with Gia last night, I could believe it'd been her. But even if it had been, her strength hadn't been enough.

"And then they took her!" Kaige let out an incoherent sound, his hands balling tight. Fury flushed his face. "When I get a hold of them—"

"We don't even know who 'them' is," Rowan pointed out, but I noticed his own face had paled.

I straightened up, flattening my voice but hating the dispassionate sound of it at the same time. "It's not hard to guess, is it? Who's taken her before? Who's wanted her dead this whole time?"

"Colt Bryant and his fucking Steel Knights," Wylder growled. "How the hell did they get this far into our territory without anyone noticing? They grabbed her right from our doorstep, the motherfuckers."

He was right. The move was bold and in some ways an open challenge, even though I doubted Colt would ever admit his involvement in Mercy's kidnapping unless we forced it out of him. Imagining setting Kaige loose on the prick in Kaige's current state gave me a small measure of satisfaction. The leader of the Steel Knights wouldn't survive that encounter.

Kaige swiveled around. "I think I remember seeing a van parked down at the other end of the street. I figured it was just someone making a delivery. Shit, I should have paid more attention."

Wylder smacked his knuckles against his palm. "The men we have stationed all over the city should have noticed something."

"There's no use in pointing fingers or placing blame," Rowan said quickly, ever the diplomat. "That doesn't help Mercy. We have to focus on her." His voice cracked slightly on the last word. Even he was starting to lose his composure.

Kaige shook his head, raising his hands to his temples. "What do you think they've done to her? They've had her for an hour already. Is she even...?"

He trailed off. I didn't want to complete his sentence, but the thought had occurred to me too. No doubt it'd crossed all our minds.

Mercy had been nothing but defiant to Colt. Of course he would want to get her out of his way as soon as possible.

"Bryant is a dead man walking," Wylder said in a chilling voice that made my gaze jerk to him. I couldn't remember when I'd last heard him quite that furious. I'd known Mercy appealed to him, but I hadn't thought he cared quite that much.

But then, I hadn't thought *I* cared as much as the knot in my stomach said I did either.

My best friend turned to me. "Whatever those shitheads have done, we need to find them before they can do worse. Can you get the license plate off the surveillance footage and run it?"

My mind leapt back to the recording, trying to remember how clear the back of the van had been in the split-second when it'd roared across the screen, but my practical side was already reminding me that there was no way Colt would have used any vehicle that could be traced to him or wherever his people had meant to take Mercy. I opened my mouth, dreading Wylder's reaction to that statement. Then inspiration hit like a lightning bolt.

Yes. I'd been prepared for something like this after all... even if this hadn't been quite what I was picturing when I'd made my preparations.

A smile had crossed my lips of its own accord. Kaige stared at me. "What the hell are you grinning about, Gideon? This is—"

I snapped my fingers, cutting him off. "Stop raving like a lunatic for a second and listen. We *can* find her. I've got something even better than a license plate to track her down."

Mercy

AS COLT'S HENCHMAN CIRCLED ME, I TESTED MY bonds again. They held firm, my wrists aching at the pressure.

Billy snickered. "Don't think you're getting out of this, Miss Katz. I'll get the answers the boss wants whether I have to carve them out of you or pull them out by your fingernails. But it's up to you how much fun we have. Now that you've seen what I have to offer, maybe you want to cough up a little something right away?"

I ignored him, shifting my weight on the chair just slightly. I had a little mobility. That would work in my favor.

Colt had made two mistakes that'd probably never occurred to him would cause him any problems: my ankles were tied, but not to the chair, and the chair he'd stuck me in was wooden.

He had no idea the drills my father used to run me through, tying me up one way or another and taunting me with words and blows until I managed to get free. Supposedly Dad had been training me for all the possible dangers of gang life, but I'd always known it was at least as much about punishing me for being born a girl.

Now I was glad I was a woman. These assholes just couldn't wrap their heads around the idea that I might have more skills than they did. That I might have trained harder than they'd ever imagined, even if it hadn't been my choice.

I just needed the asshole in the room to come a little closer.

Billy stopped in front of me with that ugly leer. Just looking into his face, remembering the glimpse of it I'd gotten in the midst of the carnage several days ago, made my hands itch to punch his tongue right down his throat.

Was he the one who'd shot Grandma? Or Aunt Renee? He'd been acting under Colt's orders, but somehow I didn't think he was sorry about it.

"Let's hear it," he said. "What big plans did your dear old dad have in the works? How many people had he reached out to?"

This again. I bit back a sigh and simply glared at him.

Unnervingly, Billy kept smiling, not thrown by my silence. "Or how about this—we want to know what you've spilled about the Nobles' operations to whoever you're still in contact with from your father's allies."

I hesitated, momentarily distracted. *Was* Ezra behind this kidnapping—because somehow he'd gotten it into his head that I'd been ratting out his business to competitors? I hadn't said a thing about the goings-on in the Noble mansion to anyone.

Or was this just a round-about way for Colt to try to get information about the Nobles from me, because he was still aiming to overthrow them?

I couldn't expect Billy to tell me that. He was still keeping his distance, toying with me. I needed him riled up.

"Why the fuck should I tell you anything?" I asked. "You're obviously a pathetic excuse for a man, getting off on threatening someone who's unarmed and restrained. And I guess you figure you can't do enough damage with your fists even like that—you need a knife to get the job done?"

Billy's eyes flashed, and the grin deflated. Excellent.

"Big mouth on a chick who can't move anything else," he retorted. "We'll see what you think of the knife when I'm stabbing it into you."

"Oooh, I'm so scared. As far as I can tell, all *you* know how to move is your mouth too."

His jaw clenched. I could see him reining in his anger, but I'd pissed him off enough that he walked right up to me. "If you're in such a hurry to get to the painful parts, I'm happy to start right—"

He wasn't a total idiot—he came up beside me rather than in front, where I might have had a hope of swinging my bound legs at him. But that wasn't the main part of my plan anyway.

The moment he was in range, the knife gleaming dangerously close to my cheek, I rocked forward with all the force I had in me. My weight landed on my feet. I whipped around, doubling over to lift the chair legs higher.

The solid wooden legs slammed into Billy's body, one of them clocking him right in the face. The cracking sound suggested I'd broken at least one bone.

Billy swore and stumbled backward, groping at his cheek, which I hoped ached twice as much as mine did. I flung myself toward the nearest wall, wrenching the chair toward it as I went. I rammed the chair into the concrete surface so hard the impact reverberated through my bones—and cracked the thin wooden arms.

I shook myself free of the chair, tugging at the now-loosened ropes. As I yanked them off my chafed wrists, Billy charged at me. Blood streamed down the side of his face, and his eyes were murderous.

My fingers closed around the best weapon I had—one of the broken pieces of wood, its splintered end sharp as a stake. I fumbled with the rope around my ankles at the same time. Billy swung his knife at me, and I smacked it aside with my makeshift weapon before flipping backward to slam my feet into his gut.

He plummeted to the floor with a pained grunt. I managed to heave a loop of the rope over my heel, which loosened the whole mess enough to kick it off—just in time for Billy to come at me again.

Springing to my feet, I dodged and swiped at his knife hand. My heart pounded so loud it drowned out every other sound. If I could knock the blade far enough away and he ran for it, I might have time to break one of the windows and flee that way. I didn't dare turn my back on him while he was wielding that thing.

I was not going to die here. I'd made it out of situations that'd looked even more dire before. This kitty cat was going to make full use of her nine lives.

"You cunt," Billy snarled. He slashed at me again, too fast for me to block. The blade sliced across my forearm, drawing a thin line of blood.

I jabbed at him again, weaving back and forth. He raised the knife, and then he opened his mouth, sucking in a mass of air.

Understanding hit me like a cold slap. He was going to holler for the other men, and in a second I'd be outnumbered with only a broken chair arm to defend myself.

In that instant, my mind narrowed down to one undeniable fact: I couldn't let him get out that yell, no matter what I had to do.

My body reacted without conscious thought. I hurled myself at Billy, heedless of the knife and his grasping hands, thinking only of cutting off his voice and ending that sadistic fucking smile before he killed yet another Katz.

He hadn't been expecting me to launch myself at him that boldly. We tumbled over, me on top of him, his shout coming out as a strangled yelp—and then I slammed the jagged end of the chair arm as hard as I could into his neck.

The start of his yelp turned into a gurgle. Hot blood

spurted up to splash his face. A little splattered my shirt. I jerked backward, leaving the stake embedded in his throat, nausea twisting my stomach.

He gripped his neck to try to stop the flow of blood, thrashing like a wounded animal, but only for a few moments. Then his arms went limp. His body twitched and stilled on the floor, blood flowing from the wound in a steady stream. All the anger and life in his eyes glazed over.

He was dead.

I'd never actually killed anyone before. I'd imagined it plenty of times, but actually going through with the act...

I couldn't say I'd enjoyed it, but I didn't feel any particular remorse either. The only emotion gripping me other than the twinge of queasiness was the sense that the bastard had deserved it. Hell, he'd deserved worse.

I could almost hear Dad whisper in my ear: "There's the killer I trained all these years."

Before I could shudder at that thought, the door burst open. Shit. The other men had heard Billy's call for help after all.

Only two of them, though, and I'd already disposed of one opponent. They froze just inside with matching expressions of stunned disbelief, taking in me, disheveled, panting, and blood-speckled, and Billy's corpse on the floor.

I might not get another chance. Snatching a second broken piece of wood off the floor in case I needed it, I bolted for the closest window. With a quick flip, I rammed my heels into the glass with all my strength.

Pain radiated through my calves, but the pane shattered. The men shouted and hurtled after me, one of them reaching to his waist—damn it, of course he'd have a gun.

I dropped to the floor and kicked out my legs fast enough to knock his feet out from under him. As he toppled, the gun jolted from his fingers. The other guy snatched at me, and I stabbed my second stake into his upper arm. Then I leapt for the window.

A few shards of glass bit into my palms, but I didn't give a shit. I curled my body into a roll and tumbled through the narrow opening, swinging my legs down just in time to land on my feet. The second they hit the ground, I was running.

The afternoon humidity closed around me, condensing in my lungs. Shouts rang out through the window behind me. I sprinted in the opposite direction from the van, figuring more of Colt's men—even Colt himself—might be hanging around by the entrance to the yard.

Footsteps pounded out onto the cracked concrete, but I'd already reached the chain-link fence. I scrambled up it and hefted myself over in a few adrenaline-powered motions.

Up ahead lay a sea of rusty shipping containers with several low brick buildings beyond them. I wove between the big metal boxes, using them for cover. Voices hollered behind me.

"She went that way! Come on!"

"What the fuck is wrong with you people?"

I couldn't take any enjoyment from their frustration while my life still hung in the balance. I pumped my legs as hard as they'd go, only taking a tiny bit of relief when I reached the first of the actual buildings. The whole area seemed to be abandoned. I wasn't familiar with this part of the Bend.

I clambered over another fence, dashed through a couple more yards, and found myself on an unfamiliar street. On instinct, I ran in what felt like the direction that'd take me farther from Colt and his goons. Eventually I'd have to figure out where the hell I was and how to get back to someplace I knew, but for now I just wanted to put distance between me and the guns.

The heat was baking my skin and sending up faint whiffs of a sickly meaty scent from the splatter of Billy's blood on my shirt. I grimaced, wiping at the sweat now soaking the back of my neck, and just kept running.

Five blocks, ten, twenty, veering in a new direction every few minutes just to make it harder for any pursuers to follow. Finally, when I hadn't heard any sounds from behind me in ages and I could see actual traffic on the road up ahead, I slowed down to take stock.

My lungs ached, and my cheek still stung where Colt had hit me. My palms throbbed, blood seeping from the glass cuts. Bracing myself, I plucked out a couple of shards that were still embedded in my flesh and glanced around.

I was standing next to a furniture warehouse with a foreclosure sign pasted on the window. A row of bland low-rise apartment buildings stood up ahead by the busier street. A couple of kids were chasing each other around the playground behind them, where only one of the swings was still attached to both its chains. I'd probably give children nightmares in my current state.

I was about to slink past them to where I could check the street sign when a car engine rumbled not from up ahead but behind me. My head jerked around, my body bracing to run... but the car looked way too familiar. I'd ridden in that deep blue Mustang before, hadn't I?

As I hesitated, Kaige's and Wylder's faces came into focus through the windshield.

I took a few steps back toward the furniture warehouse, but then I stood my ground and waited for them to reach me. My hands balled at my sides. I wasn't dismissing the idea of making a run for it until I'd heard what they had to say.

Mercy

THE MUSTANG JERKED TO A HALT IN FRONT OF THE
warehouse's parking lot, and someone shoved the back
door open. Rowan and Gideon were sitting there,
Rowan pushing over to make room. "Get in," he said
quickly.

Kaige was already rolling his window down in the
front passenger seat. His expression was taut, his dark
eyes fierce. "Are they close by?" he asked, sounding like
he was just waiting for an excuse to crack a few skulls.

I stayed where I was. "If you're talking about the
Steel Knights, not as far as I know," I said. "And I'll stay
right here for now."

Wylder peered past Kaige from the driver's seat, his
fingers tight around the steering wheel. "What the hell
are you talking about? We're getting you out of here."

"I think I'd like to do a little more talking before I
make up my mind about that."

"For fuck's—" He cut himself off with a sound of frustration.

The next thing I knew, all four of the guys were leaping out of the Mustang with an urgency that put me even more on guard. As he came around the front of the car, Wylder's gaze shot straight to my arm—to the shallow cut where a thin trickle of blood was still seeping out and then the stains on my fingers from my glass-sliced palms. Emotion flared in his bright green eyes.

Kaige barged forward, but Wylder stepped in front of him, cutting him off. The heir to the Nobles strode right up to me, picking up speed as he came.

"Hold on a second," I said, holding up my hands as if to ward him off and taking another step back.

But Wylder didn't give a shit what I wanted. What else was new? He grabbed me by the shoulder so I couldn't retreat any farther, firmly but not hard enough to hurt, which was the only reason I didn't punch him in the nose.

He scanned my face, focusing on my bruised cheek for a moment, and then down my body, tension etched all through his stance. When his attention came back to the small wound on my forearm, his jaw clenched. "Fucking bastards."

"It's fine," I said, unsettled and yet weirdly warmed by his intensity. He sure as hell wasn't *acting* like a guy pissed off because his evil plan had gone awry. No, he was practically vibrating with agitation... over the thought that I'd shed a few drops of blood?

"It's not *fine*," he snapped, examining each of my hands. "Someone grab the first aid kit from the trunk!"

Rowan hustled over with a roll of gauze. When our gazes met, his deep blue eyes searched mine, his mouth slanting at an uneasy angle. Wylder snatched the gauze from him and started wrapping it with practiced efficiency around my palms, which were barely even stinging anymore anyway. Rowan shifted his weight as if to step closer to me and then seemed to catch himself, his attention flicking to Wylder.

I couldn't blame him if he was wary of stepping in while his boss was in this mood. I wasn't totally sure what to make of it yet myself.

Wylder tied the hasty bandages off and shoved the roll of gauze back at Rowan. "We'll get Frank to have a look at them when we get back." Grasping my shoulder again, he peered into my eyes even more intently. His hand flexed and softened its hold as if he was afraid he'd accidentally wound me himself. The movement sent a tingling over my skin. "They didn't hurt you in any other way?"

"I didn't give them a chance," I said, holding myself in place against the urge to sway closer to him. All that fiery protectiveness, and something about it drew me like a moth to a flame, especially from this guy who'd made such a performance of not giving a damn about me so many times in the past.

But I had to be sure.

Kaige pushed in beside him, his face twisted with rage. "I'm going to kill those motherfuckers."

Despite myself, a smile twitched at my lips. I

motioned to the cut on my arm. "I already killed the one who did this." The memory came with only a faint jab of discomfort, quickly overwhelmed by a swell of satisfaction. I'd given that prick what he'd deserved.

Kaige's mouth fell open.

Wylder blinked. "Well, fuck me. Kitty Cat doesn't mess around."

He sounded almost proud. I had to mentally stamp out the thrill of pleasure that pulsed through me.

I shook off Wylder's grasp and pulled away from him, crossing my arms over my chest and examining him for any trace of malice. "I'm perfectly all right. You weren't expecting that, were you?"

Kaige threw his hands in the air. "What were we supposed to think when you just disappeared—that fucking van—it *was* the Steel Knights, wasn't it? What the hell even happened?"

Wylder's lips had pursed when I'd drawn back, but he was still looking at me like I was some injured bird. "I'm not surprised. You've turned the tables on those pricks before. But we *should* get out of here. We're deep in Steel Knights territory. I'm looking forward to putting a lot of bullets in a lot of heads, but let's get you out of the potential crossfire first."

"I'll tear their fucking heads right off," Kaige muttered, clenching his hands.

I wasn't seeing any sign that either of them was anything other than relieved that I was okay—and furious with the people who hadn't wanted me to be. My gaze slid to the other two men.

Gideon had come up beside Rowan, his beloved

tablet tucked under one arm, his smooth face as detached in its alien beauty as ever. I'd almost have thought it didn't matter to him that they'd happened to find me if he hadn't jumped out of the car as fast as the others. There was a stiffness to the way he held himself now as if he wasn't sure what to do with himself. I didn't know what to make of that, but then, I rarely knew what to make of the Nobles' tech expert.

Rowan was still standing uncertainly next to Wylder. When I looked at him, he swallowed audibly. His voice came out so gentle I'd almost think he'd transformed back into the boy I'd believed he was five years ago. "Let's go, Mercy. We can sort the rest out in the car."

There was still one part of this that didn't make sense. I fixed my gaze on Wylder again. "How did you even know where I was?" It was awfully convenient, wasn't it, that they'd shown up right after I'd given Colt's men the slip and known exactly where I'd be?

I wasn't expecting Wylder's lips to twitch with amusement. He glanced at Gideon with an arch of his eyebrows.

The other guy swung his tablet out, and I saw a map with a blinking light on the screen. "It was actually very simple," he said in his usual cool tone. "It seemed plausible that we might need to locate you at some point for one reason or another, so I attached a small tracking device to both of your bras."

Now it was my turn to gape. "You did *what*?"

He shrugged, as nonchalant as if he were saying he'd put on a load of laundry for me. "It was the most reasonable option. You only had two, so you'd nearly always be wearing one unless you were asleep, and the structure makes detection much less likely than most other clothing."

If it'd been anyone else, speaking any less practically about it, I'd have been totally creeped out. I looked down at my chest. I was still a little creeped out. "Can you de-tracker them?"

Kaige let out a rough guffaw. "I dunno—seems to me it came in pretty handy."

It had. If I *hadn't* been able to get away from Colt's people, I'd have been awfully grateful for Gideon's apparently nonexistent sense of personal boundaries. But still...

"We'll come back to that subject later." I glanced around, apprehension prickling down my spine. *I* didn't like hanging around in my ex's territory either, and my lingering worries had fallen away. For the guys to have gotten all the way here from Paradise City, they must have left before I'd gotten away from my captors—and why would they have already been heading out in search of me if getting me kidnapped had been their own plan? "All right, let's get out of here."

All four of the guys moved—but not toward the car, toward me, as if they thought I needed a full contingent of bodyguards just to walk the ten feet to the waiting Mustang. Oh-kay then. Kaige's hand hovered by my elbow as they ushered me to the curb, and then he dove into the backseat even though he'd been riding shotgun before.

Well, I wasn't against sitting next to him. As I climbed in after him, I noticed Wylder eyeing us as if he was debating claiming the other seat next to me. But it was his car. He marched back to the driver's seat with an oddly annoyed air.

Gideon got in beside him, and Rowan grabbed his previous spot in the back. He sank onto the seat, leaving a few careful inches between us. "I'm glad you're all right," he said quietly as Wylder started the engine.

Even though he'd gone out of his way to sit next to me, Kaige stayed strangely silent. His hands were balled into fists on his lap, the veins standing out in their backs, looking ready to pop.

"You wanted to know what happened," I said in an attempt to break the awkwardness of the moment. "It *was* the Steel Knights. They ambushed me on the sidewalk and dragged me into a van. Colt was there waiting for me."

In the driver's seat, Wylder stiffened. "Colt was there?" he said before I could go on.

"Apparently he wanted to oversee the operation personally."

The Noble heir's voice came out even more strained than it'd been when he first found me. "He's a walking dead man. That's an open challenge to our authority. He came right up to our gates and grabbed you—it's a fucking act of war."

"I'm sorry, Mercy," Kaige burst out, sounding so agonized that my gaze jerked to him. His hands had somehow clenched even tighter, his face flushed with more anger that he now seemed to be directing at himself. He smacked his palm. "If I'd paid enough attention to the van—if I hadn't suggested the run to begin with—I should have been keeping a closer eye on things—"

I stared at him for a second before my voice caught up. "It's not your fault. How could you have known Colt would do something that bold?"

Kaige and I had hooked up, and he'd been flirty with me even when he was angry with *me* before, but I wouldn't have thought he'd be this affected by me being in danger. Or was it just a matter of honor for him, having failed his duty to the Nobles?

Kaige grimaced as if he couldn't accept the excuse I'd offered, but Gideon broke in, aloof as ever. "What did they want with you? Obviously not simply to kill you, or you'd be dead."

"Thanks for pointing that out," I said sarcastically, kicking the back of his seat. "Colt wanted information... About the plans my father was supposedly making against him, and about whether I'd given anyone information about the Nobles."

Rowan frowned. "Why would he ask that?"

I hesitated and decided now wasn't the best time to tell them Colt had claimed they'd put him up to it—and that I hadn't been totally sure he was lying until a few minutes ago. Their combined reaction might blow the roof off the car. Maybe *never* would be a good time to mention that.

"Probably all part of his stupid paranoia." I paused. "He did seem to be working with someone else. He took a call while I was there... He said some things about having made a deal to get what he wanted."

A deal that still could have been with Ezra Noble.

My gaze settled on the back of Wylder's head and his fiery auburn hair, so like his father's. When would be a good time to bring *that* possibility up?

"It's not like anything your dad was planning matters anyway, considering—" Kaige stopped, snapping his mouth shut, but the unspoken words hung in the confined space of the car. It didn't matter now because Dad and the rest of my family were dead anyway.

"I didn't mean it that way," he added quickly.

I waved him off, settling deeper into the seat. I was bone-weary tired, and my brain was this close to shutting down, but I knew that wasn't really an option. "It's okay. It's true—my dad is gone. But Colt obviously doesn't see it that way. Anyway, the asshole he set up to torture the answers out of me didn't get anything before I broke free, and he didn't leave me with a whole lot of choice but to kill him, so it's not like they got anywhere."

We fell into a stretch of silence. We weren't quite out of the Bend yet, and even here on a busier street lined with shops, the buildings on either side of us were periodically marked with the spray-painted Steel Knights symbol.

The message was clear. Everything here now belonged to them.

Gideon held up his tablet to take a few photographs. "This didn't use to be Steel Knights territory, did it?"

My stomach knotted. "No. They're taking over every street they can."

"I didn't realize it was so bad," he murmured.

Maybe it was a good thing the situation had forced

the guys to finally come down here. They could witness the changing face of the Bend firsthand.

"I told you," I couldn't help saying.

"And we should have believed you before," Wylder said, the protective note still in his voice making something inside me clench. I hadn't seen this part of him before, but I liked it. I liked it more than might be wise.

"We're going to push back," Kaige said. "We're going to push back and crush them, and that pathetic excuse of a man is going to wish he never laid a finger on you."

Rowan exhaled slowly. "He's fixated on his plan to take over, and he's convinced your dad was the one who could have screwed it up. That's why he's obsessed with getting answers out of you, I'd guess. He's afraid there's some way it could still go wrong." He shook his head. "Of course, it was always going to go wrong once he messed with the Nobles."

Wylder hit the steering wheel. "Damn straight."

The assurance in their words steadied me. We were leaving the marks of the Steel Knights behind for now anyway, passing from the Bend into the brighter, posher streets of Paradise City. As we came to a stop at a red light, Wylder yanked something out of his pocket. He twisted in his seat to hand it to me, his expression offering no room for argument. "Take this."

I reached for it automatically and found my fingers wrapping around the hilt of a knife in a thin leather sheath. I stared down at it and then back at Wylder, but he'd already turned to face the road.

"You obviously need to be armed from now on," he said. "If Colt comes for you again, I want you ready."

I wasn't going to argue with that. An almost giddy warmth bloomed in my chest at the show of trust. Wylder was arming me, giving me the means to hurt *him* if I'd wanted to—knowing I wouldn't.

And it was more than that. I drew the knife from the sheath just for a moment to test its weight in my hand and noticed the engraving on the hilt. *W.N.*

My head jerked up. "This is *yours*. I mean, obviously, but—"

"And now it's yours," he said sharply before I could protest him giving me a weapon that must have been meaningful to him in some way. Presumably he didn't go around having every knife he ever carried engraved with his initials. "I'll see that you get a gun too. There are plenty of options in the latest shipment. You're with us now, and that means whatever you need, it's taken care of."

I couldn't deny that the knife felt good in my hand. I slid it back into its sheath and held it on my lap. "Thank you."

From his profile, I saw a flicker of a smile cross his lips. "As long as you use it well."

The hill topped with its sprawl of mansions loomed ahead of us. As we drove steadily closer, I couldn't help reflecting on who was waiting for us back in the Nobles' home. My mouth went dry. But I had to say *something*.

It wasn't until we'd crested the hill and pulled into the driveway that I forced the question out. "Your father came back this morning—he knows why I'm here, right?"

The click as the engine cut off sounded ominous.

Wylder's shoulders had tensed. "I assume he's heard the gist of it. I haven't had a chance to talk to him about you yet. You don't have to worry. I'll take care of that too."

"It was only—Colt made it sound as if someone had encouraged him to come after me right by your house— and those questions he had his guy ask about whether I'd spilled anything about the Nobles—"

Wylder swung around in his seat, his eyes flashing. "What are you trying to say?"

I stared right back at him, my hackles coming up. If he was going to make me spit it right out, then I would. "Maybe Ezra isn't so happy about having the princess of the Claws in his home. Maybe he already wants me gone."

Kaige sucked in a breath.

Wylder's expression went totally cold. "My father would never lower himself to making deals with scum like Colt. He'd be offended if you even mentioned the possibility. So don't."

He shoved open the door and got out without giving me a chance to respond. But I couldn't help noticing that he hadn't said his father would never turn on a guest of his son's or that he wouldn't have acted without speaking to Wylder first.

Maybe I was safe from Ezra Noble conspiring with my ex-fiancé, but that didn't mean I was actually *safe* here.

Wylder

I DIDN'T EVEN GET A CHANCE TO EAT BREAKFAST before Axel waylaid me in the hall. He stopped in front of me with a cigarette butt hanging from the corner of his mouth, but since it wasn't lit, I didn't have any grounds to get on his case about it. Which he knew. The bastard looked smug as ever.

"What?" I demanded, eyeing the other man. He was nearly half a foot shorter than me, but he'd never let that faze him. My father didn't put his trust in weaklings.

"Boss wants to see you," he said. "Right now."

Of course he did. After we'd gotten back from retrieving Mercy yesterday afternoon, I'd indicated to Dad that I had some things to discuss with him, but he'd only given me a chance to briefly cover the discovery of Titus's murderer before he'd put me off to handle other business.

Naturally, he'd call me in on his own schedule without any concern for how I might be occupying myself. I was lucky I'd been up, or Axel probably would have enjoyed dragging me out of bed.

Oh, well. I'd been mentally preparing for this meeting since yesterday. Might as well get it over with already, even if I'd rather have tackled it without the pang of hunger in my stomach.

Even if there was an insistent tug in my gut trying to convince me that I needed to see Mercy, to confirm with my own eyes that she was still here, before I did a single other thing.

I squashed down that urge with significant effort. "Is he in his office?" I asked.

Axel nodded, the glee visible on his face. He was enjoying this. "Yeah. Come on, I'll go with you."

"There's no need for that."

"I insist," Axel said with a snide smile. "I have some work to go over with him anyway."

He was probably only tagging along so that he could overhear the uncomfortable conversation Dad and I were going to have. But there was no stopping him. As Dad's right-hand man, sometimes he took undue advantage of his position, which also included getting on my nerves free of charge.

Walking through the halls to Dad's study, I mostly ignored the guy, but it occurred to me I'd better ask: "What have you told him about Mercy?"

He shrugged. "Not much. I figured that was a conversation you were better off handling."

I wasn't sure whether to be grateful that I was

getting to set the tone or annoyed that Axel was obviously anticipating the discussion going badly. I settled for both.

The door at the far end of the second-floor hall was closed. I knocked, steady and firm, the way Dad would see as a show of confidence.

"Come in," he called out from inside.

I walked straight in and came to a stop in front of his large oak desk. "I'm glad you have time to talk now, Dad."

My father looked up from the papers he was studying in the imposing leather chair behind his desk. Ezra Noble didn't believe in technology crowding his space. If you wanted to show him records of anything in here, you'd better have them printed out.

Other than the desk, the only furniture was a liquor cabinet stocked with vintages that plenty of people would drool over and a broad built-in book shelf. An oil-painted family portrait hung opposite the desk, showing my grandparents and Dad when he'd been a little younger than me.

We could have passed for twins if I'd traveled back in time to that moment. Now, a few streaks of silver had sprung up through his shock of auburn hair and faint lines of age marked the corners of his eyes and mouth. But none of that diminished the aura of authority that radiated off him.

"Wylder," he said softly. "I've been waiting for you." Dad never raised his voice, never showed any emotion on his blank face. You could never be prepared for what you'd get from him.

He had a way of speaking that was almost hypnotic, as if he could charm anyone he was talking to like a snake. His emerald-green eyes had a similar effect. I'd watched grown men reduced to stammers and quaking under the weight of his pointed stare. It could still send a shiver down my spine, though I was careful not to let that show.

"I came as soon as Axel told me you were ready to see me," I said, not bothering to mention that *I'd* been waiting for him since yesterday, and then added for politeness's sake, "Did you get the out-of-town business sorted out to your satisfaction?"

"It appears so, although a few of the minor pieces are still up in the air." He set the papers down on the corner of his desk and sat up straight, leaning his elbows on the desktop. "What is it you were in a hurry to report to me? Is there more going on beyond all this commotion with the groupies?"

How much had his men or Anthea filled him in on the details there? My aunt had promised she'd confirm my story, since she was the one he'd called in to investigate the murder, after all. He hadn't shown any surprise when I'd explained about Gia, even though the rest of us had found it hard to believe she'd been the culprit.

But then, maybe it didn't matter to him how far-fetched the scenario sounded as long as we were sure the matter was dealt with now. Gia definitely wasn't going to cause any more trouble.

"There is," I said, willing down my rising trepidation at this subject. "It's about Mercy Katz. She—"

He cut me off smoothly. "Ah, yes, the Claws heir

under my roof. Maybe you can explain why we're still entertaining her."

"She's quite a handful," Axel put in before I could reply. "Feisty little thing. You'll like her, boss."

One of Dad's eyebrows arched. "Will I?"

I cursed Axel silently, my stomach lurching. My father's interest in Mercy was the last thing I wanted.

Reining in my temper, I groped for the clearest, most dispassionate account I could give before this meeting went completely off the rails. "As I mentioned before, she's the one who made the connection between Titus and Gia. And the Claws don't exist anymore. She came to us because Colt Bryant, the leader of the Steel Knights, murdered her family and her father's closest associates."

Dad regarded me without any visible reaction. "And how does that affect us?"

It affected *me*, more than even I was really comfortable with. Even hearing him question it set off a fresh flare of anger, spurred hotter by the memory of finding Mercy scratched up and blood-splattered in the Bend yesterday. That fucking asshole had destroyed everything she had and then come back to finish the job by tearing her apart too—

I caught my hands just before they clenched and gave away my fury. Mercy was *ours* now. It was that simple. And Colt needed to find out exactly what happened to people who messed with what belonged to the Nobles.

I just couldn't put it to Dad quite like that without putting her at even more risk.

"Bryant's move on the Claws was the beginning of a hostile takeover," I said. "He's rapidly been expanding his territory throughout the Bend, and he's made it clear that he isn't going to stop there. He has plans to take Paradise City as well."

Behind me, Axel snorted. Dad raised both eyebrows. "And you feel this is a legitimate threat?"

I had to walk carefully here. I couldn't make it sound as if I doubted his hold over Paradise Bend, but I still had to make it clear that we needed to take action.

"Bryant has proven that he's ruthless and committed, and we've gotten reports of massive weapons shipments that he's brought in. He's been adding to his manpower as well, taking on new recruits. The Steel Knights' mark is all over the Bend, with none of the other gangs out there strong enough to contest his invasion into their territory. I'm sure we can stamp out his insurrection, but there'll be less bloodshed on our side if we crush him quickly and decisively before he's gained any more ground."

While I spoke, I eyed my father carefully. Mercy's suggestion that he might have encouraged Colt to snatch her off our doorstep had made me balk instinctively, but could I say absolutely for sure Dad wasn't playing some kind of long game I didn't know about? Nothing was ever completely off the table when it came to Ezra Noble. If he felt it'd advance his plans in some way that hadn't occurred to me, it was possible.

"And?" he prompted, giving away nothing.

Frustration raked through me. "Isn't that reason

enough? He's openly defying our authority. How can we let that stand?"

"Watch your tone," Dad said in a low voice, and my mouth snapped shut. I hated how quick I leapt to obey him, but I was well aware of the potential consequences of defiance. Questioning his judgment was only a short step from mutiny in his eyes, and he'd be a hell of a lot angrier about that from me than some small-time gang leader from the Bend.

"None of this explains why we're keeping this girl around," Dad said. "We're not a charity. If her father did his job right, she can fend for herself. Why shouldn't I have her escorted off the premises right now?"

I flinched inwardly. Because there were men crawling all through the Bend waiting for the chance to gut her for Colt's good favor. Because she'd proven she could stand with us, and I'd promised her my help—sworn it on my blood.

Because the thought of her vanishing from my life like she almost had yesterday set all my nerves on edge with the desire to rip apart whoever was responsible. Even if it was my father.

The strength of that reaction hit me like a cold slap, bringing me back to reality. *Nothing* could matter that much to me—definitely not some gang princess who'd turned up at our door like a lost kitten, no matter how capable she was. No matter how much space she'd somehow taken up in my head. This was just business.

It had to be, as far as Dad was concerned.

"She's had an inside view on Colt's operations, and she's eager to see him taken down after what he did to the Claws. I believe she's a valuable asset. She's proven herself loyal to us throughout the tests I've put her through. You know I wouldn't trust an outsider without good reason."

The look Dad gave me suggested he didn't actually believe he knew that for sure, even though I'd never given him any reason to doubt me. My teeth set on edge.

"Is that all there is to it?" he asked. "You have no other attachment to her?"

"No," I said, keeping my voice as firm and flat as I could. I couldn't afford for him to even consider that Mercy was more than a useful chess-piece. "I barely know her. I simply believe in making use of what we can while we can. Her father *has* trained her well. She's the one who discovered the weapons shipments. And she brought Titus's murderer to justice. Don't you think she deserves some recognition for that, not to be tossed onto the street? We wouldn't have much more honor than Bryant otherwise."

Dad rubbed his chin and glanced past me to Axel. "What do you think?"

Irritation flared through me. Why was he pulling the other man into this? Axel hadn't gotten involved in anything to do with Mercy other than to make accusations at my men and sneer at her.

Axel shrugged. "I think Colt is a fool, and sooner or later things will blow over. We've seen minor uprisings in the Bend before, and they've never come to much."

"This isn't the same as before," I said. "It's definitely not *minor*."

"What would you know?" Axel asked in a mocking voice he could only get away with because he'd been one of Dad's most trusted associates for decades. "You're just a twenty-two-year-old reckless kid."

"I'm not a kid," I snapped.

"Don't act like one, and I won't say it."

Dad shifted in his seat. "That's enough, Axel. Wylder knows the importance of keeping a cool head and evaluating a situation carefully. He wouldn't be in any position to take over the mantle of the Noble empire otherwise."

I wished there'd been a little more warmth in that vote of confidence, rather than the sense that I was the only option for an heir he had. I drew myself up straighter.

"It's not only the situation in the Bend. Yesterday, Colt and some of the Steel Knights grabbed Mercy off the sidewalk just outside the mansion, totally disregarding the protection we've been offering her. You couldn't get a more open challenge than that. If we let him get away with it, it'll look as if we're too weak to defend our own."

"She's hardly our own," Dad said with an edge I didn't like, but for the first time he did appear slightly annoyed. My concerns that he might have been involved in the kidnapping somehow faded. I could tell he hadn't even known about it—and he didn't like the disrespect of the act, even if he didn't care about Mercy particularly. "You confronted him to get her back?"

I had to bite back a smile of pride. "We didn't need to. I told you she's proven herself capable of handling herself. She got away from his men on her own, with more information about his plans."

Dad studied me with an air that made my skin tighten. "You admire her," he said after a moment.

A denial leapt to my tongue, but if I argued too vehemently, I'd only be proving my investment. "She's stronger than many of the men we've initiated, and I appreciate her dedication to seeing Bryant fall. I think that's only natural."

"Are you sure that's all it is? I don't want to invest my resources in a fool's errand over some pretty face that's caught your eye."

And he wouldn't want me getting invested in any "pretty face" at all. A memory flickered through my head: a slumped form cowering on the floor, my father standing over her, firm hands gripping my arms when I tried to throw myself forward—

Nausea coiled around my stomach. My expression had stiffened. I spoke with perfect calm. "I have only what's best for the Nobles and our dominion over Paradise Bend in mind. I've seen what the Steel Knights are doing firsthand."

Dad didn't answer, only staring thoughtfully into space. That was actually a good sign. If he'd been sure I was wrong, he wouldn't hesitate to say it.

I pushed my advantage. "Dad, let me take care of this. I won't let it interfere with any other business you have underway. My inner circle and I will spearhead the mission to crush Bryant—we can handle it. All I need is your go-ahead and the use of some of the men when they're not occupied under your command. It'll be a chance for me to show that there's more than one Noble to fear in Paradise City."

I could tell I'd convinced him. Triumph bloomed in my chest before he even opened his mouth.

"That sounds like a reasonable proposition," he said, picking up his papers again. "I expect to see the situation dealt with quickly and efficiently. And make sure you don't bring too big a war to our doorstep. We want our enemies subdued, not multiplying."

I suppressed a grin. "Of course. You can count on me."

Dad made a gesture of dismissal. I moved to go, relief washing through me. But I hadn't quite made it to the door before he spoke again. "Oh, and Wylder?"

I glanced back, dread unfurling through my chest. "Yes?"

"I'd like to speak with the Katz girl myself. I'll send Anthea to get her when I'm done with this. Make sure she's ready."

My heart lurched. I almost blurted out a ragged *No!* Instead, I clamped my jaw shut.

Of course he'd want to talk to her himself. It was only natural. As long as I hadn't fucked up, there was nothing to be worried about. No reason at all for my gut to be churning twice as hard as it'd been a few minutes ago.

I nodded, holding my emotions in check with an iron grip. "Sure, Dad. I'll let her know."

6

Mercy

Frank finished taping the last bandage in place and gave me a quick nod. "Everything's healing well. I think you can handle them from here."

I glanced down at the thin layer of gauze wrapped around my palms and the cut on my arm and then shot him a smile. "I'll try not to show up bleeding again any time soon."

The middle-aged guy who handled the Nobles' basic medical needs let out a chuckle at that. He offered me an energy drink from his kit.

Before I could reach for it, Kaige swiped it from his hand. "I'm going to have that."

Frank frowned at him. "It's not advisable to be buzzed on those things all the time."

A cocky grin stretched Kaige's mouth. "Define 'all the time.'"

The older man sighed and left, but Anthea shook

her head where she was standing by the stove. "You're going to ruin your appetite, and then what am I doing all this work for?"

"Aww, Auntie Anthea, you love cooking for us," Kaige drawled.

She skewered him with the kind of look that could penetrate steel. "I'm not *your* aunt. You're lucky I like my actual nephew enough to put up with the rest of you. Why don't you make yourself useful and get out the plates?"

Kaige headed over to the cupboards without complaint, and I swiveled on my stool to appreciate the excellent view of his sculpted backside. Next to me, Gideon was typically occupied with his tablet. Rowan jumped up at the other end of the island to grab some knives and forks. My stomach grumbled, the mouth-watering smell of the frying bacon reminding me how much I was looking forward to this breakfast.

The five of us had gathered in the kitchen on Anthea's insistence. She'd shown up first thing this morning, apparently as soon as she'd heard about the whole kidnapping thing, and fussed over me for several minutes before insisting we all needed a good meal. I didn't know where Wylder had gotten to—Rowan had thought he'd seen him heading to Ezra's office—but he could join us when he finished whatever business he was taking care of.

Anthea glanced over her shoulder at me. She was wearing one of her typical housewife-style floral dresses, the red waves of her hair pinned back from her face with a couple of silver clips, but the domestic vibe was totally deceiving. It hid a sharp, conniving, and fierce woman I hoped never to be on the wrong side of again. I still wasn't totally sure how I'd ended up on her good side.

Presumably the fact that I'd saved her from a murder attempt by a crazy gang groupie had something to do with it. The marks from when her car had crashed into the telephone pole still dappled her forehead and arms, but she'd recovered quickly.

"How are you feeling?" she asked me with genuine concern. It was bizarre to think that just a few days ago, she'd absolutely hated my guts and been trying her best to get me kicked out of the mansion. "Are you hurting much anymore?"

I flexed my hands. The small cuts from the window glass stung but didn't throb like they had yesterday. "Just a bit. They're getting better."

"Good. Now eat up. I'm not having you get weak on my watch." She set a plate of bacon, home fries, and an omelet oozing melted cheese in front of me. My stomach just about jumped up my throat to inhale it faster.

Kaige reached for one of the home fries, but Anthea batted his hand away with her spatula. "No, that's for only Mercy. Let her eat. She needs to get her energy back after everything that asshole ex of hers put her through. You'll get your own plate."

She looked at me fondly, and I found myself smiling back at her. When Anthea wasn't trying to poison me, she could be surprisingly nice. Wylder had called her his honorary mother, and she could definitely bring out the motherly vibes when she wanted to.

Not that I'd know much about motherliness, considering mine had vanished when I was six years old. The only piece of her I had left was the little silver bracelet she'd given me back then, tucked in my pocket as always like a good luck charm.

I popped a piece of bacon into my mouth and nearly swooned. "It's perfect," I told Anthea, swallowing the salty, chewy-yet-crunchy strip. "If you ever want to switch callings, I'm pretty sure you could make a killing running a diner."

Anthea snorted and turned to start dishing out the other plates. "No, thank you. I'll stick to poisons and not-really-accidental deaths. We all need our happy place."

As the guys returned to their seats around the island, Gideon propped his tablet next to his plate and shoveled a forkful of omelet into his mouth, barely seeming to taste it he was so absorbed in the screen. My gaze couldn't help tracking the tempting flick of his tongue over his lip ring.

It really wasn't fair that a guy so detached from the world outside of computers was so delicious.

"Let's talk strategy," he said. "Like Wylder mentioned before, we need to move in fast. Colt has been working at an astronomical speed to get his grip on the Bend. We have to cut down on his power."

Rowan waved his fork in the air. "But how? I'm sure he's got lots of underlings working for him. We can't just go straight at him."

Kaige let out an angry rumble. "Too bad. I'd *like* to punch him into a pulp."

Gideon rolled his eyes. "I'm sure we'll get to the part where you use your fists. But first I think we should weaken his defenses and reduce his resources."

"And how exactly are we going to do that?"

"Figuring out who his strongest allies are would probably be a good start," Rowan put in. "For him to think he's going to challenge us, he needs a large army. He's probably formed alliances with some of the smaller gangs to strengthen his position. But it might not be hard to win them back to our side."

I frowned. "That's something that bothered me. He's managed to take control over most of the Bend. I can't see most of even the small-time gangs rolling over without protest."

"It is odd," Gideon said.

Just then, Wylder stalked into the kitchen with his fists balled at his sides. He looked so grouchy he might as well have brought his own personal thundercloud with him.

I wasn't the only one who noticed. "Jeez, what's up with you?" Kaige asked before downing another mouthful of bacon.

Wylder's eyes briefly dropped to the space between Kaige and me at the island, and his gaze darkened. "I'm fine," he said brusquely, as if any of us were going to believe that when he said it that way.

His energy had seemed strange ever since they'd found me. Like something inside him had gotten wound up too tight and he hadn't figured out how to unravel it.

I wasn't sure I wanted to be around if whatever it was snapped.

Of course, he'd also been oddly protective of me the whole time. The knife he'd given me—one of his personal weapons—formed a solid weight in my hip pocket. It felt weirdly intimate, as if he was touching me there through it. The thought made my insides heat.

Ignoring his boss's mood, Kaige shifted his stool a little closer to me and squeezed my shoulder while still looking at Wylder. "You'll be glad to know this one's fine too. Frank already checked her over again." Shifting his gaze to me, he leaned a little closer with a teasing arch of his eyebrows. "We wouldn't want our kitten in anything but tiptop shape, right?"

The hunger in his eyes, which had nothing to do with breakfast now, sent a deeper flare of heat through me. There was a softer edge of his flirting than there'd been before, more gently playful than aggressively seductive. After all the back and forth between us, maybe he wasn't so sure of himself. But Kaige being uncertain was actually kind of cute.

I couldn't help thinking back to the way he'd picked me up with those bulging arms and set me on the hood of his car to ravish me. I did like him fierce too.

A smile touched my lips even as I had to hold back a squirm at the memory, and Kaige's grin widened. "And smiling too. Gotta have that beautiful smile."

My stomach really shouldn't have fluttered at such a small compliment, but it did.

"We're all glad you're okay," Rowan said.

Annoyingly, something in his voice provoked

another flutter. I shouldn't be getting at all mushy over the guy who'd already broken my heart once, even if he'd had my back a little in the past few days.

Wylder stalked past us to the counter without a word. My gaze flicked to Gideon, and I decided to flip it into a joke. I kicked him gently in the shin, making him finally look up from his tablet. "Maybe not all of you. Somehow I think Gideon might have been happier without me here complicating all his data."

Gideon blinked at me with those cool gray eyes of his, and a brief flicker of emotion passed through his angelic face. "Actually," he said matter-of-factly, "I'm finding your kind of complication can be gratifyingly stimulating."

That was a compliment, right? My body had certainly reacted as if it was, some of the heat from before settling between my thighs. Stimulation and gratification—I could definitely do with more of the latter to go with all of the former these guys had been supplying.

Kaige laughed and gave my ponytail an affectionate tug. "She is all that and more."

"Fucking damn it!" Wylder slammed his hands against the counter. I practically jumped out of my seat, and the tablet wobbled in Gideon's grasp. We all stared at the Noble heir, who whipped around to glare at all of us, his gaze searing. "Where is my brandy?"

"What brandy?" Rowan asked. His eyes mirrored the surprise that had shown up on everybody's face.

"*My* brandy," Wylder said in an irritated voice. "I left it in the kitchen."

"I put it back in the liquor cabinet by the bar," Anthea said.

"Well, you should have asked me before you did that," he snapped. "I could really use a drink right now."

Kaige rubbed his jaw. "It's nine in the morning, man."

Wylder spun on him. "Who the hell asked you? You know what? I can barely hear myself think around here."

"Did everything go all right with your father?" Gideon asked tentatively.

Wylder bared his teeth. "I can handle my father just fine, although it doesn't help that everyone keeps bringing him up. Why don't you all get out of here and let me have a little breakfast in peace?"

Oooh-kay then. Prince Wylder had clearly gotten up on the wrong side of the bed this morning. The other guys exchanged a glance and got up from their stools.

"Do you want me to—" Anthea started to offer, gesturing to the frying pan.

"No!" Wylder snapped. "I can figure out how to feed myself. Just go."

She made a tsking sound with her tongue, but she headed for the door with the others. I stood up too with every intention of leaving.

"Where do you think you're going, Kitty Cat?" Wylder asked in a growl of a voice when I was halfway to the door. The others had already vanished into the hall.

I turned, folding my arms over my chest, my skin

pricking with an unsettling energy that wasn't exactly unpleasant. "I thought you wanted us to leave."

He prowled toward me, every bit of muscular power in his well-built body on display. "I didn't say *you*."

"You kind of made it sound like all of—"

He stopped in front of me, close enough that I could feel his breath as he fingered the hem of my T-shirt. His gaze stayed fixed on me, utterly predatory. "Why are you in such a hurry? Missing their attention already?"

I glowered at him. "What are you even talking about?"

He waved toward the open door. "I think you like having them all focused on you. Fawning over you like you really are some kind of princess."

Oh, for fuck's sake. I leaned closer, holding his gaze, every nerve alight with the electricity building between us. "I *am* a princess. The Claws Princess, as you like to remind me so much."

"And you love that too." His face tipped even closer to mine, those gorgeous green eyes flashing. "It's my attention you crave the most, isn't it? You like to pretend you don't care, but I know you better than that by now."

I snorted even though an eager shiver had rippled through me at his words. "Spoiler alert: not everything is about you."

"No, but this is."

I cocked my head, my neck straining a bit as I glared up at him. "Maybe this is about you. What are you so pissed off about anyway? Annoyed that I ruined your valiant rescue effort yesterday by rescuing myself?"

His jaw clenched. "I would have torn through every one of those assholes."

"But instead you're tearing into the rest of us. Nice." I exhaled sharply and started to turn. "Maybe I *should* just go—"

Wylder grabbed my elbow and jerked me back toward him, his fingers scorching my skin. I shoved at his chest instinctively, and he shoved right back— pushing the door closed and me up against it. "I didn't say you could leave."

"I don't answer to you, you prick."

"Then it's about time you started."

"You have some nerve," I spat out, and then his whole body was against me, pulsing with heat. It was all I could do not to melt right into him.

"You're so fucking sexy when you're furious," he said, and then his mouth crashed down on mine.

I should have pushed him off me. That would have been the sensible thing to do. But sensible wasn't exactly my specialty, and the truth was, my entire being had been craving this moment since the first time Wylder had touched me—hell, since the first time he'd *looked* at me.

It felt as inevitable as gravity or a magnetic force. We'd been bound to collide eventually. Why the hell should I deny it?

Especially when it felt this fucking good.

His mouth moved against mine, furious and urgent.

I gripped his shirt and kissed him right back, refusing to back down.

His tongue traced the seam of my mouth before flicking inside. Mine tangled with it, dueling for dominance. I felt the grin on his face as our mouths mashed together. Neither of us had any plans to give up control.

So it was probably a good thing that it turned out we both wanted the same thing.

Wylder twisted the lock on the kitchen door and then swung me around to set my ass on the nearest countertop. The cool granite bit into the backs of my thighs for just a second before he heated everything up again by pushing between my legs.

I grinded against him, giddy at the feel of the hard bulge already pressing against the fly of his jeans. My hands pulled at his hair before slightly massaging his nape.

He groaned against my mouth, and that only turned me on more. I liked this version of Wylder who wasn't Mr. Cool and Cocky but lost in his lust, even if I was lost here with him.

His hot tongue delved into my mouth again and mimicked the action of a cock, doing shallow laps at first and then moving deep inside. I moaned and began to rock against him, seeking more of him. Wylder's hand skimmed down my chest and rolled my nipple between his deft fingers. I hissed encouragingly at the contact.

Panting, he broke the kiss. He brought his other hand to my cheek with startling tenderness considering the rage in his voice as he traced the bruise Colt had given me. "I'm going to kill him myself."

My own anger flared through the flames of desire. "He's mine to destroy."

Wylder held my face and looked straight into my eyes. There was something so intense and determined in his it felt like a promise. "Fine. Then we'll do it together."

His gaze broke from mine, but only so he could suck a path down the side of my neck. His fingers squeezed and kneaded my breasts as if he couldn't get enough of them. An embarrassing whimper tumbled out of me, and then another when his mouth finally descended on a nipple and sucked on it through the thin cotton of my top. My body thrummed.

It wasn't enough. I needed all of him this time.

Wylder seemed to have the same idea. He tugged at the zipper of my jeans and then pulled back to see my expression. In answer, I drew his hand to my throbbing cunt.

He squeezed tightly, making me clench with a wave of pleasure. "Fuck," he said under his breath. "You're delectable."

He tugged at my jeans so viciously I was almost afraid he'd rip the denim apart. Part of me wanted him to. He wrenched his own jeans down and freed his cock. It sprang to attention, huge and gleaming with precum and a Prince Albert piercing at the tip.

Fuck me.

My mouth watered at the sight. What would it be

like to feel the metal rolling against my tongue as I took his dick in my mouth?

I reached out and rolled the ring between my fingers, spreading the slickness of his precum. Wylder's eyes closed, and he let out a grunt. But as I continued to move my hand up and down his shaft, he pushed it away with a growl. "Not right now. We're coming together this time, and I'm going to be balls deep inside you when we do."

If I'd been wet before, those words made me gush. He took a condom from his back-pocket and ripped the foil with his teeth before rolling it on. With one almost frantic thrust, he filled me to the brim.

I gasped at the fullness of his thick cock. He didn't give me a chance to get accustomed to his girth as he started to pump into me, but I was ready for him anyway. The stretch sent a delicious burn of bliss all through my torso.

As he stroked even deeper, I pushed my hips toward him. My fingers scraped his back. Our wild breaths mingled together, our bodies jerking and slapping against each other as our breaths fractured. It was savage and raw, nothing even remotely gentle about it, but somehow I felt closer to him in that moment than I had to any lover before.

Sweat trickled down my back. I arched my spine, curling one of my legs around Wylder so that he could find even deeper access. The new angle made him hit a spot so good my eyes rolled heavenward. I matched his rhythm, his thrusts plunging deeper still as he sent me careening toward my orgasm.

I looked up at him in the same instant that he looked down. There was a wild urgency in his green eyes. "You're mine," he snarled. "*Mine.*"

I didn't think it was just lust in his voice. There was something more than that, something that made my heart wobble.

Before I could examine that impression too closely, Wylder bucked into me harder and faster than before, setting off a chain reaction of sensations inside me. Pleasure blazed through me and exploded in my core. I leaned in and bit him on his arm to muffle my scream.

Wylder jerked inside me, his muscles contracting. "Oh, fuck," he muttered. With a hitch of his hips, he emptied himself inside me.

We stayed locked together for several seconds. I was still clutching his shirt, trying to catch my breath. Wylder closed his eyes as if he wasn't ready for the moment to end.

Then he opened them again, and something hardened both in his gaze and his stance. The fire in those emerald orbs died in an instant. Something cold took its place, and a chill washed over me in turn.

He pulled out of me, yanking off the condom and heaving up his jeans in rough movements.

I pulled my panties up, watching him. "Let me just remind you that *you* were the one—"

"Don't even go there." He zipped himself up and then discarded the used condom in the trash. Then he jerked around to face me, his expression so emotionless it was hard to believe he'd even touched me, let alone fucked me so desperately.

"My dad wants to talk to you," he said flatly.

That'd come out of nowhere. "About what?"

"He wants to discuss the situation with the Steel Knights and your position here. You'd better get changed so you're ready when he calls on you." And just like that he walked out of the kitchen, without giving me so much as a backward glance.

Mercy

"Jackass," I muttered as I made my way upstairs. But as much of a jackass as he'd been, Wylder was right about one thing: I couldn't very well present myself to Ezra Noble in my current ravaged state, smelling of his son.

I'd never had a problem enjoying sex as something purely physical before. Why the hell should it matter that Wylder had gone cold and distant the second our passion had flamed out?

But it was impossible to forget how he'd looked as he touched my cheek and swore to kill Colt, the intensity in his eyes as he'd pumped away inside me, his usual cool, commanding mask giving way to show something deeper inside.

But maybe I'd been mistaken about that. He hadn't even asked me if I was okay or if it was good for me. Maybe the smug bastard already knew how much I had liked it. My pussy throbbed at the memory as if it wanted more of him. Traitorous body.

Well, it was done now, and it'd been fan-fucking-tastic sex while we'd been having it. I'd just focus on that and let the Noble heir do whatever he felt like doing with himself now. *I* certainly wasn't doing him again while he was being such a prick.

Ducking into the second-floor bathroom, I checked myself in the mirror. As I'd expected, my hair was a total mess. I washed my face and then quickly hopped into the shower, hoping a quick shampoo and rubdown with soap would help me look presentable.

When I came back to the guest bedroom where I'd been staying in the mansion, I found Anthea waiting for me by my bed. She pointed at the neatly pressed pile of clothes on the covers. "My brother has summoned you," she said, somehow managing to sound both wry and serious at the same time. "I thought you might need this."

"Thanks so much," I said gratefully. I had been wondering what I was going to wear to meet Ezra. The only clothes I had now were thrift store tees and jeans that weren't going to generate much respect, and most of those had cooking oil stains on them courtesy of hostile groupies.

While Anthea waited, I quickly changed into the gray slacks and pearl-pink blouse she'd brought me. The outfit was too feminine and business-y for me to feel totally comfortable in it, but she knew her brother better than I did.

If I thought Wylder was a piece of work, his father

was a whole other level of dangerous. He was the power behind the Nobles, the one who'd held them together and even expanded their reach beyond the boundaries of the county over the past couple of decades. What was he going to think of me?

I found myself staring down at the tee I'd just taken off, the fabric scrunched in my fist. My gaze lingered on the faint pattern of the oil stain that hadn't quite washed out.

Anthea must have noticed it too. Her lips thinned. For a second, she looked oddly uncomfortable.

I braced myself, half-expecting some cutting remark to come out of her after all, to discover that her sudden turn-around on me could turn back just as quickly. Instead, she shook back her hair and sighed.

"Look," she said. "About before, the things I said to you, the things I did... I was only looking out for Wylder and his boys, all right? It wasn't anything personal. I didn't know you. Most of the women who turn up here don't have anything on their minds except getting as prominent a Noble as they can on the hook. It took me a while to see that there's a lot more to you than that."

Was that... an apology, from the deadly Anthea Noble? I managed to catch myself before I outright gaped at her. A smile tugged at my lips, a strange warmth unfurling in my chest.

No matter what an ass Wylder decided to be, I did have at least one friend here now. Which was one more than I'd ever been able to count on in my life before.

"I know," I said. "I wish you'd seen it a little sooner,

but—I've got bigger things to worry about than staying pissed off about that. Besides, you do make a really good breakfast. I'm happy staying on your good side and forgetting about the rest."

Anthea laughed and gave me a sly look. "I wish I'd figured it out sooner too. You are going to make life around here much more interesting—I think in a good way." She dragged in a breath. "Assuming Ezra doesn't find any fault in you. Are you ready to go? He won't like it if we keep him waiting very long."

In my newfound ease with her, I realized there was one thing I wanted to ask her, and not out in the hall where any of Ezra's underlings might overhear. "Anthea —Colt was talking as if someone had put him up to taking and torturing me. Do you think there's any chance Ezra would have done something like that?"

I cringed inwardly as I asked, worried she'd get offended, but instead she knit her brow, her gaze turning thoughtful. At least she seemed to be seriously considering it, unlike Wylder who'd given the idea a kneejerk rejection I didn't totally trust.

"I can see why you might wonder," she said after a moment, "but I honestly don't think so. If Ezra were upset with you or wanted information out of you, he'd have his own men handle it. He wouldn't trust any other gang, especially one from the Bend, to do the job to his requirements. Why would he? Colt has nothing he wants, and he certainly wouldn't feel the need to bargain with a man he considers below him."

That all made sense. Even Wylder hadn't seen Colt as a real threat for a long time, so it was hard to believe

Ezra would be so frightened by him he'd make a deal rather than simply crushing him. I'd have to see how this meeting went, but a weight lifted from my chest. I swept my fingers over my hair one more time and nodded. "That's good to know. All right, let's go."

Anthea led me down the hall toward the opposite wing of the house. I willed my heart not to beat too fast. Even if Ezra hadn't been behind my kidnapping, he was still no one to be trifled with. "So, what's he like? Your brother?"

Anthea hummed to herself. "It's hard to put Ezra in a box. I can spout a whole lot of adjectives, but they really won't do him any justice. You'll see when you meet him."

That was really encouraging. I held back a grimace. I'd only seen the head of the Nobles a few times at a distance when my dad had pointed him out around town. I'd heard the stories, though—horrifying ones about what happened to people who crossed him.

Anthea glanced at me, and her expression softened with a hint of sympathy. "Look, you should be fine. You solved a very large problem we were having and protected me while you were doing it. You just have to be a little careful about what you say."

I wet my lips. "Okay. Careful how?"

"My brother is very particular, so tell him only the things that he's asked of you. He has a way of twisting your words and then holding them against you. We don't want that happening now, especially with how things stand with the Steel Knights."

Oh, great. "I'll, uh, keep that in mind," I said.

Anthea looked sheepish. "Did I come off a little intense? I swear I'm only trying to prepare you."

"No, no, this is good," I said. At least she was trying to warn me about him, which was far better than Wylder abandoning me in the kitchen. What the hell was that about anyway? If I didn't know any better, I'd think that the sex we'd had was a scenario I'd concocted in my head. If only it hadn't been so fucking good.

We passed three girls who I recognized immediately from the groupie room. One of them—one I'd sent running with a few threats the other day—glared at me.

"They don't know what really happened between Gia and you," Anthea said, her voice low. "But they have their ideas, none of them good."

Let them think whatever they wanted. I walked by without giving them another glance, but one of them spit right at my feet.

Anthea whirled in on them. "Do we have a problem?"

Their eyes widened. One of the girls shook her head. "No, we were just—"

"Then you'd better clean that up." Anthea pointed to the wet spot on the hardwood floor. When they all stayed frozen, she glowered at them. "Well, get on with it."

One of the girls twitched and fished a tissue out of her pocket, kneeling to dab at the spit. Anthea clearly had a reputation around here. She was still a force of fury, only thankfully it was no longer directed at me.

"Get out of here," Anthea said when the girl was

done, and the three of them took off down the hallway toward the staircase.

Anthea gazed after them, frowning. "I know not to underestimate *them* now too."

Memories of Gia flashed through my mind: the fury twisting her pale face when she'd attacked me the other night, the mess of blood and brains after Wylder had shot her in the head. My stomach turned. That wasn't what I needed to be thinking about when I was about to face Ezra Noble.

"Anything else I should keep in mind about Ezra?" I asked as we started walking again.

"Well... if my brother bothers you too much, imagine him with a carrot on his head."

I stared at her. "*What?*"

"Trust me," she said as if she were confiding a secret. "It really works."

I still wasn't sure if she was being serious, but even if she was only making a joke to lighten the mood, it'd worked. I found myself chuckling thinking of the most dangerous person in all of Paradise City with a carrot balanced in his auburn hair.

We turned a corner and headed toward the back of the house. "You'll be meeting Ezra in what he calls his 'audience room,'" she said. "He has it set up specifically for meeting with people he doesn't trust enough to bring into his study. Don't let that get you down. He can count the number of people he'll let into his actual workspace on his hands without running out of fingers."

Fair enough. Why would a man like him invite a stranger into his inner sanctum?

Anthea opened a door at the end of the hall and ushered me into a large, sparsely decorated room. A picture window looked out over the back lawn. Other than a watercolor painting hanging opposite it, the walls were bare. A buttery leather armchair stood on one side of a glass coffee table, looking every bit a throne. A matching sofa sat opposite it, with a few scattered chairs behind that.

"Have a seat," Anthea said, motioning to the sofa, and then pressed my elbow reassuringly. "Don't worry, you'll be good."

After the hurricane that'd been sex with Wylder, this situation did nothing to calm my nerves. I inhaled deeply and sank onto the sofa, which was almost disturbingly smooth and soft. Like it was meant to lull whoever was sitting on it into a false sense of security. Anthea stayed standing beside the coffee table.

The door on the other side of the room opened, and a man stepped in. At the sight of him, my pulse hiccupped.

I'd forgotten just how much Wylder resembled his father. Ezra had identical bright green eyes and auburn hair other than a few streaks of gray in it, as well as similarly sculpted features and broad shoulders. The most noticeable difference was the way he moved. I'd seen Wylder stalk and prowl across a room, but his father made his way over to his chair with the air of a watchful wolf, absolutely animalistic and feral.

I started to stand up from my seat in case he expected the gesture of respect, but Ezra just motioned me to stay put. He settled into his own chair, poised so regally it was even easier to picture it as a throne. His piercing gaze took me in. "So, here's the Katz heir in my home."

"Thank you for having me here," I said quickly.

"It's not by my choice."

The weight of his stare tangled my tongue. "I mean —thank you for taking the time to see me."

"You're here to see me," he said, arching one eyebrow.

Shit. I was saying all the wrong things already. Now I knew exactly what Anthea had meant about Ezra Noble twisting one's words. What had she said? Focus on only what he asked me, nothing else. I could do that.

"That's true," I said, and simply waited.

Ezra let the silence hang for long enough that my skin started to itch. Then he leaned slightly forward. "I hear you're the one who solved Titus's murder." I could hear the skepticism in his voice.

I drew myself up a little straighter. "Yes, I did. It was one of the groupies. She thought that—" I stopped myself. My gut told me that I shouldn't mention the fact that Gia had been convinced that Titus was trying to kill Kaige. But Ezra was still waiting for me to finish. "She thought that he was a threat to her, so she decided to take him out first."

"I see," he said. "And why did you end up here in the first place?"

That was familiar territory. I'd been expecting this question and had the answer ready. "I guess you've also heard about how Colt Bryant, my ex-fiancé, slaughtered my father and the rest of my family. I have to make him pay for that betrayal, but I knew I couldn't take him on without help. The Nobles are the most powerful family in Paradise Bend, and you have a stake in keeping the lesser gangs in line. Coming here seemed like the obvious choice."

"That's why you approached my son?" Ezra asked. Was his gaze even more penetrating than before? I fought down the urge to rub my arms as if he might be able to spot traces of my hookup with Wylder on my skin. Who knew how he'd react if he found out I'd caught that much of Wylder's attention—for however long his interest had lasted.

"Only because you weren't available," I said, keeping my voice as even as I could. "I came here looking for you right after the massacre, but I found Wylder. At first he was reluctant to help me, but I struck a bargain with him. Finding out who killed Titus and clearing Kaige's name was my way of proving I deserved his— and your—help." I assumed Wylder had already told him about our deal.

"She consistently came through on every occasion we tested her," Anthea put in, conveniently leaving out my meltdown during their freezer test. The less Ezra heard about *that* embarrassing incident, the better.

"Very impressive," Ezra said in a tone that suggested it wasn't impressive at all. He folded his hands together on his lap with a flex of his fingers. "What about your fiancé, Colt? Why do you think he went rogue? Did he give you any indication of what he was going to do?"

He had used the term fiancé—without the "ex"—for some reason. I didn't like the implication. He definitely didn't sound like someone who'd had inside dealings with the man.

"Apparently he believed that my father was out to double-cross him, so he decided to attack first," I said. "As far as I know, he's delusional. My father showed every sign of looking forward to the alliance between the Claws and the Steel Knights. And I had no idea my *ex*-fiancé was planning anything violent until it happened."

Ezra chuckled coolly in response, probably noting my emphasis. "I'm certain it's a sore topic for you."

Was he trying to ruffle me? I kept it short and sweet. "He's attempted to kill me several times. Any ties of loyalty or commitment between us are gone."

But Ezra managed to turn that around on me too. "And how can I be sure your loyalties to us will be steadier?"

I bit my tongue before a snarky remark like "How about don't try to murder me?" slipped out, but I didn't know what to say instead.

Anthea coughed, stepping in. "I've told you that Mercy saved my life. She did everything she could to warn me that Gia had messed with my car, and then she risked her own life to prevent a probably fatal accident. And I hadn't gone easy on her before then. *I* have no doubts about her sense of loyalty."

Irritation flickered across her brother's face at the interruption, but when he spoke again, his voice was even. "You can be sure I'm keeping that in mind, Anthea." His attention stayed fixed on me. "I'm curious about your position in the Claws. You're technically the heir, but I've had no reports of you working alongside your father. How much did he let you get involved?"

I winced inwardly, but I had to go with the truth. "He didn't let me. He never brought me in on anything directly related to his business dealings. But he made sure I was capable of holding my own among his men with intensive training starting from an early age."

"And yet you were only a prop," Ezra said.

I bristled. "Not by my choice. I kept myself as aware of everything that was going on as I could."

"So you went against his wishes?"

I had run myself into a wall. I shot a pleading look at Anthea, but she only offered a fleeting grimace. Ezra Noble was really good at what he did.

"Only when it was absolutely necessary," I said, trying to keep my voice level. "I did my best to meet my father's expectations, but he was never going to be happy with a girl as his heir. I wanted to be ready in case I needed to step up. He severely underestimated me and my capabilities, choosing to trust an outsider instead—and in the end, that's what killed him."

"What would you have done differently that night?" Ezra asked.

Oh, I'd thought that through hundreds of times, how I could go back and do things differently. Unfortunately, every time I came to the same conclusion. "I didn't have a chance to get the upper hand in the moment. If I'd been on more equal footing with Colt with a proper position in the Claws, maybe I'd have been able to pick up the signs of the coming betrayal ahead of time. What I *wish* I could have done is stab that bastard in his neck, gouge out his eyes, and then hang up his body in the middle of the Bend for every Claws member to spit on."

Ezra Noble might have looked faintly impressed. "As I suppose he would deserve. And you're ready to swear full loyalty to the Nobles now?"

"You've given me protection. You've given me hope when I had none. I owe you everything I can offer for that."

"Wylder has said he'll help you in your crusade against Bryant." Ezra shifted in his seat, giving me the impression of an eagle about to swoop in to his prey.

I chose my words carefully. "Those were the terms of our deal. He's a force I'll be grateful to have on my side."

Ezra considered me for a long moment. I didn't think I'd managed to get through to him as much as I'd have liked to, but hopefully it'd been enough.

"Very well then," he said finally—and maybe a little reluctantly. "I accept you as a new initiate of the Nobles. But be aware that I'll expect you to face all the same dangers my men do. Are you ready for that?"

He looked like he wanted me to say no. In this one thing, I was going to disappoint him.

"I am," I said, feeling like I had just signed my soul away with invisible ink.

Mercy

An energetic rapping of knuckles against my bedroom door brought me over. I opened it to find Kaige standing outside. He took in my questioning look and tipped his head toward the hall. "You're coming, aren't you?"

I blinked at him. "Coming where?"

His forehead furrowed. "Didn't— We're going into the Bend to start reminding the Steel Knights who's boss."

"What, now?" At his nod, I marched past him into the hall. "Of course I want to be there for that."

I might have believed it was a miscommunication, but when we found the other three guys around the back of the garage, examining a couple cases of pistols, the hardening of Wylder's expression told me I'd been left in the dark on purpose.

"You don't need to come along," he said shortly,

already turning his attention back to the guns. "We can handle this without you."

What the hell? He'd been a jerk about our hook-up, but this was something else entirely.

I set my hands on my hips. "I'm sure you *can*. But I'm also sure this is my fight even more than it's yours, so I'm fucking well going to be part of making it happen."

"The four of us know how to work together as a team. You'd just get in the way. Go find something else to entertain yourself with, Princess."

Oh, so we were back to "Princess" again, were we? My teeth set on edge at the sting of his comments. The other guys glanced between us, tense and uncertain.

Then I registered exactly what Wylder had said. "Four? Gideon's going?" I realized how insulting the disbelief in my voice might sound a second too late and quickly backtracked, catching the tech genius's gaze. "I mean, usually you'd want to stay back here and focus on the data, right?"

"I insisted on coming along because I want to see what's going on in the Bend firsthand to supplement that data," Gideon said, cool and even. "I don't expect to be involved in much of the fighting. I know my limitations."

I spun back toward Wylder. He could lash out at me all he wanted. I'd already survived his wrath before. If it took a little more work to shut off the part of myself that cared what he thought of me now, oh well.

"If he can insist, then I can insist too," I said. "And I

do. Insist. Colt is mine to crush, and I plan to be there every step of the way, whether you like it or not."

The glare Wylder shot me showed he didn't like it at all. "Wylder," Kaige said tentatively, and his boss let out a huff. Maybe he'd decided it'd be too much hassle arguing more.

"Have it your way, then. Just stay out of *our* way. And that means making sure you can defend yourself." Wylder motioned to the guns. "Take your pick."

I hesitated, taking in the array of pistols and lingering on the sleek one he'd already picked up. "You mean—"

"I promised you a gun, and I'm a man of my word. Get on with it."

Well, if he was going to be that pissy about it...

I pointed at the one in his hands. "I want that one."

Somehow his scowl got even deeper, but he shoved it toward me. "Then it's yours. Come on, everyone, let's move out."

The guys all grabbed a gun for themselves, even Gideon. I tucked mine into the back of my jeans like they did. I'd handled a gun plenty of times, but my dad had never let me keep one on me, so I wasn't used to carrying one.

He'd probably been afraid I'd get too tempted to put a bullet in his head. There'd been times when I might have.

We tramped into the garage and headed to a car that turned out to be Rowan's, which was a good choice for a mission to the Bend—unlike Wylder and Kaige, he'd gone for something low key rather than obviously expensive. The silver Toyota sedan had plenty of room for all of us and looked to be a model at least a few years old rather than shiny and new.

Rowan drove us into the Bend with ease. Of course, he'd spent much of his formative years growing up there if not as many as I had. It used to be his home too.

Wylder sat in hostile silence the whole way, only speaking up a couple of times to give an instruction. But when Rowan stopped down the street from a trio of men wearing the Steel Knights' red bandanas around their upper arms, the Noble heir straightened up with an eager expression.

The guys were circling a girl who looked barely eighteen and absolutely terrified. Their voices wafted through the open window to me with the hot summer air. "Nice tits you got there. What are you hiding under that pretty skirt of yours?"

I bristled and reached for the car door, but Wylder shook his head. "Stay inside. You don't jump in unless it's absolutely necessary."

Rowan killed the engine and got out of the car alongside Wylder and Kaige. I stayed where I was only because Wylder might have a bit of a point about my presence throwing off the guys' dynamic. I didn't want to be the reason one of them got messed up. Next to me, Gideon was snapping pictures of the buildings around us with his tablet. My hands balled on my lap.

The Steel Knights looked up and noticed the guys approaching them, frowns crossing their faces. "What the fuck do you want?" one of them called out, swinging a bat that was covered with nails.

"Ideally you, lying in several pieces on the ground," Wylder said in an easy tone, as if he were talking about nothing but the weather. "I think it's time you remembered who actually owns this county, and it's not the Steel Knights."

The girl took the distraction as an opportunity to make a run for it, but one of the Steel Knights yanked her back by her hair. As she shrieked, he looked toward Wylder and the rest with a challenge in his eyes.

I growled in anger. What an absolute shit-prick.

Kaige barreled towards the Steel Knights instantly, sending two of them flying to the ground. One of them cocked his gun at him, but before he could pull the trigger, Kaige ripped it out of the guy's hands and threw it away. He slammed his fists into the sides of the guy's head hard enough to make him yelp.

The one who'd grabbed the girl pushed her away and started to make a run for it. But Rowan was faster. He sprinted up to him and drove his heel into the back of his knee to topple him. The man reached for his gun and shot at him blindly. Rowan easily ducked and twisted the gun away from his hand while he stepped on his wrist. The man groaned in agony.

Where had my easy-going high school sweetheart learned *those* moves?

The guys didn't take out their own guns. They didn't want to kill these assholes—not today. They were sending a message, and they needed the losers to go deliver it to their idiot friends. And to Colt.

The girl dashed off. One of the men on the ground stood up shakily. He reached for his bat and brought it crashing down on Kaige's arm, but the jerk of Kaige's wrist sent the weapon smashing into its owner's face in turn. Blood gushed from his forehead. He swore and took off.

Rowan dragged what looked like the leader of the bunch over and threw him at Wylder's feet. Bending down to the battered man's level, Wylder yanked his head up by the hair and looked him straight in the eye.

"What do you fucking want from us?" the man groaned.

"You've forgotten who the boss is around here," Wylder said in a chilling voice. "This is your only *gentle* reminder. The Nobles are clearing the trash from our streets. And if anyone asks who gave us that authority, tell them you talked to Wylder Noble himself."

He picked up the nail-studded baseball bat and then drove it into the man's palm, drawing blood and a scream that echoed down the street. I had no sympathy for Wylder's victim, especially not after the way that prick had assaulted the girl. He could consider it payback.

Rowan ripped off the bandana from the man's arm and handed it to Wylder, who took something out of his pocket. At first I thought he was reaching for a gun, but then I realized that it was a lighter.

Wylder placed it under the bandana and set it on fire. He dropped it on the ground, watching as the hungry flames curled around the Steel Knight symbol, devouring it. It seemed so prophetic that goosebumps ran down my arms. This was the beginning of the end.

When the bandana was all but destroyed, Wylder

stepped on it with his heel deliberately and said, "Remember this the next time we meet." He kicked the guy in the ribs for good measure and left him groaning on the pavement.

Kaige and Rowan got into the car after Wylder. We still had more work to do.

We stopped again a few streets down in front of a vandalized laundromat. Kaige stepped out first, eyeing the four Steel Knights who were hanging out on the sidewalk, probably looking to deal. None of them had any weapons in sight, but I suspected they had at least a knife or a gun on them.

Kaige casually strolled up to them. "You need something, big guy?" the closest one asked.

"I don't know. I was looking for Cunt Town and my GPS seems to tell me it's here," Kaige said with a smirk.

"You son of a bitch," the man growled and raised his fist. Wrong move. Kaige caught him easily and twisted his hand. I heard the crunch of bones breaking.

The other guys stared at Kaige in shock and fury. "You're not going to get away with this," one of them said.

Before we knew what was happening, he whistled shrilly. Kaige punched him hard, again and again, until he shut up.

The other Steel Knights tried to bolt, but Wylder and Rowan moved to intercept them. "I don't think so," Wylder said with a cruel smile that somehow electrified me even though I knew how unpleasant his viciousness could be. "No one's leaving here without paying their dues."

A couple of the guys swung at them—and the third managed to dart between them while they were occupied, dashing past the car.

Oh no, he didn't. I didn't give a fuck what Wylder had ordered me to do.

I shoved open the door and leapt out. Flinging myself after the escapee, I latched my fingers around his arm and wrenched him back toward me—and into my fist. The snap of his breaking nose was the most satisfying thing I'd heard all day. A weird, woozy exhilaration swept through me.

I stomped my heel down on the guy's shin and kneed him in the gut for good measure. When I turned around, Wylder and Rowan were striding over to me, the guys they'd been dealing with slumped on the ground. I braced myself for Wylder to berate me.

Instead, his eyes slid to the man I'd knocked down and back to my face. His jaw worked. "We got them all," he said. Not a "thank you" or a "good job," but I'd still take it over a "I told you to stay in the car."

Just as he motioned toward the Toyota, several motorcycles roared down the street, more men with red bandanas riding them. A black muscle car followed them.

I tensed, my gut lurching. I'd know that shape anywhere. I'd been *inside* it more times than I could count.

My voice came out thin. "That's my father's car."

Kaige rejoined us, and we held our ground around the Toyota. The motorcycles formed a semi-circle around us, but if we'd jumped into the car and gunned it, we could have crashed through them. I could tell from the set of Wylder's shoulders that he had no intention of running scared, though.

The car pulled up across the street from us. The windows were tinted so it was impossible to see who was inside. Then the door opened and Colt stepped out.

My blood started to boil, both at the sight of him and the fact that my murderous ex had commandeered Dad's car. I took a step forward automatically, but Kaige caught me by my elbow.

More of Colt's men leapt out of the car. I recognized one of them as one of my father's associates, Mr. Jenner. The sinewy-limbed man with graying jowls had come around the house once a month or so to report to Dad and take new orders.

I gaped openly at him. He had switched sides already? Un-fucking-believable.

Colt stayed where he was by the driver's side door. "I heard there was a major disturbance going on and thought I'd better deal with it myself. I'm going to ask that you go back to your pretty palace in the city and leave my men and my streets alone."

Wylder scoffed. "*Your* streets? All of Paradise Bend answers to the Nobles. The fact that you've forgotten that is exactly why we're here."

Colt feigned a look of surprise. "I had no idea the Nobles were even interested in the Bend. I thought you deemed all of us beneath you."

As he spoke, another car had parked behind his. A few men got out, staying a little to the side of the confrontation. More bodyguards, I assumed, but something about their stern expressions and confident poses sent an uneasy tremor through me. They weren't wearing the Steel Knights bandanas on their arms.

Who the hell were *they*?

"You are beneath us," Wylder said flippantly. "And that's where you should stay—under our heels. Do you think we don't know everything you're planning? Consider this a warning and back off *now*."

Colt's eyes flashed. The newcomers didn't stir, seemingly content just to watch. They looked almost bored.

No, they weren't bodyguards. I frowned. It was almost as if they were supervising the situation rather than participating.

My ex-fiancé crossed his arms over his chest and flicked his icy stare toward me just for a moment before turning back to Wylder. "Am I to take it that you're siding with the Claws, then?"

"We're enforcing the power of the Nobles and the respect we're due," Wylder shot back.

"The Steel Knights have been instigating violence all over the Bend," Rowan said more evenly. "That isn't good for anyone—except maybe you, for now."

Colt chuckled darkly. "When was the Bend ever free of violence?"

"There used to be a lot less," I snapped.

Beside me, Kaige flexed his substantial muscles. "And it doesn't belong to you. You don't get to make decisions like that."

"Yet," Colt said. "I'm not a ruler. I definitely do not rule these men, if they happen to take offense." He gestured to the biker gang members flanking him. The threat was clear.

"But they wear marks of loyalty to you, so we'll hold you responsible all the same," Wylder replied. "And that includes my father. But if you'd like to have Ezra Noble and his full force cracking down on you within the hour..."

Colt's smile froze on his face. "I'm sure that won't be necessary today. You're always welcome to visit the Bend as you please. I have nothing but respect for the Nobles." He shifted his gaze to me again. "Rats are a totally different thing."

He made a brisk gesture, and some of the motorcycles eased out of our way. "You're free to leave."

Wylder's jaw ticked, but he didn't say anything. Picking a fight after Colt had stood down would make us look like the bad guys in this scenario, and we'd have a hard time winning anyway when we were so grossly outnumbered.

"I appreciate your recognition of what we're owed," Wylder said, and motioned to us. He stood there with his gun in his hand, never letting his attention waver from Colt while the rest of us slid into the car.

Only when Rowan had ignited the engine did Wylder come around to his seat. We cruised through the opening between the motorcycles—not too fast so we didn't give the appearance of running away. Colt even waved at us mockingly, but I saw the way his gaze remained on me, full of venom.

"Why did he let us go?" Kaige asked.

"He's not ready to go against us yet," Wylder said.

"He knows the implications if he so much as even laid his hand on any of us. Even Mercy as long as she's with us."

"Did you notice the strange men who joined him at the end?" I asked.

"Yeah." Gideon rubbed his forehead. "What the fuck was up with them?"

My gut said it was nothing good.

Wylder looked deep in thought. "He's definitely brought in more people for backup. I'm not sure who they are, but I don't think they were from around here. He's biding his time while he gathers more manpower."

"I don't like it," Rowan said.

"Me neither." Wylder grimaced. "I don't know what he thinks he's got up his sleeve, but we'd better shut him down before he pushes this power grab of his even one step farther."

Mercy

OF COURSE, TAKING COLT DOWN WAS EASIER SAID than done, especially now that we'd seen he had some kind of mysterious backup dudes. The fact that Wylder was barely acknowledging my presence even when we were all having a conversation didn't help matters. I'd thought that stepping up and holding my own with them in the Bend might shake him out of his pissy mood, but if anything, he'd gotten worse.

He set his pawn down on the chessboard in Gideon's office firmly enough to make the other pieces wobble and looked around at the guys, his gaze skimming right over the spot where I was leaning against Gideon's long computer desk. "We haven't been able to pick up any word at all about who those new assholes were?"

Rowan shifted on his feet uneasily. "The most I could gather from my connections is that there are a bunch of them, and they started showing up around Colt in the past week. And everyone seems kind of scared of them, although no one's mentioned anything they've actually done that's scary."

Wylder let out a frustrated sound and turned back to the board, just as Gideon slid his bishop over to claim one of Wylder's knights. "I checked my databases and couldn't find any matches," the tech guy said, and lifted his chin toward the board. "Give up."

"You haven't won yet," Wylder muttered. There was no sound except the burbling of the massive aquarium's filter as he appeared to consider both the chessboard and the problems in the Bend.

"They had a vibe that was a lot more pulled together than any of the smaller gangs in the Bend anyway," I said. "They're obviously not from this area."

"Thank you so much for your brilliant insight," Wylder said, still without bothering to look at me, his sarcasm razor-sharp. "Why don't you go find something else to do, Princess? We can figure this out without your 'contributions.'"

Kaige raised his head, his forehead furrowed, and touched my forearm just for a second as if in reassurance. "*I* wouldn't have known that."

I glared at Wylder for a second and then focused on Gideon, since all he ever cared about was the facts anyway. "Have the Nobles had any run-ins with organizations farther out in the state, people who might want to get back at you?"

Gideon leaned back with a swipe of his slim fingers through his ragged blue hair. "I can't think of any major conflicts since I've been keeping track of things."

"It could be based on a conflict from a while ago," Rowan said. "Before any of us were really active in the gang. The Nobles have gathered a lot of power over the past several decades—it's hard to do that without stepping on people on the way up."

"Don't you think *I* would know if one of our neighbors had a major issue with our family?" Wylder said, as cutting as before. "Stay on track, and stop getting distracted."

Distracted by me and my supposedly useless comments, he meant. I bristled, but we did need to hash out the Colt problem, and that wasn't going to happen if I called him out in front of his friends. He'd probably double-down no matter what I said, but he definitely wasn't going to let himself lose any face in front of them.

"So what do *you* think then?" I demanded, because I wasn't going to just sit and keep quiet either. I plopped into one of the cushioned revolving chairs that Gideon had by his workstation.

"I think you shouldn't even be part of this conversation," he shot back, finally meeting my gaze with eyes hard as stone. "It's Noble business."

"I'm working with the Nobles now. Your own father initiated me." And the prick in front of me had told me I was one of them now just a few days ago. How had one quick fuck changed his attitude so completely?

"Let's go over everything that we saw yesterday first," Gideon said, diverting any further argument. He pushed away from the chessboard and grabbed his tablet off the desk. "Bryant had at least one motorcycle club backing him up too. Based on the iconography I spotted, they're local, operating out of a clubhouse in the southeast part of the Bend."

"But they were wearing the Steel Knights insignia too," Kaige pointed out. "They've really thrown in their lot with that jackass."

My stomach sank as I remembered what else I'd seen. "And there was at least one guy with Colt who used to be part of the Claws. I guess some of them have joined him now that there's no leadership." Let's be real, the Claws were essentially dead. I couldn't resurrect them all on my own.

"I guess that's not surprising," Rowan said, unexpectedly gentle.

Gideon fixed his cool gaze on me. "You said that while Bryant was holding you, he got a call and acted as if he might be following someone else's orders."

I nodded. "I'm not totally sure, but he wasn't talking to them like he was in charge of the conversation. He's obviously the one directing all the local outfits we've seen joining up with him. Maybe those outsiders have something to do with a larger gang from someplace else that's supporting him."

"Some chickenshit gang that won't confront us directly." Wylder scowled. "We'll string them up like chickens, then."

Gideon frowned at his tablet. "The question is why."

None of us spoke. Without knowing who these

people were, it was hard to narrow down the possi-
bilities.

Finally, Wylder shoved himself to his feet. "Like
Rowan said, the Nobles have gained a lot of power.
When you've got that, there are always people who want
to take it from you for themselves simply because they
see an opening. We'll just have to close that opening fast
—show them, whoever they are, that betting on Colt
Bryant is a bad gamble. We need to hit the Steel
Knights again, but harder and where it'll really hurt."

"I'll draw on all my resources to predict his next
moves so we can interrupt them," Gideon said.

"Sounds great," Wylder said. With the meeting
dismissed, he strode out of the room.

I hurried after him, ignoring Kaige's questioning
glance. The Noble heir was walking so fast he'd already
made it halfway down the hall. I had to jog to catch
him. He didn't stop until I'd planted myself right in
front of him.

"What is wrong with you?" I asked.

Wylder's jaw twitched. He looked like he was ready
to kill me, or maybe kiss me as furiously as he had in the
kitchen the other day. The memory of that moment and
the way it made my pussy tighten just pissed me off
more. I didn't know if my anger was directed at him or
myself.

Wylder had made things more than clear. He didn't
want anything to do with me. Time for my body to get
the memo too.

I glowered at him. "Answer me. I feel like I'm

talking to a wall. Why are you treating me like I'm useless? I've proven myself about a million times over by now."

Wylder's gaze smoldered right back at me. "And why should I care about that?"

I barely restrained a growl. "*You* told me I was part of the Nobles now. What happened to that?"

"Just because you've wormed your way into my home doesn't mean I have to entertain you," he replied, his voice cold.

"I'm not asking you to. I just want to be a part of everything that's going down against the Steel Knights." I folded my arms over my chest. "You know I'm capable. You told me yourself. Why are you treating me like this now?"

Wylder hesitated, and for a second I thought I might get an honest answer out of him. Then his lips curled with a sneer. "It's not my fault you bought into all that bullshit. I've gotten what I wanted from you. Now I'm done with you. Deal with it."

He spoke as if I were a doll he could use and throw away. Despite my determination not to care, pain and humiliation lanced through me.

Before I could think of what to say in response, Wylder pushed past me. "And I have more important things to take care of than your hurt feelings, Princess. Bryant, for starters. We can handle him just fine without you. You're only going to end up slowing us down."

He stalked off without a backward glance, leaving

me burning with an uncomfortable mix of anger and shame.

He couldn't really mean even half of what he'd just said, could he? I remembered so clearly the way he'd acted when the guys had found me after I'd escaped from Colt, how carefully he'd looked me over, how much restrained fury had radiated from him. A man like Wylder didn't get that worked up over a woman he just saw as a one-time lay to use and discard.

And the way he'd held me in the kitchen, his promise that we'd destroy Colt together...

No, I couldn't believe all that had been an act. But the words he'd just hurled at me still jabbed deep. There had to be something else going on with him, some other reason he was acting like such a jerk... but he didn't trust me enough to tell me.

So in a way, I might as well be back where I'd started. Fuck. Fuck him, fuck this whole place.

I'd still be the one to make Colt pay, no matter what Wylder Noble had to say about it.

10

Kaige

Leaning against the metal frame of the fire escape, I stretched my arms above me and contained a deep sigh. After the events of the last week, I wanted to take a nap, preferably for several days.

It didn't help that I barely slept most nights. Sometimes I never bothered going to bed, because when I did I just kept tossing and turning. The hammock in the yard was a better bet to get in a few winks, but I wasn't tired enough to resort to that yet.

I lit the joint I'd rolled before climbing out here and took a long drag. The pungent smoke immediately tingled into my lungs and loosened my muscles.

The thought of the meeting we'd just had niggled at me, but what could I contribute to our plans against the Steel Knights? I was more brawn than brains. The others would come up with an effective strategy to take down Colt.

No, it wasn't the lack of answers that bothered me most about the meeting. Why had Wylder been laying into Mercy like that? The sense that I should have spoken up for her more itched at me, but it'd made so little sense after he'd finally accepted her into our group, I hadn't been sure if I was missing something. It wouldn't be the first time.

Whatever it was, I hoped that they'd be able to sort it out, or at least that Mercy could knock some sense into the dickhead. I hadn't liked the way he was talking to her at all.

Just as the evening darkened completely into night, a faint mew reached my ears. I grinned and fished the bag of cat treats out of my pocket. When I rattled it, the stray tabby I'd gradually made friends with came scampering up onto the fire escape landing near me. I tossed her a couple of treats, and she snapped them up, purring loud enough to wake the dead.

A window slid open farther down the landing. Mittens startled but then went right back to purring when she saw who it was. Somehow she'd warmed up to Mercy in just a few minutes when it'd taken her months with me.

But then, maybe I couldn't blame the cat for that. Mercy leaned out, strands of her dark brown hair falling loose from her ponytail in a way that made me long to brush them back behind her ear. And then kiss her. And then a whole lot more than kiss her. This woman was the most perfect combination of beautiful and kickass I'd ever met.

Right now, though, she looked like she might be

considering kicking *my* ass. She paused, worrying at her lip, which drew my gaze straight to that lush mouth. I yanked it back to her eyes before she caught me leering. "Hey."

"Hey." She glanced around. "I—I just wanted to get a little space. I'll leave you to it."

"No, no, there's plenty of space out here," I said before she could duck back inside. "Look at me. I barely take up any!"

I spread my arms, showing off my expansive chest and shoulders—we both knew I was actually the biggest guy around here now—and Mercy's lips twitched with a smile like I'd hoped they would. Her gaze stayed wary, though. "If you're sure...?"

I guessed we hadn't been on the best of terms lately. Which was my fault for flying off the handle at her over stupid Gia's lies. I restrained the urge to grit my teeth in frustration at myself and beckoned her out. "Absolutely. And I know Mittens could use your company too."

She looked down at the cat who'd started rubbing herself against the window ledge, still purring, and laughed. "Well, I can't turn *her* down."

As she clambered through the window, I moved to crush my blunt under the sole of my combat boots, but Mercy stopped me, reaching for it instead. "Can I have a drag of that?"

I raised my brow. "This is pretty potent stuff."

She just scowled and made a gimme gesture, so I handed it over. I expected her to cough, but she took a long, slow drag and hummed contentedly. I really should have known her better by now.

"You know, no other woman could have managed to stick with us for as long as you have," I had to say. When she raised a brow, I added, "I don't mean anything sexist by that."

"Women are much stronger than you think," she said with a faraway look.

Something about her tone made my gut twinge. "I'm sorry for how I acted before," I blurted out. "For how angry I got and how I talked to you after Gia made her accusations. And all the other stuff. You didn't deserve that. I mean, it's impressive that you were strong enough not to let it faze you too badly, but you still shouldn't have had to put up with it."

Mercy shrugged. "Your first loyalty is to Wylder, and you were following his orders, defending him when you thought you had to. I didn't enjoy it, but I'm not mad at you over it."

That was a relief. It didn't feel like I'd said enough, though. I groped for something else to say that might completely fix things between us. "I shouldn't ever have called you weak, that's for sure. Just because of that one thing with the freezer—I mean, we all have at least one weakness."

Mercy cocked her head. "Oh, yeah? What's yours?"

I gave her a crooked smile. "I can't sleep. Why do you think I down all those energy drinks? Gotta keep myself alert."

"Did you ever think it could be that all those energy drinks are what's stopping you from sleeping?"

"People might have mentioned it once or twice," I muttered, and reached to take the joint back. "But if I don't have any, then I'm sluggish and I *still* don't sleep. So I'll take what I can get."

She hummed to herself. "I don't think that's quite on the same level as melting down over small spaces."

I debated for a second before letting the question tumble out. "Have you just always had a thing about tight spaces, or did something happen...?" Rowan's reaction in the moment had given me the impression he knew more about the situation than we did—and that there was more to it than a simple phobia.

Mercy swiped her hand across her mouth, her expression darkening, and I immediately regretted the question. "Never mind. You don't have to—"

"No, it's fine," she said, but there was an artificial flatness to her even tone. She squared her shoulders. "I've told you before that my dad wasn't happy he only had a girl for an heir. When he wasn't training me, which he only did because he couldn't stand to have a total wimp as a kid, he came up with ways to take his frustrations out on me. One of his favorites was dumping me in a pit he had in the basement floor, about the size of a coffin. He'd shut me in there for hours on end."

The hairs on the back of my neck stood on end. I'd thought my parents were fucked up, but they'd never buried me alive, for Christ's sake. "That sounds horrible."

"Oh, it was. He mostly used it for torturing people who crossed him, and he never cleaned it up, so there was dried blood and piss and vomit down there. And it was totally dark once he got the concrete slab that closed it in place." She looked down at her fingertips, and I remembered the faint scars interlaced across them that were only visible in brighter light. "It was mostly when I was a kid. I'd scratch the hell out of my fingers trying to get out, crying and begging him, but he'd just laugh and leave."

"Fuck," I said, at a loss for any other words. I could imagine a younger version of Mercy being locked up in that pit, crying out for help, clawing hopelessly until her fingertips bled.

But she'd survived it. She'd survived it and come out fierce and otherwise unshakeable. She was even stronger than I'd realized.

My stomach had twisted into one huge knot. "I'm so sorry, Mercy. I know the words aren't enough, but I am."

She gave me a tight smile. "It's fine, you didn't know."

"Doing that stuff to a kid—didn't anyone ever try to stop him?" Of course, nobody had helped me either.

"He didn't do the worst stuff in front of other people," she said. "And I didn't really have anyone anyway. Well, except Grandma. She took care of me and saved me from Dad's wrath whenever she could, but she couldn't completely stop him. And that bastard Colt had her killed as if *she* was any kind of threat to him." Anguish tensed her features. She ducked her head.

I had the strongest urge to run my hands over her hair and pull her to me, as if that would comfort her.

Why shouldn't I try? If she was still too wary of me to be okay with it, she'd shake me off.

Tentatively, as if she were a wild creature I might accidentally spook, I reached for her. My fingers grazed the side of her head. When she didn't flinch at my touch, I stroked them over the silky strands.

Mercy raised her head, and I let my hand fall, but I thought she scooted a tiny bit closer to me. We sat for a moment in silence, watching as the stars came up. Then Mercy looked at me again and cleared her throat. "I had sex with Wylder."

I froze at her confession, something ugly rearing in me. For a second, all I saw was red. I wanted to smash my fist through a wall or maybe Wylder's face.

But I didn't own her. I'd thrown her away. And Wylder had clearly noticed all her assets from the moment she'd joined us just like I had. Why shouldn't she hook up with him if he'd gone for it?

He had the name—he was a hell of a lot smarter than I was, and almost as good a fighter. Not that Mercy probably cared about that part. Argh.

I rubbed my forehead, forcing my breaths to stay even and shoving away the images that tried to rise up of Mercy staring at Wylder with the same expression she'd made when she'd come with me inside her, her eyes glazed with pleasure. When I dared to look at her again, she was watching me closely, her eyes flitting over my face as if to detect any sort of emotional upheaval I might be having.

There was a fucking hurricane inside of me, but I managed to hold it in. Then I remembered how he'd been treating her lately. A scowl crossed my face. "Before or after he started laying into you left and right?"

A startled guffaw slipped out of her. "Before," she said wryly. "He's got another thing coming if he figures I'm going to go for it again after the way he's been acting. I don't know—it was a spur of the moment thing, and ever since he's been acting like I have the plague. So that's been fun. It's not like I made any promises or commitments to him or whatever. I just thought you should know. You can make whatever you want of it. *I* don't see why I should have to be tied down to one guy anyway."

Wait. Was she implying... that she'd want to hook up with *me* again?

I couldn't help noticing how luscious her lips looked as she sucked the lower one under her teeth. I wanted to grab her and plant my mouth right on her until she was moaning for my cock.

But with everything she'd revealed tonight and all the messed-up history between us, I balked in a moment of indecision. In that moment, Mercy stood up. She leaned against the railing, gazing out over the lawn.

I got up too, meaning to tug her closer to me, but then her stance abruptly stiffened. "What?" I asked, following her gaze.

She pointed. "There's something in the grass there, right across from my bedroom window. Do you see it?"

I did. In the hazy light at the edge of the security lamps' range, a dark shape showed against the green of the lawn. I couldn't tell what it was from here, but something about it set my nerves on edge. "Yeah. Should we check it out?"

I almost wished she'd say no, but Mercy was already hefting herself over the railing. She eased down the other side of the landing and then took the several-foot drop to the ground below like it was nothing.

With all my bulk, I wasn't pulling off a move that nimble. "Wait for me," I told her, hoping she'd listen, and hustled inside to take the stairs.

When I came around from the front door, Mercy was where I'd left her, thank God. We headed over to the strange shape together. An unnerving smell trickled into my nose, sour and almost meaty. My stomach turned.

Then the form in the grass came into clear enough focus for me to recognize it for what it was.

A cat's body lay on the lawn, flies buzzing around it. It'd been sliced open down the middle with its guts spilling all over the place, its skull smashed open—and its tail completely gone.

There'd been a cat's tail stuck to Mercy's window less than a week ago. I'd told myself it must have been Gia, but Gia was gone, and someone had left this here since the last security patrol. My jaw clenched with a surge of protective rage.

Whoever was targeting Mercy so gruesomely, they were still around.

11

Mercy

ANTHEA CAREFULLY PRODDED THE CAT'S MANGLED body with a stick. A renewed waft of the rotten flesh stink drifted up, and my stomach twisted all over again.

"It's not a fresh kill," she said. "How long ago was it that you found the tail on your window?"

I rubbed my hand over my face, trying to clear my head. The security lamps cast a faint yellow glow over this part of the lawn that only made the situation more eerie. "I found it when I woke up the same day I figured out things about Gia."

"Then I'd guess the cat was already dead or killed shortly after the perpetrator cut off the tail. They were saving the rest until now." Anthea's nose wrinkled.

Kaige was pacing back and forth on the lawn, his muscles flexing with tension I knew he must be dying to let out. "Who the hell could have done this? Why are they doing it?"

"It obviously wasn't Gia," I said. Unless her ghost had come back from the dead to haunt me.

Anthea didn't suggest that possibility. She sighed and looked around the lawn again, but after Kaige had called her out to make use of her forensics expertise, she'd already gone over the whole area thoroughly. "I haven't found any evidence pointing to the perp. They were careful about it. All I know is that from the looks of the entrails, they left the cat whole until just before they placed it here."

Kaige let out a growl. "It's obviously a threat toward Mercy. Katz—a dead cat. Even *I* can figure that one out."

"There was a creepy drawing someone shoved through my window too," I said, remembering with a jolt. "A couple of days before the tail. It was a girl with cat ears and her neck sliced open."

"I'd say it's very likely it was all the same person," Anthea said. "There are a lot of sickos out there, but they tend to indulge their inclinations alone." She tossed the gory stick aside and swiped her hands together, her voice getting that deadly tone that made me glad *she* no longer had it out for me. "It doesn't matter. We protect our own. Whoever thought it was a good idea to harass Mercy like this is going to die."

At the rustle of footsteps, I glanced up. Rowan was hurrying toward us from the house with a concerned expression. "I saw you from the window. What's going on out here?" Then he spotted the cat and stopped in his tracks. "What the hell?"

"Mercy's stalker is upping his game," Kaige said

grimly, and paused. "Or her game. It couldn't have been Gia, but what about the other groupies? If one of them could have killed Titus, who knows what the others might get up to?"

"I won't discount the possibility," Anthea said. "You can be sure I'll interrogate them thoroughly." Her eyes gleamed as if she was looking forward to it. I wouldn't be surprised if she was. "Our known enemies seem like the most likely option, though."

Of course. "Colt," I said, a surge of anger racing through me. No matter where I went, he couldn't stop hounding me.

"That bastard," Kaige snapped. "I'll tear him open like he did that cat."

"Let's not do anything crazy when we don't have definite answers," Rowan said. "Shouldn't the security cameras have picked up whoever did it?" He glanced toward the house.

I frowned. We'd been too distracted the day of the cat tail to end up checking. "You'd think so, wouldn't you?" I glanced at the cat and restrained a shudder. I needed to get away from it, away from the reminder of what some insane person apparently wanted to do to me. Raising my chin, I stepped back and took on a brisk tone. "I'll go talk to Gideon. I wanted to check how things are going with his investigations into the Steel Knights anyway."

Rowan shot me a worried glance. "Are you going to be okay?"

He sounded genuinely concerned, but I wasn't about to open up to the guy who'd already crushed my heart once, no matter how much he'd eased off on me recently.

"Yeah," I said. "Nothing happened to me. It's the cat that got torn up."

Anthea gave the furry corpse a sympathetic grimace. "Poor thing."

Kaige moved as if he was going to offer to come with me, but even though I'd been feeling pretty comfortable with him on the fire escape just a half hour ago, our discovery had left my skin twitching. I needed space, and he wasn't the best at giving it.

"Why don't you make a larger sweep of the property and see if you turn anything up?" I suggested, not really thinking it'd accomplish much but aiming to keep him busy.

He perked up a little with the thought of taking action. "Good idea. I'll grab a flashlight and get right on it."

I set off for the house before anyone else could try to join me. It wasn't that late yet, and I suspected that Gideon regularly stayed up to the wee hours tapping away at his keyboard and tablet. He didn't like to leave work unfinished—that much I'd gathered.

We weren't exactly friendly, but at least he wasn't the type to play games. I could count on getting straight answers from him and a minimum of bullshit.

I knocked on his office door and got a distracted-sounding "Come in." When I pushed it open, I found him exactly where I'd expected, poised in front of his multiple monitors with his fingers racing over the keyboard and his eyes flicking from screen to screen. A fresh cup of the coffee he made so precisely was steaming away in easy reach.

His gaze darted to me just long enough to see who'd come in, then veered back to his work. "Did you need something?" he asked in his usual disinterested tone.

I kicked the door shut and sank into the wheeled chair at the end of the desk closest to me. "A couple of things, actually. First off, could you check the surveillance footage for the east side of the house?"

Gideon's hands paused over the keyboard. He gave me a longer, analytical look. "What for?"

"Someone left a dead cat on the lawn across from my bedroom window," I said. "The one that used to be connected to the tail that was stuck to my window almost a week ago, it looks like. I'm hoping the cameras will show who did it."

A hint of something more intense sparked in Gideon's eyes. He frowned and swiveled back toward his computer. "They should have. Pretty much every inch of the outside property is covered by those cameras."

He brought up a few feeds on different monitors and rewound them all at the same time. We quickly spotted Kaige, Anthea, Rowan and me gathered around the spot. The camera showed a clear view of the area all around the cat—there was no way someone could have dropped it there without coming into view.

Gideon flicked his tongue over his lip ring in a way that momentarily distracted me from our quest. "Let's see... The last patrol in that area would have been two and a half hours ago, so if we go back through that whole time frame, we should—"

He cut himself off, pausing the video. He'd rewound to the spot where one of the Noble men was clearly visible ambling along in his circuit of the grounds. I hadn't noticed anyone on the video before then.

"Is the cat already there and he just didn't notice?" I asked.

Gideon squinted at the screen and zoomed it in. "No. It's not there yet." He sounded puzzled and a little annoyed. "It didn't appear out of nowhere. They must have just been really fast. If I go forward through the footage a little more slowly…"

He fast-forwarded, and we both peered at the screen. Nothing much changed other than the leaves on the one tree in frame swaying with the breeze. Then— out of nowhere, despite what he'd said—suddenly there was a dark shape in the grass.

Gideon's mouth tightened. Without saying a word, he rewound and played the footage at that spot again, this time flipping through it what appeared to be frame by frame.

I hadn't seen wrong. One moment, the lawn was empty. The next, there was the cat. And no sign of anyone near it.

"What the fuck?" I said, leaning forward as if looking closer would change anything.

Gideon frowned and flipped back and forth through the footage there a couple of times. Then he swore.

"What?" I demanded.

He motioned to the tree. "Watch the leaves. Damn it. I never thought—fucking *damn it*."

He sounded so frustrated I didn't dare ask anything else, just watched.

The footage played, the branches swayed in the breeze—and then they seemed to give a slight hitch as if there'd been a hiccup in the recording.

I blinked. "Someone... cut out part of the footage?"

"Something like that," Gideon said, his voice now taut. "No one could have messed with the actual footage after it'd been recorded. I have *that* system perfectly secure with multiple backups. But the cameras are digital. They send the feed to the hard drive over the network. My best guess is, whoever did it was able to briefly interrupt that signal."

"That's possible?"

"Yes. Almost impossible to avoid unless you hard-wire all the cameras, which Ezra didn't want because then they can be interfered with physically." Gideon sighed. "Most people don't know how or have the tech to do it. And they must have moved fast so that no one would notice anything more than a website taking a little longer than usual to load."

His hands clenched. "I'll tell Ezra to increase the on-the-ground patrols. And that we'll need to add a few cameras with full wiring so we're covered in both ways. I should have insisted on that to begin with."

His obvious agitation sent a twinge through my chest. I'd seen how much he prided himself in his thoroughness. "It isn't your fault. I get the impression Ezra doesn't listen to much of anyone other than himself anyway."

Gideon's gaze jerked to me as if he was startled to hear anyone talk about the big boss so flippantly. Then his stance relaxed just a tad. "You might have a point there. Still, it's an oversight that obviously needs to be rectified now." He glanced at the time. "Or early tomorrow morning. Ezra won't be happy if I disturb him this late. I suppose it's unlikely this person will strike again in the same day. Maybe you should switch rooms, though. Just in case."

Was he actually... concerned for my safety? I guessed he had seemed a little relieved to find me safe and sound the other day.

"Good point," I said. "I'm not going to bed just yet, though. I did also want to ask if you've made any progress figuring out how we can strike at Colt. I'm especially enthusiastic about getting on with that now, since he's the only one I can think of who'd have much motive to be leaving me bloody presents."

A pleased gleam came into Gideon's eyes, and a small smile curled his lips. Oh, good, at least I'd given him one thing he was happy to talk about.

"I've made significant progress, actually," he said. "I'm still sifting through the data so that I have as accurate a picture as possible, but I've already seen clear evidence that the Steel Knights are going to receive a shipment that's very important to them soon."

"A shipment we could interrupt," I said with a smile of my own. "Sounds perfect."

"I think so. Just a matter of determining exactly

when it's coming in and where." He shot a look at the screens that was just shy of maniacal. "While they're playing stupid pranks on the lawn, we're going to come down on them so hard they won't know what hit them. I'm keeping a close eye on all the activity around the major highways."

A prickle of memory passed through my mind. "It won't be coming on the roads."

Gideon raised an eyebrow at me. "What are you talking about?"

"Anything particularly important, Colt would have his people delivering it at the docks on the river. He's got some people there under his thumb—it's easier to avoid random checks or something."

Now it was Gideon's turn to blink at me. "How do you know that?"

I leaned back in my chair. "I *was* engaged to him for a year, you know. He didn't talk business much with me, but I was around him a lot. I listen well."

"Huh." Gideon's hand darted over his tablet. "I'll take that into account, then. We wouldn't want to ambush them right in the docks area, of course. Too easy for us to end up surrounded. But the most likely route through to the main Steel Knights holdings in the Bend from there would be..." He brought up a map on one of the larger screens and drew his finger through the air to trace a few streets.

I considered it and then shook my head. "Not quite. There's a pocket of Black Jacks territory through there, and they're one outfit that won't have thrown their lot in with the Steel Knights no matter what.

There's a longstanding rivalry between them because of something Colt's dad did ages before Colt even inherited the leadership. He's tried to make peace— tried to open a conversation with them just a few months ago, but they just sent him back the head of his messenger."

Gideon eyed me for a moment with an appraising air. It was hard not to feel like I'd be coming up short under that piercing stare. But then his smile returned, a little wider this time. "It seems like it's a good thing you stopped by. I should have asked you to weigh in with your inside knowledge of the Bend to begin with."

From him, that was practically a love letter. Weirdly exhilarated by the praise, I grinned at him. "If it helps reduce Colt and his men to smithereens, I'm all in."

Something shifted in Gideon's expression that I couldn't read. He jerked his gaze away, but when he spoke, his voice didn't sound quite as cool as before. "I wonder if we could make use of the Black Jacks against Bryant then."

I hummed to myself. "I don't think there'd be much point. They're a pretty small outfit—they wouldn't add much to what the Nobles can do on their own. And they seem to prefer to stick to their own business. They'd push back against Colt if he came into their territory, but they haven't come out of theirs to attack him. Unless he strikes against them directly, I don't think we'd get more than grudging help out of them."

"Better to rely on our own power, then." Gideon slid his thumb along his mouth, drawing my attention there again. "I just have to make sure that I can narrow down the arrival window before they actually bring the goods through."

"I'm sure you'll figure it out with plenty of time," I said. "You always seem to be one step ahead of everyone else."

He looked surprised, and then his eyes softened. "Everyone except you, it's starting to seem. But thanks for your confidence."

I never would have expected it, but the vibe between us had gotten almost... comfortable. Maybe we could be friendly after all. Me and Wylder's closest friend...

The question tumbled out before I could second-guess the impulse. "Do you know what's up with Wylder lately? He's been acting kind of... strange with me." I hesitated to use the more accurate words like "asshole" and "prick," considering Gideon's loyalty to his boss and best friend.

Gideon's smile vanished. "I have noticed that," he said after a moment. "I don't know what to tell you."

I held up my hands. "I get that you don't want to criticize him behind his back or whatever. I'm not asking you to. But you know him a lot better than I do. I was just wondering if I should push back against the attitude or ignore it or...? Whatever will mean the least amount of mind games going forward."

Gideon hesitated again, and I could tell he knew something I didn't. He sucked in a breath. "All I can say is that I'm honestly not sure what would work—or if there is anything—but you probably shouldn't take it personally."

I snorted. How was I supposed to not take it personally when Wylder personally insulted me straight to my face? But when Gideon didn't elaborate, it appeared the conversation was over.

"Okay," I said, getting up. "Thanks all the same— and for checking the footage for me. It was... actually kind of nice chatting with you."

As I reached for the doorknob, Gideon spoke. "Mercy... You should know this much. I don't believe his current attitude has anything to do with your competence or his enjoyment of your company. You haven't done anything wrong."

Somehow, hearing that from him was weirdly reassuring even if I didn't know what to make of it.

"Thanks," I repeated, meaning it, and left his office with my emotions even more jumbled up than before.

Mercy

THREE NIGHTS LATER, I FOUND MYSELF WITH THE guys in Rowan's car heading into the Bend again— although this time Gideon was with us only via speakerphone.

"The timing of the ships is rarely exact," he said through a faint hum of static. "You'll want to make sure to get into position within the hour."

"We're only twenty minutes away now," Wylder replied. "It shouldn't be a problem." His voice still held a bit of the edge that had crept into it when we'd had yet another argument about me coming along before we'd left.

This time, Gideon had cut it short by saying that my knowledge of the Bend made me invaluable and that Wylder would be an idiot not to have me there. It might have been funny seeing how quickly Wylder shut up at the unexpected criticism from his right-hand man if I hadn't been so annoyed that he was still acting like a jackass to begin with.

"What about the other car?" Gideon asked. Ezra had ever-so-generously allowed Wylder a contingent of Noble underlings to assist with the mission.

Rowan glanced in the rearview mirror. "Only a block behind us."

"Good, good." I could picture Gideon skimming through footage and data on his various screens with his smooth face in that perfectly focused expression of determination. "We're still not sure exactly what the shipment *contains*, so—"

"We went over this already, Gideon," Wylder said, his voice softening a little with a fond tone I didn't often hear in it. He might have wanted to toss me in the trash, but there was no denying his bond with his best friend. "All the extra details, we'll figure out once we're there."

Gideon made a disgruntled sound as if he didn't see that as a solid strategy.

As we drove on through the glow of the streetlamps outside, Kaige reached across the back seat to give my hand a quick squeeze. The affection in the gesture sent an unexpected wobble through my pulse.

When we'd talked the other night on the fire escape, he'd seemed to honestly regret his harsh behavior—and I really did understand that instantaneous aggression in defense of his people was just Kaige's default setting. And something I kind of liked about him, if *I* was being honest. The thought of him seeing me as one of his people now sent a flood of warmth down through my torso to tingle between my thighs.

Not that he was going *there* any time tonight. But... maybe later we could pick up where we'd left off. Just to blow off some steam when we needed it.

Abruptly, Gideon muttered a curse.

Wylder's posture snapped straighter. "What is it?"

"There's a cop car cruising around within a few blocks of the ambush spot. If there's gunfire, they'd hear it for sure. There must have been a call for some other reason—this isn't their typical route."

"We'll handle it," Wylder said with the smooth confidence I'd once—and, okay, still—found so goddamned sexy. He glanced back at Kaige. "Are you good to provide a diversion?"

Kaige grinned, his eyes lighting up. "My second favorite job."

That sounded a little ominous in terms of what the diversion might involve. But Wylder was already gesturing to Rowan, who pulled over to the curb. Kaige was pushing open the door before the Toyota had even rolled to a stop.

"You know where to find us after," Wylder said. "Be quick about it."

Still grinning, Kaige gave him a thumbs up and disappeared into the night. I looked at Rowan, knowing Wylder was less likely to give me a real answer. "What's he going to do?"

Rowan's mouth slanted into a crooked smile. "Create a disturbance that'll lead the cops far enough away for us to pull off the job. Knowing him, it'll prob-ably involve at least one explosion."

Oh goodie.

As we sped down the last short distance to the ambush spot, my pulse thumped in my veins. I was so ready for this. A real strike against the Steel Knights, a chance to knock the sneer right off Colt's face. And while he was reeling, maybe I'd get the chance to evis-cerate him before much longer.

The Bend's dock area was a sprawling compound arcing around a curve in the river. It had only one exit and just a few routes that made sense to take when driving away from the spot, and Gideon had picked a place for us to lie in wait that should put us right in the truck's path or at least where we could see if it took an unexpected turn before it reached us.

Rowan parked by the curb in a dark patch beneath a broken streetlamp. The other car with our extra men stopped farther down the street.

I settled deeper into my seat. We were going to have at least a bit of a wait. We'd given ourselves lots of extra time since we didn't want to miss the shipment. My fingers automatically traced over the small lump of my bracelet from my mother in the opposite pocket from my knife. I definitely wasn't anyone's *Little Angel* now. What would she have thought if she'd known I'd end up here?

Or maybe, given who my father was, this was the best she'd have ever hoped for me.

"We're in position," Wylder said to Gideon. "I'm switching to the headset now. Ping me if you see anything of concern." He ended the call and adjusted the mic in his ear.

"You can make out the edge of the wall around the docks down at the end of the street there," I said, raising my chin toward it. "The entrance is just to the right. We should see the truck carrying Colt's cargo well before it gets here."

"Assuming you were right about him avoiding the Black Jacks' area," Wylder said, his voice hard again. "You'd better hope your expert advice didn't screw this up for us, Princess."

It'd used to irritate me when he called me Kitty Cat. Now I wished he'd go back to it.

"I still contributed more to this plan than *you* did, Prince Noble," I shot back.

"I'm sure we'll have a better chance regardless if we're focused on the plan rather than jumping down each other's throats," Rowan said in the mild way he had that made any argument seem silly.

Wylder let out a faint growl, but he shut his mouth after that. I couldn't help remembering how much I'd wanted to deep-throat a certain part of him just a few days ago. A flush I didn't approve of at all swept through my body.

Even if it'd turned Wylder into an even more epic prick than before, it'd still been an amazing fuck.

A boom thundered in the distance. My head jerked toward the rearview mirror, but I couldn't see anything out there.

"That must be Kaige," Wylder said with a satisfied air.

Explosions—right. It'd definitely been audible here but far enough away that we could hope the cops would be out of hearing range of anything we got up to once they followed Kaige on his little chase.

Another boom reached my ears, this one even more distant. I strained my hearing, listening for another. A random car rumbled past us down the street. Hinges creaked somewhere nearby. I must have been braced there several minutes when a huge figure emerged from the darkness and yanked open the door across from me.

My heart just about flipped over before I recognized Kaige. He was grinning like he'd never stopped from the moment he left the car, which maybe he hadn't. "Mission accomplished," he announced, sliding into the seat.

A curiosity I couldn't deny tugged at me. "What did you blow up?"

He chuckled. "A few cars. Rich asshole types like we normally drive, so I'm sure the owners deserved it."

Wylder snorted. "How Robin Hood of you."

"Hey, gotta think of the common people."

Rowan raised his hand to catch our attention. "Movement," he said, motioning to the windshield.

A beige delivery truck rounded the corner several blocks away. We all tensed in our seats, Rowan's hands tightening around the steering wheel, Wylder getting out his gun.

"Get ready," the Noble heir told the other car over his phone. Then he swiveled to look at me. "Since you're only here to share your insights, you stay in the car unless it's absolutely necessary. I don't want you getting in the way. Understood?"

I bristled, but the truth was, he had a bit of a point. I'd never been allowed to be part of any of the operations my father had run. I didn't have anywhere near the level of experience these guys had in this kind of organized mission, even if I could hold my own in a fight.

"Fine," I bit out. "But the second it looks like you need me out there, I'm jumping in."

"Oh, don't worry. I highly doubt we'll *need* you," he drawled.

I resisted the urge to smack the back of his arrogant head, only for the sake of not screwing up the operation.

The truck drove on toward us. I braced myself for it to take an unexpected turn and for Wylder to snark at me as we course-corrected, but the vehicle stayed on the route we'd expected. As it reached us, I found myself holding my breath.

The second it passed us, the guys sprang out of the car. At the same moment, the other Noble car tore into the middle of the road, blocking the truck's path.

The driver tried to veer around them and then lurched to a halt at an angle. Wylder and the others dashed over. Shouts echoed through the street, followed by a sputter of gunfire.

I peered through the rearview window, watching the bodies fade in and out of the shadows. Had they gotten everyone in the truck? Was it already over?

A creeping sensation ran up my arms. That seemed too easy.

But it appeared that we really were done already.

Wylder came into view by the back of the truck with a pleased smirk. He raised the door to the cargo area and hopped in to check out the goods.

Since the danger appeared to be over, I figured he couldn't snark too much about me joining them now. Keeping my gun in my hand out of caution, I stepped out of the car and walked over. "What were they bringing in?" I asked.

Wylder leapt back out and yanked the door shut. He was in a good enough mood with the success of the mission to forget that he was supposed to hate me now. "Some kind of drug," he said, clapping his hands together triumphantly. "We'll have to take a closer look at it when we're back on our home turf. For now, all that matters is it's in *our* hands, not—"

Tires screeched, and three cars raced around the nearest corner. Bullets thundered from their open windows.

"Take shelter!" Wylder hollered, already diving around the side of the truck. I ducked down next to him, my breath catching in my throat.

I'd been right that everything had gone too easily, but I wasn't exactly happy about that fact. Where were Rowan and Kaige? I couldn't see them anymore—they must have found something else to shield them, right?

I peeked around the rear of the truck. Men were spilling out of the cars now—at least a dozen of them with red bandanas around their arms charging up the street toward us. Almost everyone already had a gun out, pointed towards us. Fuck.

A bullet whizzed past my head as I pulled back just

in time. I cocked my own gun, a tremor running through my body. I'd killed a man before, yes—but just the one, and not with a bullet. I'd never shot at anything other than paper targets and tin cans.

I could do this. I was Mercy Katz, Princess of the fucking Claws, and I was going to take down as many of the treacherous motherfuckers out there as I possibly could.

Wylder had already shouldered past me and was shooting at the incoming Steel Knights. A few of the other Nobles hustled over, returning fire at the enemy. As I watched, Wylder put a bullet right in the center of one guy's forehead as easily as if it were a target on his shooting range. He didn't show the slightest reaction to the killing.

Why should he? This was his job—and he was damn good at it.

Engines roared somewhere beyond my view. More men ran at us from a side-street in the other direction.

"Get up front," Wylder called to me. "Hold them off. We can't let them take the truck back."

The truck seemed to be less of a problem than making sure they didn't take our lives, but I followed his orders anyway. I dashed around the cab.

Rowan stepped forward. I had a moment's relief seeing that he was okay, but he wasn't looking my way. He raised his gun and took two men down with swift, clean shots, his expression intent. It was surreal to see the boy I had grown up with kill without a moment's hesitation.

He glanced over and saw me watching, but I

couldn't look away. What looked like guilt flashed across his face before it was replaced with determination.

Who was I to judge him anyway? I was a killer, just like them. And if we didn't kill these assholes, they were definitely going to kill *us*.

Three more Steel Knights hurtled into sight. A jolt of recognition hit me—I knew the guy in the middle. I'd seen him hanging around with some of the other Claws lackeys by my house now and then. Jenner wasn't the only one who'd switched sides and given his loyalty to the man who'd destroyed us.

I fired a few shots and managed to catch one of the other Steel Knights in the shoulder, but my heart was beating so fast it was hard to keep my arms steady. They were everywhere. How the hell were we going to get out of this?

I glanced at the door of the truck's cab next to me, still hanging open with the dead Steel Knight guard slumped on the pavement beneath it, and something clicked in my head. They were all here to protect their shipment. If we got the shipment away from them, we'd have won.

I might not be a fantastic shot yet, but I sure as hell knew how to drive.

More shots rang out on both sides. I dove into the cab and found the driver had dropped the keys on the floor—probably as he'd been riddled with bullets. He was still sprawled halfway out the other door. I kicked his slack body the rest of the way out, reached to yank the door shut—and a Steel Knight appeared, his gun cocked and pointed at me.

"Don't move, or I'm going to blow your brains out," he said.

Oh, hell no to that. I froze as if I were complying. The second his gun hand wavered, relaxing with the thought that he had me, I kicked him right in the face as hard as I could.

He staggered backward with a violent curse and then jerked with two bullets that caught him in the chest. As he collapsed, Kaige dashed into view, his eyes wild. "You okay?"

"Yeah," I said breathlessly. "Just going to get this thing out of here."

"I'll cover you."

He ran around to the passenger side, getting in another few shots as he went. I yanked my door shut and jammed the key into the ignition. As Kaige lunged into the cab with me, a bullet punctured the window next to me, whizzing by so close I'd swear it grazed the wisps of hair along my forehead.

I should have been terrified. Any sane person would have been. But instead what swept through me then was a surge of adrenaline so potent I let out a keening battle cry. Then I rammed my foot down on the gas.

The truck heaved forward with more speed than I'd anticipated. Kaige swore and grabbed the side of the door for dear life. I whirled the truck sharply to the left and the right, clipping a couple of Steel Knights in my way. Then I aimed it toward the small gap between the Noble car and the sidewalk. "I hope Ezra thinks this shipment is worth a little damage."

Kaige fired out the window and glanced at me. "What are you—"

The wheels on one side of the cab jumped the curb. The other side smashed into the trunk of the car. I spun the steering wheel, missing a telephone pole by inches. The truck shuddered—and then we were past the whole mess, speeding down a nearly empty stretch of street so fast the wind whistled past the broken windows.

"Holy shit," Kaige said in a voice that was nothing but awe. "You're insane." He let out a delighted guffaw and leaned out the window to fire a few shots to pick off people behind us. "The Steel Knights are on the run now. The ones we didn't kill, anyway. Wylder and Rowan are heading to Rowan's car."

A giddy smile stretched across my face, the crazy thrill of the moment still reverberating through my body. "Get them on the phone, then, and find out where the hell Wylder wants me to take this thing."

But as I slowed to take a corner, not wanting to flip the truck in the process, my exhilaration faded a little. The memory of the Claws guy rose up in my mind.

How could any of our people have taken the Steel Knights' side after what Colt had done? Were they really that despicable?

Or was it possible they didn't even know what had really gone down on the night of my rehearsal dinner?

Mercy

BY THE TIME KAIGE HAD DIRECTED ME TO A SMALL, inconspicuous warehouse on the outskirts of Paradise City and we'd parked the truck inside, Rowan had caught up with us in his car. He and Wylder ambled into the narrow loading bay, Wylder jerking the garage-style door shut behind them.

I looked them over quickly, trying not to let him see me checking for wounds. I didn't want to show I cared, but I was relieved to see that other than a scrape on Rowan's forehead and a ruddy blotch on Wylder's arm that was on the verge of bruising, they appeared to have made it through the shoot-out uninjured.

"Did all of the Noble people get out okay?" I asked, assuming they'd been in touch with the men from the other car.

Rowan nodded. "One of them took a bullet to the

thigh and another had his ear clipped, but nothing Frank can't deal with."

Kaige chuckled as he opened up the back of the truck. "We gave out a hell of a lot better than we got."

He climbed into the truck and opened up a crate that must have been one Wylder had opened earlier, its lid came off so easily. He picked up a baggie of pale gray powder and made a face. "Is this whole truck full of this stuff?"

"It looks like," Wylder said. "I'm guessing it's that new drug we've started hearing about on the streets. They're calling it Glory, right? Bryant would have been counting on getting a lot of funding for his operations out of selling this load. Not anymore." He grinned viciously.

Kaige opened the baggie with unusual care and took a quick sniff. "Holy shit, I can already tell that's strong stuff." He shook his head, his expression darkening. "So what are we doing with it? I vote that we incinerate the whole load."

Having seen his fondness for weed, I was surprised he wasn't advocating we all party with it, but maybe harder drugs weren't his thing.

Wylder motioned for him to get out of the truck and shut it again, sticking a padlock on the door for good measure. "For now, we hang on to it until we decide the best way to make use of it. No point in destroying a potential resource."

Kaige grumbled wordlessly but didn't say anything else.

"At least losing all this should slow the Steel Knights

down a lot," I said. "And it showed their supporters that the Nobles are stronger." The thought of the former Claws guys who'd sold their souls to my father's murderer made my stomach roil. Every former Claws member who'd joined the Steel Knights had better be regretting their choice.

"Right," Rowan said. "This was a pretty big shipment. I wonder if the Steel Knights are the ones who've been doing most of the distributing of the stuff. If so, they'll be low on stock now."

"Well, that's even better," Kaige said, swiping his hands. "We screwed over Colt and got all this crap off the streets. That's even more of a victory than we expected. I say it calls for some celebrating."

Wylder's gaze darted to me for just a second, and I could tell his momentary hesitation was because of my presence among them. But I wasn't going to bow out because he had his head up his ass. I wanted to focus on the good things about tonight, not the parts that'd unsettled me.

"I'm in!" I said. "What are we doing?"

Kaige's face lit up. "We haven't gone to the Gilded Walls in *forever*. And there isn't much else that'll be open."

"Sounds good to me," Rowan said with a questioning look at his boss.

Wylder looked as if he'd restrained a sigh, but then he smiled. "Let's do this. Gilded Walls it is."

"It's the best place," Kaige told me excitedly as Rowan drove us there. "The husband's from India and the wife from China, so they serve both kinds of food and all this fusion stuff. I could eat a whole table of it."

I laughed, letting my gaze skim over his massive torso. "I'll bet you could, and the table too."

He caught my gaze and waggled his eyebrows suggestively. "And I know just what I'd like to eat for dessert."

I couldn't help licking my lips. I might just be up for that.

Wylder stirred in the front seat, but if he had a problem with Kaige's insinuation, he didn't say anything about it.

The restaurant was tucked away between two larger, flashier places, its sign a little faded. True to its name, a gold leaf pattern was etched on the walls. Even at a little after midnight, a couple of the tables were occupied. The rich, spicy scents that hung in the air immediately had me salivating.

A bronze-skinned man with close-cropped black hair hustled out of the back as we ambled through the cozy room, flashing a brilliant grin. I guessed this was one of the owners.

"Sir," he said to Wylder. "It's a great privilege to have you joining us again. I'll see to your service myself." Perks of being a Noble, I guessed.

Wylder clapped him on the shoulder. "Thanks, Rahul. You always take good care of us. You know our favorites."

I spoke up quickly, remembering what Kaige had said about the offerings. "Can we get tandoori chicken too?"

Rahul bobbed his head. "But of course. It's one of our specialties."

I beamed at him. "Perfect. Make it extra-spicy. And I mean by *your* standards, not your typical customer. I can handle it."

He gave me an assessing look and then a pleased smile. "As the lady wishes."

"Bring another plate of that for me," Kaige put in. "If Mercy likes it, it must be good."

I arched an eyebrow at Kaige. "I'm not sure *you* can handle it. Have you had proper Indian spicing before or only the watered down stuff?" There'd been an authentic place just down the street from my house, and as a kid I'd been determined to build up my tolerance, maybe to prove there were a few things in the Bend I could totally conquer even if I couldn't protect myself from my dad.

"Hey, I like things spicy." Kaige nudged me with his elbow. "That's why I enjoy you so much."

The owner led us to a table a little apart from the others near the back. "Will you be having any wine tonight?"

Kaige perked up even more. "Hell, yeah."

Wylder made a vague gesture. "A bottle of the best stuff you have on hand that'll go with the food."

"And I'll have a glass of the Abree Vineyards Merlot," Rowan said.

As Rahul hurried off, Wylder shook his head at Rowan. "All your wining and dining experience, and you still go for that cheap crap when you're with us."

Rowan shrugged. "When I'm drinking for fun rather

than to impress, I might as well go for what I actually like."

He glanced at me just for a second and quickly jerked his gaze away. It didn't click until Rahul came back out with a fancy-looking bottle that he set in the center of the table—and another much more modest-looking one that had a logo so familiar my heart skipped a beat.

Oh. It was the stuff we used to drink back when we were teenagers. One of the cheapest wines in the store, when Rowan could cajole someone into picking it up for us, and I'd always said I thought the flowering vine that curled around the company name was pretty.

We'd been sharing a bottle of that merlot the night we'd lost our virginity to each other in the quiet little clearing in the park that we'd made our own. It'd felt like a room all to ourselves within the ring of trees and bushes. I had a flash of memory of that younger Rowan grazing his fingers down the side of my face as he smiled at me adoringly...

I shook away all those thoughts. That might as well have happened to two different people, so much had changed since then.

Funny that he still went for the same wine, though.

The appetizers came out quickly, and we all dug in. I hadn't realized how famished I was. I could have gorged myself just on the spring rolls, dumplings, and pakoras, but I knew I had to save room for my tandoori.

When the steaming hot-plate arrived, I could tell I'd made the right choice. I took one bite of a leg, the juices of the tender chicken mixing with the perfect fiery punch of spice, and was in heaven.

"Okay," I said. "I vote that we have all our dinners here from now on. And maybe breakfasts and lunches too."

Kaige grabbed a piece and took a bigger bite than I'd have recommended when he didn't know what he was in for. He swallowed and sputtered, blowing out air over his tongue as he reached for the wine-glass and downed it entirely.

I laughed. "Are you sure you can handle *that* spicy?"

"Yes," he said with a look of determination as he eyed the next piece. "I'm not scared of meat."

"There's fear and there's knowing your limits," Rowan teased, reaching for the platter of orange chicken instead.

Wylder chuckled. "As long as you all survive the meal to fight alongside me tomorrow." Then his jaw tensed as if he'd realized that comment might sound like it included me.

I rolled my eyes at him. "Don't worry, I won't let it go to my head."

Kaige took a couple of bites. Once he got accustomed to the heat, he started to gulp everything down. I watched him in amusement.

"Do you like it?" I asked.

He nodded. "A lot actually. I told you before, I appreciate a challenge."

"Speaking of challenges..." Wylder raised his wine glass in a toast. "To putting the fear of Nobles into the Steel Knights tonight."

"To taking them down completely," Rowan added. "Tonight was only the beginning."

With a *bang* that rattled my ear drums, the glass in his hand shattered.

The world slowed down as I watched three men storm into the restaurant, red bandanas on their upper arms. They cocked their rifles at us, and we all dove under the table on instinct. I fumbled for the gun tucked in the back of my jeans, glad I hadn't left it in the car.

The Steel Knights opened fire. Their bullets careened across the table, a few hitting the waitress who'd just walked out of the kitchen. I flinched, horror welling up inside me as the young woman hit the floor, her head lolling.

These pricks were just adding to the list of how much they had to pay for.

"When they reload," Wylder murmured, his expression grim, and the guys nodded. I flicked off the safety on my pistol, my heart thudding.

At the rasp and click of the men reloading their weapons, the guys leapt into action as if they'd always been prepared for this. I bobbed up from beneath the level of the table too, but our adversaries had already taken shelter behind the counter that held the cash register. Kaige fired a couple of shots anyway until Wylder hissed at him. No point in wasting the ammunition.

We exchanged a few shots back and forth, mostly staying below the table. My pulse was outright thundering now.

"What the fuck are they doing here in the City?" Rowan muttered.

"Has this ever happened before?" I asked.

"Never," Wylder said, obviously seething. "*Never* have any of those two-bit gangs from the Bend tried to attack us on our home turf."

Colt had gotten bolder than we'd imagined.

Wylder gritted his teeth. "We're not accomplishing anything other than blasting all Rahul's hard work to bits. We should be able to make it to the kitchen and head out the back without them getting in a good shot if we move fast enough. Ready?"

I should be after what we'd already been through tonight, but somehow I didn't feel it. We'd planned to fight during the ambush. Being attacked during a moment of relaxation had shaken me much more. But I wasn't going to admit that to Wylder. I *had* to be ready.

"Whenever the rest of you are," I said.

"You two go first." He tipped his head to Rowan and me. "Kaige and I will cover our retreat." That last word came out bitterly. He dragged in a breath. "And... *go.*"

Rowan and I dashed toward the doorway to the kitchen, staying low. Kaige and Wylder hurtled after us, turned to keep their guns trained on the Steel Knights.

A bullet whizzed by over my head. The guys fired several shots, one of which struck its target from the yelp that reached my ears. Then we were bursting into the kitchen area where Rahul and a woman who must have been his wife were huddled by the fridge.

"We'll pay for whatever damages those assholes caused," Wylder called to the two of them as we sprinted toward the back entrance. "And we'll make *them* pay for intruding here."

We burst into the alley out back—just as two more Steel Knights charged at us from either side.

One of them collided with Rowan, grasping his gun hand. The other tackled me to the ground. My tailbone jarred against the cracked concrete, and pain shot up my spine.

I gasped and tried to wrench my gun around to aim it at my attacker, but he slammed my arm against the ground. It slipped from my fingers. I managed to yank my other hand free and clawed at his eyes.

When he jerked away from me, I got an opening to ram my knee straight into his crotch. He groaned and doubled over, but it wasn't quite enough. As I heaved myself away from him, he swiped at me with a knife.

I threw myself backward just in time to save myself from being gutted. The knife still slashed across my stomach, slicing through the fabric of my skirt and drawing a stinging line across my skin.

My breath hitched, but the attack reminded me of my own other weapon. I snatched the knife in my pocket, dodged my attacker's next jab, and jabbed my blade at his neck.

The knife sank in with a sickening burbling of blood and crunch of cartilage. The man toppled over to reveal Wylder just behind him, looking like he'd been on the verge of shooting him. The other Steel Knight lay bleeding in the alley, Kaige standing over him.

My eyes locked with Wylder's. In that instant, I could have sworn he was about to slam me up against the back wall of the restaurant and fuck me until I was screaming my release, spectators be damned. Then his gaze dropped to the blood seeping through my torn shirt, and his expression hardened.

"Are you okay?" he snapped, making the question sound more annoyed than concerned.

I clapped my hand to the cut. It still ached, but it wasn't deep. "Just a scratch," I said, and couldn't help adding. "This time I took care of myself."

"Yes, you did," Kaige said. "Now let's all get the hell out of here!"

We dashed around the building and dove into the car. As Rowan hit the gas and the Toyota shot down the street, I sagged into the back seat.

It'd been a close one, but we'd gotten out. Somehow I couldn't summon much sense of victory now.

Colt had crossed a line tonight, and I wasn't sure where it ended or how far he'd be willing to go next.

Rowan

THE TABLE TAP BAR WAS ON THE GRUNGIER SIDE AS my typical meeting spots went. The smell of booze and sweat hung thickly in the dimly lit space. Bodies gyrated to gritty rock music on the dance floor off to the side. The gin in my gin and tonic definitely wasn't top shelf.

But I went where the people I was trying to win over wanted, and tonight Ezra had me on a very precarious assignment, so I wasn't going to raise any complaints. I'd come out to a town about an hour outside Paradise City to talk with a representative for a gang called the Demon's Wings, which operated out of a city farther west.

After hearing about the attack on Wylder right within our turf, his dad had decided we needed to bring more manpower to bear so we could crush the Steel Knights once and for all. If Colt could make new connections, so could we. But first we—or rather, *I*—had to persuade them we'd make it worth their while. My work bringing in the waterfront project seemed to have convinced Ezra that he could entrust me with that responsibility.

For both his sake and all of ours, I intended to prove him right.

I checked my watch. I always liked to be early to a meeting just so I could get a feel of the place, especially when it was one I'd never been to before. The Demon's Wings rep should be here soon, though. I scanned the figures around me in case he already was here, waiting for me to spot him, but none of the young, college-partier type clientele seemed a likely fit.

I wasn't just here to negotiate with the guy, of course. Ezra had also pointed out that since we didn't know for sure who Colt had turned to, I should first feel him out to ensure they weren't already backing the Steel Knights.

The Demon's Wings were close to the Nobles in power and influence. We'd never had any conflicts with them. I couldn't think of any reason they'd bother throwing their lot in with Colt, but there were a lot of things about this situation that didn't make much sense, so we couldn't discount the possibility entirely.

Most likely, the real problem was going to be the price. Nobody would step up in our battle unless they got something in return. I just hoped whatever they asked for, that price wasn't too steep.

I was just raising my glass to my lips again when a smashing sound made me flinch in my seat. Images flashed through my head—gunshots, the glass in my hand shattering. The two men springing at us in the alley beyond the restaurant the other night. Mercy clutching her stomach, blood seeping out from under her fingers.

With my pulse suddenly beating twice as fast, I jerked around in my seat. But it was nothing. Someone on the dance floor must have dropped their shot glass. The guy from the bar was already coming around to sweep it up. He had to shoo away some of the idiots still dancing around the area obliviously.

I turned back to the table and took a deep breath. Sweat had broken out on my brow. For a second, I closed my eyes, willing down the surge of horror that had flooded me out of nowhere.

It was *nothing*. And Mercy was fine. The wound she'd taken had been shallow, not even requiring stitches. I'd seen her just before I'd left, taking up Kaige's invitation to play a game of pool.

Remembering that didn't exactly make me feel better. I couldn't deny the twinge of jealousy that wavered through my other emotions.

I'd tried so hard to dismiss what I still felt for her, but I couldn't ignore it anymore. The thought of her in danger set off a jolt of panic, the sight of her wounded made my heart ache, and knowing she'd enjoyed at least one of the other guy's companionship in ways that used to only be reserved for me had that jealousy twisting my gut.

Nothing that had happened all those years ago had been her fault. I'd known that all along. It'd just been easier to lump her in with the rest since I couldn't have her anyway.

And now... Now it didn't matter. After the way I'd abandoned her, how could she ever look at me with the same affection? I'd lost her when I left her, and that hadn't changed.

She was never going to be mine again.

I swallowed down the pain of that knowledge and checked myself over. Shit. When I'd startled, my drink had splashed the sleeve of my dress shirt, leaving a wet blotch. So much for keeping a professional appearance.

I grabbed a napkin and pressed it to the spot, soaking up as much of the moisture as I could. Despite the mechanical whir of an air conditioning system, the air was warm, but I pulled on my suit jacket to cover the stain anyway. Better I was a little uncomfortable than look sloppy.

As I tugged the jacket sleeves straight, a burly man I placed in his early thirties—a little older than most of the crowd—strode into the bar. His polo shirt and slacks didn't stand out as much as my suit did, but he still looked more business-minded than anyone else here. And I spotted a tattoo poking from beneath the shirt's raised collar.

I stood up, and his gaze fixed on me. He sauntered over casually and confidently. I felt my back pulling straighter automatically to match his assured air.

"You must be from the Demon's Wings," I said when he was close enough that I could talk under the music, and offered my hand. "I'm Rowan Finlay, Mr. Noble's representative. It's a pleasure."

The man shook my hand firmly. "Eric Vale. I can speak for Mr. Herald as needed. Does this place work for you?"

Did he think I was going to risk the alliance by kicking up a fuss within a minute of greeting him? I pushed a mild smile onto my face. "I think it serves our purposes just fine. Let me cover the first round of drinks. What are you having?"

At the pleased gleam that entered Eric's eyes, I knew I'd already won some points with him. "A Jack and Coke would be perfect. Thanks."

I flagged the waitress. I'd given her an advance tip to make sure the service she gave us would be quick and attentive. She took my order with a bright smile and had the drinks to us before Eric had quite settled into his chair. Money greased a lot of wheels no matter what kind of establishment you were in.

I waited until Eric had sipped his drink, taking a tiny one of my own. "So," I said. "Let's get down to business."

Eric eyed me. "Yes, I'm interested to hear exactly what this business is. We were surprised when Mr. Noble reached out."

Clearly I needed to win a bunch more points before this negotiation would swing in my favor. I smiled again. "I know the Nobles and the Demon's Wings haven't had the closest of ties, but we've been aware of your presence for quite some time, and Mr. Noble has been impressed by how efficiently Mr. Herald runs his organization. When he decided to form a new alliance, the Demon's Wings were his first choice."

Not just because of what we knew of their reputation but also because we'd determined they'd had no contact on record with any gang in the Bend, but I didn't mention that part.

The other man raised his glass as if in a toast. "We appreciate the respect shown in that gesture. We've had plenty of respect ourselves for what we've heard of things in Paradise City. That doesn't explain why you're looking for an alliance now, though."

"Of course. How much do you know about the hierarchy in Paradise Bend?"

I watched him carefully as he rubbed his chin. I didn't see any sign of hidden animosity or guilt.

"Not a great deal," he admitted. "Your grip extends over the whole county, doesn't it? Collecting your tithe from the smaller-time groups that have their own bits and pieces of action here and there, like we do."

"Yes, exactly. Unfortunately, one of those groups has been creating a lot of disruption in the county."

Eric's eyebrows rose slightly, but he only looked curious, not as if he was already aware of what I was talking about. I started to relax a little, surer than ever that the Demon's Wings had no association with Colt.

"And what does that have to do with us?" he asked, swirling his drink. "Surely Ezra Noble can handle a few pissy street rats?"

"Naturally," I replied. "But there's something to be said for crushing certain sorts of rebellions as quickly and forcefully as possible. As Mr. Noble has expanded his reach to territories beyond Paradise Bend, he can't bring as large a force as he'd like down on them without leaving certain other properties vulnerable. So he has a proposition for Mr. Herald."

"I'm listening."

"All we're asking is that Mr. Herald send a contingent of his men, whoever he can spare, for one or two operations in Paradise Bend. In exchange, Mr. Noble would return the favor at whatever time Mr. Herald requires. You have our back, we have yours."

"But conveniently we have to extend ourselves first," Eric said.

I didn't let the skeptical comment faze me. "We recognize that, and so Mr. Noble is also offering a partial stake in a particularly lucrative property he's been overseeing the development of not far from your own territories. I've brought the paperwork for you to bring to Mr. Herald so he can look it over."

I retrieved the contract from my briefcase and passed it across the table. Eric studied it for a minute, unable to suppress the hint of a grin that touched his lips. I relaxed even more and allowed myself a gulp of my second gin and tonic. I just about had him.

"This is certainly generous, worthy of a man of Ezra Noble's reputation," he said, folding the papers and tucking them into his pocket.

"And our offer of manpower doesn't come with an expiration date," I said. "The Nobles never forget their debts. Rest assured that we'll be ready if you call on us."

Eric nodded. "Well, I think I've heard enough to bring this to the boss. It looks good, but it is pretty sudden. I hope you'll understand if before he commits, he'd want a more immediate, ah, contribution."

I cocked my head, ignoring the kernel of dread that was expanding in my stomach. "What sort of contribution?"

A smirk I didn't like at all curled the other man's mouth. "Oh, nothing all that substantial. Just a small token to seal the deal. I'm sure Mr. Noble has heard of Jasper Herald's taste in women."

15

Mercy

I didn't know the Noble underling who stopped me in the hall, but his words set my nerves jangling in an instant. "Mercy Katz? Ezra wants to see you in the audience room."

I gave him a thumbs up, but my heart had sunk. The Noble leader hadn't bothered to speak to me since the shoot-out in the Gilded Walls. I knew he hadn't been keen on going after the Steel Knights to begin with. It'd been my crusade, and that crusade could have gotten Ezra's only heir killed the other night.

Somehow I had the feeling he wasn't super happy with me at the moment.

Kaige had mentioned that the Nobles were putting feelers out to form an alliance so they could make a definitive strike against Colt, though. Maybe then this would all be over. I had no idea what Ezra might want to speak to me about right now, though.

When I walked into the audience room Anthea had shown me what felt like a year ago, I found Ezra already in his throne-like chair. He wasn't alone. Anthea stood on the opposite side of the coffee table, her arms crossed tightly over her chest, and Wylder was poised by his father's right hand. Both of them looked way too tense.

Axel and one of Ezra's other main men lurked at the back of the room. A prickle ran down my spine. Basically, the only person in the room I could count on to be on my side was Anthea—and she also probably had the least power out of any of them, family name aside.

Ezra nodded to the sofa across from him without so much as a hello. "Sit down. We have a lot to discuss."

I sat, eyeing him carefully. "What are we discussing today?"

Ignoring my question, he shifted his attention to my waist. "How has your wound been healing?"

I touched the scabbed-over scratch from the Steel Knight's knife. "Frank says it's healing fine. It wasn't deep."

"I appreciate how energetically you participated both in that altercation and during the ambush of the truck," he said.

He did? I managed not to gape at him, but it was a near thing. "Um, thank you. I've always promised I'd hold my own. I might not have a lot of experience on the ground, but my father put me through plenty of training."

"That much is clear. And that's why I think you'd be the right fit for this job."

I glanced at Anthea and then Wylder but got no clue what he might mean from their equally grave expressions. Wylder's mouth was set in a scowl that was typical when he had to pay any attention to me these days. I resisted the urge to grimace right back at him and focused on Ezra again. "What kind of job? If there's something I can do to help take down Colt, I'm ready."

Ezra raised his eyebrows toward Anthea. "Look how enthusiastic she is. I don't think this should be any problem at all."

"You haven't told her what the job is yet," his sister replied evenly, but those words and the sense that there'd been an argument about this between them earlier set me even more on edge. What was going on?

Ezra returned his chilly gaze to me and gave me a chillier smile. "You're aware that we've reached out to another organization to add to our numbers for a more powerful offensive against the Steel Knights? What happened last Friday was a direct call for war, and we can't leave it unanswered."

"I heard you were looking to make an alliance," I said. "Has that gone through?"

"Nearly. What do you know about the Demon's Wings or Jasper Herald?"

Both names were vaguely familiar. It took me a few moments to place them. "They're the main gang in Rallum—Jasper is the boss." My father had mentioned them once or twice. He'd kept an eye on all the major powers in the nearby counties as well as our own.

Somehow Ezra's smile got both colder and wider at the same time. "Very good. They're the organization

I've reached out to. I've been able to strike a tentative deal with them to receive the reinforcements we need for the next phase of our plan. But he's asked for a minor... gift up front to seal the deal."

I still wasn't seeing how I fit in. "I guess that makes sense. Would you like me to deliver the gift?"

He let out a soft chuckle. "Miss Katz, you *are* the gift."

My back went rigid. "*What?*"

"Only temporarily," Ezra said, looking way too amused by my reaction. "He wants us to send him a woman for one evening. He'll take you to dinner, you'll entertain him and see that he's happy, and that's all there is to it."

Anthea made a strained sound. "I think the problem is the *type* of entertainment he enjoys."

That sounded ominous. I held my instant revulsion at the idea of being offered up like a choice piece of meat in check and asked calmly, "Is there a particular reason you chose me?"

"Of course," Ezra said. "Jasper Herald has very particular interests when it comes to the women he spends time with. He likes a girl who can fend for herself and put up a fight."

Even more apprehension trickled through me. Why would I need to be putting up any fights on this date?

Ezra went on as if he hadn't said anything odd. "We already know you can hold your own, so you shouldn't be intimidated by him. And you're aware enough of the situation with Bryant that you can easily talk up our cause while you're with Mr. Herald."

"It would just be dinner?" I clarified.

Ezra inclined his head. "That's all he's asked for. He'll send a car to pick you up, and it'll bring you back to this house when your date is finished."

"If there's anything to bring back," Anthea muttered. "With his reputation when it comes to women—" She cut herself off at Ezra's glare and revised her statement to simply, "He's a volatile man. I don't like this."

"I'm well aware of your feelings on the subject, but you have become rather protective of Miss Katz beyond what she appears to require. I'm sure she can make this decision for herself."

Wylder stirred, speaking up for the first time in a bored tone. "*Mercy* is the volatile one." As I bristled, he went on. "Wouldn't it make more sense to send one of the groupies? That's what they're here for anyway. They'd probably jump at the chance to fawn over this Jasper guy."

His voice stayed blasé through the entire remark, but understanding settled over me. He was trying to protect me too, without showing that he was. If he'd really hated me as much as he'd been acting like he did lately, he'd have relished the chance to send me off to what Anthea clearly thought was my potential doom.

Just how big a sicko was this dude when it came to women?

Ezra waved his hand dismissively. "They'd make a fool of themselves and put us in a bad light. Our alliance with the Demon's Wings depends on this 'date.' I've heard from multiple sources—including you—about

Mercy's capabilities. It's time she put them to more use on our behalf." Ezra looked at me with a challenge in his eyes. "Unless you're rethinking your commitment to the Nobles?"

Understanding hit me. This wasn't just a job—it was a test of my loyalty to him. Ezra cared at least as much about making sure I'd follow his orders as how much Jasper would supposedly like me.

How would he react if I refused?

"I'm not rethinking anything," I said quickly. But no way in hell did I want to cater to some sleazy and potentially violent gangster—sleep with him and endure whatever else he might do to me. Anthea had implied he might even *kill* me.

And how would I really be able to defend myself without screwing up the deal and ruining the whole point of the "date"? It sounded like this asshole liked women to fight back so it was more of a challenge to finally overpower them. I suppressed a shudder of horror.

I groped for something else I could offer Ezra instead. "If you're looking for more allies, I might have an easier solution, one that won't require making any deals with people outside Paradise Bend. There are a lot of lower-level Claws members still out there in the Bend. A few of them have gone over to Colt's side, but there have to be lots that are still loyal to my father. I could reach out to them, get them to fight alongside us—"

Ezra scoffed so loudly my mouth snapped shut. "Do you think the people who rolled over for the Steel

Knights while Bryant took control of the Bend will be any real help to us? Wake up, Miss Katz. If you ask for my opinion, those worthless bastards should be crushed too, right alongside the Steel Knights."

"Exactly," Axel said from behind me. "We're better off without them anywhere near us."

I didn't have any way to argue that. As I hesitated, Ezra leaned back in his chair, his gaze getting even more penetrating. "Well? Are you willing to take this job for me? Or despite all your talk and the fact that I initiated you into our ranks, should I assume you're not actually serious about your dedication to me and the Nobles?"

"I was just taking a second to think," I said.

"Actions speak louder than words," he said. I got the impression he was trying to push my buttons, waiting for me to snap. But I wasn't going to give him an excuse to dismiss me like he'd just written off everyone else left from the Claws.

For a second, I let myself picture telling Ezra Noble to fuck off and walking right out of here, out of this mess for good. In some ways, it was a satisfying image. Hell, Wylder had been encouraging me to take off and leave the Steel Knights to them for days. I could give him what he wanted and not put my neck on the line in this way that made my skin want to crawl off my body.

But I only considered it for a second. That was how long it took before the screams of my dying family echoed up from my memory. That gurgle as Grandma had slumped on the floor, gasping her last breath...

My hands clenched at my sides. Neither father nor son was going to get rid of me this easily. Colt had stolen too much from me, and I wasn't going to let any other asshole take my revenge away as well. Nothing would really be okay until I'd destroyed that bastard with my own two hands.

I lifted my chin and stared right back at Ezra. "And I'm a woman of action, so that's not a problem. If this is what you need, I'll go on a date with Jasper."

"And agree to all his conditions?" Ezra said.

More like his whims, from the sounds of things.

I shrugged as if it was nothing at all. "Yes. Just tell me when it's happening."

Mercy

Two hours later, Anthea showed up at my bedroom door with the dress Ezra had approved for my date, which it turned out was happening tonight. So much for having a chance to really prepare.

Anthea handed it to me, and I unfurled it in my hands. It was slinky emerald-green satin, with spaghetti straps so thin a brisk breeze might snap them and a slit from the ankle-length hem to halfway up the thigh.

Lovely. Ezra might as well be gift-wrapping me.

"I don't want you to go," Anthea said quietly. "The things I've heard about Jasper Herald..." She winced.

"If he's bad enough to freak even you out, I don't want to go either," I said. "But I gave Ezra my word. I'll... I'll figure something out if things get bad."

"You have proven very resourceful so far." She gave me a sympathetic smile. "At least let me help you get ready? Maybe if you're stunning enough, Jasper will forget he wants to do anything more than stare at you."

I snorted. Not fucking likely. But I motioned for her to stay anyway. Having the company would distract me from the horror that might be waiting for me tonight.

I changed into the dress quickly, making a face when I saw just how low the neckline dipped. Then Anthea spent a good part of the next hour spritzing and then curling my hair and slathering my face with makeup.

At the end of it, I almost couldn't recognize the girl in the mirror. She looked like a femme-fatale, something I decidedly was not. But it was still me in the mirror.

"Wow," I said. "Are you sure you're not also a wizard?"

Anthea rolled her eyes, but her smile looked pleased. She swiveled me back toward her and gave my mouth one last touch-up with the lipstick. Then she took a little velvet box out of her purse and handed it to me. "As a final touch. In case things do get particularly bad."

I opened the box with some trepidation, but all I found inside was a gold hair pin with a gleaming pearl mounted on it. "I can stab him with it? I think the heels of the shoes I'm supposed to wear with this dress might do more damage."

Anthea laughed and plucked the pin from the box. She fixed it into the now-buoyant waves of my hair. "Stab, yes, but that's not all there is to it. You know I specialize in subtler methods. The sharp end is laced with a poison that'll slow any man down. It should give you a chance to get away from him if it comes to that, without having the murder of a crime boss hanging over your head. Just be careful while you're taking it out of your hair."

"No kidding." I touched the smooth metal surface. I wasn't supposed to take any weapons with me, but Jasper would never know the difference. Hopefully he wouldn't make me use it. "Thank you."

My gaze dropped to the jeans I'd taken off. I wasn't supposed to take any bag or purse with me, just present myself like, well, a present. Which meant I had nowhere to keep my childhood bracelet on me. After how many times my belongings had been messed with here, I didn't like just leaving it in my room either.

I fished it out of the pocket and held it out to Anthea. "Would you hold onto this for me until I get back? I want to be sure it's safe."

Anthea read the inscription and raised her eyebrows at me. I let out an awkward laugh. "It's the only thing I have left from my mother."

Her eyes widened. "Of course. I'll defend it with my life." She tucked it carefully in her purse with an air as if she'd meant that statement completely literally, which knowing her, she probably did.

Just then, the door burst open. Kaige sauntered in as if he was perfectly at home in my bedroom.

Anthea gave him a reproachful look. "You should knock."

"So I keep telling him," Gideon said, coming in after him. He was followed by Rowan. As the door thumped shut behind them, the three of them stopped in their tracks to stare at me.

Rowan recovered his voice first. "Wow, Mercy, you look…"

He didn't seem to know how to finish, which was strange for the guy who'd always been quick with his words. I abruptly noticed the hollowed quality to his eyes, as if he hadn't slept much last night. Had he known what Ezra was planning?

Would he really have been that worried about me?

"Like a siren who came out of the sea to murder us," Kaige finished for him, walking around me to take in the full view with avid eyes. "Like, seriously, I'm already dying here. I honestly wouldn't be too upset if you decided to drag me down into the sea with you."

I rolled my eyes but couldn't help the blush that crept up my face. "You don't mean that."

Kaige stepped closer. "Hell yeah, I do. I wish you were getting dressed for me, and we were the ones going out. Not that fucking asshole Jasper Herald."

With that comment, the mood in the room shifted to something more somber. "So, what are you all doing here?" I asked to try to break the gloom. "Did you just come to ogle me?"

"Not at all," Gideon said briskly. He sat on the edge of my bed and tapped on his tablet. "We thought you should go into this evening with every possible advantage. The records I've been able to dig up on him are… not ideal."

"He's a fucking lunatic," Kaige clarified, scowling.

A shiver ran down my back. "What exactly did you find?"

Gideon hesitated for a second before he spoke. That seemed like a bad sign in itself. He cleared his throat. "At least three sex workers he's hired were never heard from again. And those are just the ones where I could find enough of a paper trail, which means the actual number could be many times higher."

"I've heard of several who ended up with major injuries, even though they survived," Anthea said. "He definitely likes to play rough, and he doesn't care whether his partner is into it. He might even prefer that she isn't."

Rowan winced at those words. I tried to put them out of my mind. My goal, going in, was to avoid sleeping with Jasper by any means. Then he wouldn't get the chance to act out those urges. I just hadn't figured out how I was going to manage it yet.

"Isn't there some way we can convince Ezra to take a different tactic?" Rowan burst out. "This is sick."

Emotion rippled through his voice. Apparently my safety did mean a lot to him.

I tried not to let that shake my nerve as I squared my shoulders. "I have to go. If it means we get to crush the Steel Knights the way they deserve, it'll be worth it."

"We figured you'd say that," Kaige said with a hint of a growl in his voice. "That's why we're going to make sure you've got everything you could possibly need going in."

Oh. They'd come to help me prepare just like

Anthea had. A weird warmth flooded my chest, but I couldn't help asking, "Does Wylder know about this?"

"Wylder doesn't need to know," Gideon said coolly. "It wouldn't look good for him to act as if he doesn't trust his dad's judgment anyway. But we can lend a hand... as friends." A sly gleam entered his eyes that made them hard to look away from.

Kaige touched my arm, drawing my attention back to him. "Let's go over all the self-defense techniques that might come up. Since you can't carry any weapons to your meeting, you'll have to depend on yourself and your core strength. Never turn your back on him. If you have to get him off you, use your elbows and knees since they can hit hard without risking much injury to you. And always, always, aim for the groin."

"I know all of that already," I reminded him. "I've spent my whole life learning how to defend myself."

"It can't help to get a reminder. And you'll need to be extra smart about it after the wounds you've taken recently."

I glanced down at my palms, which now showed only pink lines where I'd cut them escaping from Colt. If I could survive my ex-fiancé, I could survive Jasper too. "I haven't stopped training. I bet I've been in the gym more than you have." I hadn't had a whole lot of other things to do between missions while Wylder was shooting death glares at me every time we were in the same room.

"Well, good." Kaige rubbed his mouth. "We found some pictures of the guy. He's big—not as buff as me, but he'll have a lot of weight on you. You'll want to rely on speed and agility rather than strength."

I nodded. "Thanks for the tip."

"Just... Just come at it smart, not hard, and you'll be fine. I know you've got lots of experience putting pricks in their place."

The corner of my mouth twitched, and I managed to smile at him despite the dread coiled in my gut.

Rowan spoke up, his voice low. "From what I gathered during my meeting with Jasper's representative, Jasper is a take-no-prisoner kind of guy, like Ezra himself. His man alluded to his violent nature, so it's obviously a fact he doesn't try to hide much. In fact, I got the impression he revels in it, which means he won't be worried about shocking you or trying to keep a low profile."

"Wonderful," I said with a grimace.

"My research has turned up some more details on his recreational activities," Gideon said. "It seems he has a wide variety. He gets season tickets for the Rallum Opera House every year."

Kaige gaped. "Opera? Are you serious?"

"This doesn't seem like a good time for making jokes." Gideon skimmed through the data he'd gathered. "He has an extensive collection of classic cars, the jewel of which is a 1967 Lamborghini Miura. But what I found most interesting is this bit of info I doubt he'd like anyone knowing about."

He turned his tablet around so that we could see the screen. It showed a list of what looked like bank transactions.

"What's this supposed to mean?" Kaige asked.

"Payments he's made that I traced to a local domina-trix. One who specializes in dominating male clients. It seems Jasper enjoys receiving violence nearly as much as he likes dealing it out. From what I can tell, he's one of her regular patrons and her most well-paying."

"So our Jasper boy likes his ass spanked by a woman in tight leather, maybe even calling her his mama." Kaige chuckled. "Who would have thought?"

"It's not that uncommon for men in positions of power," Rowan said. "They have to be so in control in every area of their life that they need some kind of outlet now and then."

"Too bad it's Mercy he's looking to control tonight," Anthea muttered.

She was right. I was touched that the guys had come to pitch in however they could, especially when I doubted Ezra would have approved of me getting extra help. But so far what I'd heard hadn't told me much other than that I needed to prepare for the worst. Still, it meant a hell of a lot that the three of them were here.

"Thank you guys," I said. "Really. I couldn't be more prepared now."

I gave Rowan's shoulder a quick squeeze, yanking my hand back before the flutter that started in my chest could expand, and stepped closer to Kaige to kiss him on the cheek. He hummed in a way that suggested he'd have bent me over and explored my mouth with his tongue if Anthea hadn't nudged him away just then.

"We'd better get going. It's almost time for the car to arrive." She shot me one last fierce look. "You'll get through this. He has no idea what he's dealing with. That's always our greatest strength."

As women, she meant, and after the events of the past few weeks, I knew how right she was.

I dipped my head gratefully. She, Kaige, and Rowan filed out. Gideon got up, dismissing the app on his tablet, and then paused by the door. He turned to face me.

"If you want to just skip town and forget all this shit," he said, deadly serious, "I can arrange a car for you and the stuff to make sure no one ever tracks you down. You'd be out of here in less than ten minutes."

I blinked at him, not at all surprised that he *could* do that but startled that he'd offered it to me. Not for the first time, I had to wonder just how much was going on behind that detached, ever-logical front that I'd never guessed.

"No," I said without even needing to think about it. "I appreciate the offer, but I'm seeing this through."

An even more unexpected smile flitted across his face, amplifying his unearthly appeal. "I thought you'd say that. That's why I like you."

Did he? My body moved of its own accord. I leaned in to press a quick kiss to his lips like the one I'd given Kaige's cheek.

Only it didn't turn out that way. The second my lips brushed his, Gideon grabbed me by the waist and kissed me back hard. I found myself gripping the front of his shirt, throwing myself into the sensation, the heat of his mouth and the cool pressure of his lip ring sending all kinds of sparks over my skin.

I flicked my tongue against the ring like I'd watched him do so many times, and he made an urgent sound in the back of his throat. It was so different from the calm and collected Gideon I was used to that my insides melted into jelly.

He kissed me for a second longer and then wrenched away from me as if the separation took a massive effort. His breath held a faint rasp.

Whoa, that had really been something.

Gideon stared at me, so many emotions darting through his expression that I couldn't identify any of them and then fading away until he looked as impenetrable as marble. But when his gaze dropped to my lips, heat flared through them without the slightest contact.

"I could have smudged your lipstick," he said, as if that practical concern was all that mattered, but the unevenness of his breath told me he hadn't really been so unaffected. Hell, he'd been the one who'd grabbed *me*.

A smile twitched at the corners of my mouth. "I'll check it in the car. I can take care of a few things on my own."

"I know." He reached for the door knob, his gaze still locked with mine. "For the record, I don't think this asshole Jasper has the slightest chance of getting in your way."

Then he stepped out, leaving me alone. But only for a matter of seconds before Axel's voice called from the foyer loud enough to reach me.

"Katz, get your ass down here! Your ride's just arrived. Time to go."

Mercy

I SMOOTHED THE SKIRT OF MY DRESS AS I STEPPED OUT of the car Jasper had sent. The black marble walls of the posh bar it'd stopped in front of gleamed, and I caught a hint of jazz seeping through the broad front window.

The man who'd driven me motioned briskly to the door. "Mr. Herald is already waiting for you. Let's not keep him waiting."

He'd already patted me down for weapons before I'd gotten in the car. He'd been brisk and efficient about that too, but his detachment hadn't comforted me. It'd given me the impression of him carefully checking over a package he was supposed to deliver for his boss's exclusive use.

He ushered me into the bar and over to a large booth at the back of the room. Everything inside had a reddish cast to it from the mood-lighting. It made the three men waiting for us at the table look even more ominous than they would have anyway.

The two who sat at the closest ends of the booth, dressed casually but with a noticeable lump of a gun at their hips, got up at our approach. Their eyes lingered on the plunging neckline of my dress before skimming over the rest of me. One prowled around me, and I could practically feel him ogling my ass. I resisted the urge to ram my elbow backward and "accidentally" clock him in the gut.

But most of my attention stayed on the man still seated at the back of the booth, his eyes roving over me just as avidly from there. This was Jasper Herald.

My first thought was that he resembled a pig. He'd slicked his graying hair close to his scalp, but no amount of gel could hide the fact that it was thinning, letting hints of the pale, pinkish skin beneath show through. The swell of his portly frame filled out an expensive-looking suit tailored to his bulk, and his wide nose was slightly upturned. He wore a thick gold chain on his neck and a Rolex watch on his wrist.

He smiled broadly at me and got up when he must have been satisfied with his men's close examination. They hadn't blinked twice at Anthea's hair pin, thank God.

"You must be Mercy Katz," he said in a jovial voice that sent a shiver over my skin. Did he think *I* was happy to be here? He held out his arms as if he expected me to give him a hug in greeting.

Uh, no, that would definitely set the wrong precedent for this "date." I lowered my head in acknowledgment instead. "That's me. Mr. Noble sends his regards. I'm looking forward to spending the evening with you."

The last bit was a lie, of course, but I was trying to keep Jasper a little placated. My attempt clearly fell short. His smile stayed in place, but a cold glint entered his eyes as he lowered his arms.

He settled for taking my hand and kissing the back of it. Cloying cologne wafted off him. I had to tense my muscles to keep from recoiling, especially after he flicked his *tongue* over my knuckle before withdrawing.

What the fuck? Was he just trying to get a reaction out of me, or did he think there was something sexy about that?

I retrieved my hand as graciously as I could manage, clenching my fingers against the impulse to wipe his saliva off on the thigh of my dress. My smile felt rigid on my face, but at least it was still there.

"I hope you enjoy this establishment," Jasper said. "It's one of the many properties I have a stake in within and around this city."

"It's very atmospheric," I said. "I like the music."

His smile managed to widen. "Excellent. I have a feeling we're going to have quite a memorable night. If you'd join me upstairs? There's a private suite reserved for my use where we can indulge in each other's company undisturbed by the other customers. It even has its own bar for our use."

And it'd mean he could have his way with me without anyone seeing. I bit my tongue against spitting out a "Hell no" that would have ruined Ezra's deal before the night had even started. "Sure, that sounds wonderful." On opposite day, maybe.

Either Jasper didn't pick up on the lack of enthusiasm in my tone or, I wouldn't be surprised, he didn't give a shit. He might even have preferred me to be unwilling. He set his pudgy hand on the small of my back and guided me toward a set of wrought-iron stairs. They led to a landing with a row of doors overlooking the rest of the bar. His hand stayed against me the whole way up the stairs, making my flesh crawl with every step.

This wasn't a man who took no for an answer. Everything Anthea and the guys had uncovered confirmed that. I just had to figure out how to divert him before he got to the point where I couldn't tolerate what he was doing.

The landing was lit with small hexagonal spots of light. I hadn't spent a lot of time in places this swanky, and I might have appreciated the interior design if not for the man next to me. I could feel his impatience coiling around me as his gaze stayed on me. He wasn't even watching where he was going.

Uneasiness churned in my stomach. I turned to him, giving me an excuse to twist out of range of his hand, and attempted the sort of practiced smile I'd seen Rowan dazzle people with. "So, Mr. Herald—"

"Call me Jasper, sweetheart," he said. "And let's save the conversation for when we've gotten comfortable."

I nodded stiffly and kept my mouth shut.

At the end of the landing, a server dressed in a tux was waiting for us. He showed us into a room with a plush divan, a low, black lacquered table in front of it, and a bar that was stocked up with all kinds of alcohol.

The server swept his arm toward the divan, "Please take your seat. I'll have your drinks ready shortly. Do you have any preferences?"

"Something strong and sweet, easy on the ice," Jasper replied, looking right at me. His gaze traveled up my body. He was almost salivating by the time he got up to my chest. Bile rose up my throat at the look on his face. "What'll you have, darling?"

I'd have him cutting out the sweet talk if I'd had a real choice about it. I settled for picking a drink— nothing too strong, since I wanted to keep my mind and my reflexes sharp. "A mojito, please, easy on the rum."

Jasper clucked his tongue chidingly. "Don't be silly. I can more than afford to treat you right." He glanced at the server. "Give her a double shot."

Well, fuck, then I'd just have to drink it very slowly. Were there any potted plants around I could toss a little into when he wasn't looking?

But when would Jasper not be looking at me? There wasn't much else in the room to draw his attention.

The vile man put his arms around my waist, his thick fingers digging into my dress as if he was trying to touch my skin through the fabric. In my head, I imag- ined smashing his nose into the floor and driving the stiletto heel of my shoe into the back of his skull. I'd take a million more shoot-outs and ambushes rather than end up on a mission like this again.

He sat me down on the divan beside him, his arm

draped around my back. The server worked at the bar station and produced two cocktails for us.

"For you, sir, with some of our best vodka," he said with a smile.

Jasper took the drink from him, took one sip, and spit it back into the glass with a disgusted sputter. "What is this atrocity?" he roared.

The other man's expression froze with panic. Before he could reply, Jasper grabbed his wrist and twisted it. There was a sickening crack, and the man screamed. A wave of cold washed through my body.

He'd broken the man's wrist over a drink he hadn't liked.

"There," Jasper said in a cool voice. "This might be reminder enough for you to take more care when catering to important clientele. Now go and make me something better."

My heart lurched at the sudden change in his behavior. It was like watching his skin peel off slowly, revealing his true visage. The jovial front he'd put on downstairs had fallen away completely to show the gang boss beneath, a killer with no repentance. And all that portliness hid more strength than I'd assumed.

The server started back toward the small private bar, his other hand cradling his broken wrist, a faint sound of pain slipping past his tightened lips. My pulse stuttered. I couldn't sit here and watch him try to put together another drink one-handed. What would this prick do to him if he wasn't satisfied with that one either?

"Jasper," I said, restraining a cringe as I set my hand

on his chest. Jasper looked down at where my fingers rested. I wondered if I'd made the wrong choice, if he had problems with other people touching him, but then his jowls quivered. His lust practically rolled off him.

"Yes, sweetheart?" he said, rubbing my shoulder in slow circles that made me want to hurl.

I batted my eyelashes at him. "Why don't *I* make a drink for you?"

He raised his eyebrows skeptically.

I patted his chest, containing my revulsion. "I'm very good at it. You'll see." Before he could stop me, I walked to the bar and dismissed the server, who left without protest. I hoped he could get medical attention quickly.

I considered the ample selection and grabbed a few different bottles. Even at my father's events, I'd rarely gotten to play with alcohol this top shelf. Too bad I was going to have to play to Jasper's preferences rather than having fun experimenting.

A splash of this and another of that. A squeeze and a sprinkle, and a small scoop of ice. "Strong and sweet, easy on the ice," I said as I went. Swaying my hips, I let the dress work the rest of its magic. Jasper's attention stayed rapt on me.

When I was satisfied with my work, I sashayed up to him, careful not to show a hint of fear. "A special blend just for you."

He raised the glass to his lips, still eyeing me. I sank into the divan, trying not to hold my breath. After the first sip, he paused. Then he sipped again. A renewed smile crept across his lips that both relieved me and tied my gut in a knot.

A happy Jasper wasn't necessarily less violent than a pissed off one, just harder to anticipate.

"Drink up," he said, nodding to my mojito. "We're only just getting started."

We'd see about that. But I picked up my glass and gave the appearance of taking a larger gulp when I'd only let a small bit of the liquid into my mouth. The extra rum gave it a sourness that turned my stomach.

Jasper shifted closer to me on the divan, moving to slide his arm around my shoulders. Impatience radiated off him. He might not even let me get through the one drink.

"That was a nice car you sent for me," I blurted out, remembering what Gideon had dug up about Jasper's love of classic vehicles. If I could get him talking about something else he was interested in, I might at least buy myself some time. "Very clean lines."

Jasper cocked his head, an eager spark lighting in his eyes. One point to me. "Oh, I have much nicer than that back home. Are you a car enthusiast?"

I shrugged demurely, forcing a giggle. "Oh, I don't know a whole lot about them, but I know when I like the look of one. They just don't make them like they used to back in the '60s and '70s anymore, do they?"

"No, they don't. Perhaps another time I'll have the chance to give you a ride in one of my beauties. Let me tell you about them, and you can pick your favorite."

As Jasper rambled about his various cars, he polished off his drink and I quickly mixed him another.

I brought my glass over to the bar with me and managed to pour quite a bit of it into the ice bucket when he momentarily looked away. When I returned, though, his enthusiasm for that line of conversation was winding down.

"How did you end up with the Nobles, darling?" he asked as he took his refilled glass from me. "Ezra says your father ran some kind of operation of his own in Paradise Bend."

I plastered another smile on my face. Trust Ezra to have used that tidbit of information to rouse Jasper's interest. "Unfortunately my father was killed by another organization that betrayed him. I came to the Nobles because I knew they'd set things right."

Ezra *had* wanted me to talk up the cause a little. I strained my mind for the best way to approach it. "The Nobles always come through on their word when they give it," I added, in case Jasper had any doubts about Ezra repaying him for his help. "And the assholes responsible need to be dealt with quickly. I wouldn't be surprised if they start looking farther afield for territory to steal before long."

Jasper's eyes hardened. He'd caught my insinuation. "I'm not afraid of any street rats."

"No one was, and that became their weakness. These people benefit from being dismissed—it gives them time to shore up their power until they have a chance to turn the tables." I hoped he didn't realize that applied to *me* as well. "But the Nobles are smart enough to see the danger in leaving a supposedly minor threat to grow. They're going to crush them once and for all. If we have you on our side, it'll be done so much faster."

Jasper simply hummed to himself. Then he threw back the rest of his drink.

"Do you want another?" I asked, already reaching for the glass.

He shook his head, his gaze turning into a leer. He wrapped his hand around my bicep—just loosely for now.

"Come here, girl," he said.

I could tell I'd bought all the time I was going to get, but I couldn't help grasping for another chance to delay. "Shouldn't we talk a little more first?"

His grip tightened. "I think I've had enough talking. I know all I need to know about you."

He leaned in, his lips seeking mine, and my heart lurched. My hand formed a fist I wanted to smash into his face, but the consequences of that could ruin everything I'd worked for. Anyway, he'd probably like seeing me panicked and flailing, getting the chance to—

A lightbulb went off in my head. Thanks to Gideon, I might know everything I needed to about the man in front of me too.

I jerked back, managing to snap my arm from his hold, and looked at him sternly. I made my voice as domineering as possible. "Watch where you touch me. You didn't ask for my permission."

Jasper gaped at me, stunned. My heart thumped faster. I was taking a huge risk, but this man did apparently enjoy being dominated. Why the hell couldn't I be the one calling the shots, then?

Unless I'd gone too far, or he was only in the mood for that at particular times, or—

But he didn't lunge at me. He stayed still, waiting to see what I'd do next. A faint flush had crept into his cheeks. Was he a little turned on already?

I had to keep going before I lost the moment.

"Good boy," I said, standing up. "If you want to touch me, you have to work for it. Do you understand?"

Jasper's pupils dilated. "What kind of 'work' do you want from me, sweetheart?"

Good question. I pointed to the bar. "It's your turn to mix me a drink."

"I don't think so," he said, but his voice wasn't quite as forceful as before. I studied him carefully as he got up and walked toward me. When I circled him, always staying just out of reach as I swayed with the music, his expression became even more avid. He was enjoying the chase.

"Look but don't touch," I said, waggling my finger at him.

"Surely I can do something to be rewarded," he suggested, practically drooling. Oh, he was into it now.

I shimmied a little farther away. "Dance with me. We'll see how much you can impress me." Would I really be able to get away with turning him down?

Jasper slowly followed me, moving his hips from side to side and matching his steps to the rhythm of the music. We made a couple of circuits of the room before I could see his lust overcoming his enjoyment. Tamping down on my disgust, I continued to smile at him seductively.

It was better if he thought this dance was going to end with sex. I knew I was walking a very dangerous line. One wrong move and...

He reached to tug me to him, and I darted out of his reach, shaking my head. My nerves were jangling, but I spoke with the most commanding tone I had in me. "You're a naughty boy, Jasper. And you know what happens to naughty boys? They get punished."

Jasper's breath caught. Ugh, was that a bulge behind the fly of his slacks? Yep, he was already erect.

"Come on, girl," he said, his eyes gone dark with desire. "Don't make me wait for it."

"But the anticipation is part of the fun," I cooed. "And I need to see you've earned it."

"Oh, I can earn it, all right."

He stepped toward me, and I forced myself to keep dancing without touching him. His anticipation wrapped around me. I wasn't out of this yet. How could I—

Then he groped at my breasts, and I acted on pure instinct. Spinning around, I slammed my hand between his legs, squeezing his balls hard between my fingers. "What did I tell you about punishment?" I said with a hint of whisper.

Jasper's eyes widened, and I pressed harder. A sheen of sweat broke over his brow. He moaned, and then with a jerk of his hips, I felt him come in his pants.

Holding in a shudder, I stepped away before the wetness could slip through the fabric and onto my palm. I wanted to run to the washroom and scrub my hands until the skin was red, but instead I drew myself into a haughty posture. "Well?"

Jasper was still recovering from his orgasm, panting hard. Then he began to chuckle until he was practically roaring with laughter. I watched him warily.

"You, my dear," he said as he got a hold of himself, "are a force to be reckoned with. There aren't many who can please me in certain ways I enjoy so well. Ezra had better take care of you."

"Yes," I said, smiling thinly. "He had."

"He certainly made the right choice sending you." His eyes narrowed for a second, and his voice turned hard as steel. "You won't mention our encounter to anyone."

I could only imagine what the consequences of blabbing his secret would be, but I had no interest in gossiping about it anyway. I widened my eyes innocently. "All we did was have a few drinks and a good time."

"Good girl." Jasper smiled a cruel but pleased smile and looked down at the wet spot spreading across the crotch of his pants. "I think we're finished here. Ezra can count on the Demon's Wings' support. The deal is done."

Wylder

I LEANED BACK ON THE LEATHER CHAIR AND TOOK A small sip of my brandy as Mozart's No 40 in G Minor played in the background. Normally, the music would have cleared my head. Tonight, I couldn't shake all the pictures my imagination kept conjuring for me.

Why did Mercy have to be so fucking stubborn? She should have taken off for someplace safe days ago. But no, she'd stuck around even with everything I'd been doing to push her away, and now she was out on a "date" with that psychotic prick Jasper Herald.

Date was a polite word for what was open sex bartering. I couldn't believe Dad had agreed to it. Why the hell had *Mercy* agreed to it? After the agony I'd put myself through, seeing the betrayal and hurt flash across her face every time I insulted her and having to hold myself back from telling her I didn't mean any of it, she'd walked straight into the lion's den anyway. Straight into the lion's *mouth*, more like it.

One thing was for sure: there was no other way the night would end except for Mercy sleeping with him. The only question was how much of her would be left afterward.

The glass cracked in my hand, a trickle of the amber liquid seeping over my fingers. I blinked down at it. I'd started gripping the glass so hard I'd fractured it. Shit.

A tiny thread of scarlet wound into the spilling brandy where the crack had nicked my skin. I watched it, remembering the time I had cut myself to promise Mercy that I was going to help her crush Colt Bryant if she cleared Kaige's name.

She'd held up her end of the deal, and I was making good on my promise. Wasn't that enough? Why did she have to get involved and put herself in the line of fire? Why couldn't she let me protect her?

Dad obviously didn't trust or respect her as much as he should have someone he'd initiated, let alone as much as she'd earned. He wouldn't have sent her on this mission otherwise. He was probably hoping she'd come back shattered so he wouldn't have to deal with her anymore.

If she survived tonight, he'd just find something worse to throw at her. We still had a battle with the Steel Knights ahead of us, and Lord knew it was going to be bloody no matter how many men we had on our side.

Unless I could come up with a way out of it. The beginnings of a plan had occurred to me after the night of the ambush, thinking of how I'd had to send Kaige to draw away the cops. Why not turn one of the biggest pains in our asses into a tool and save us all a whole lot of trouble?

I'd wanted to get the details totally solid in my head tonight, but I was too distracted. I straightened up, dropping the glass on the side table and going to wash my hands. Maybe it was never going to be perfect. I'd already delayed talking to Dad about the idea while I tried to get it there, and look what Mercy had gotten herself into in the meantime. I needed to convince him *now*, before she could find herself in an even worse mess.

And things could get a lot worse for her. I should know.

When I got to Dad's study, I found him sitting in his usual spot behind his desk, engrossed in a book. Some treatise on business strategy or politics, probably. He was dressed in his usual business clothes, an immaculate tie and shirt pressed to perfection. Sometimes I wondered if Rowan took his fashion cues from my father.

He glanced up at me, as unreadable as ever. "Wylder. I assume everything went smoothly before Mercy left for the date?"

I sat down in the armchair closest to his desk. "I wouldn't know. I didn't see her before she left."

That wasn't true. I'd watched her from the second floor as she'd gotten into the car and been driven away. She'd looked absolutely stunning in the emerald-green dress that'd hugged her in all the right places. She was all sinful curves and softness, and it should have been my hands on them, not fucking Jasper Herald—

I had to catch my fingers before they dug into my palms and bit back the question I wanted to ask. Had he heard anything from Jasper's people yet? I couldn't betray even that much interest.

"I'm sure she's enjoying his company," Dad said, setting his book down with a smile.

My jaw ticked. Mercy wouldn't want some aging crime boss's greasy paws all over her. But I knew Dad was trying to set me off. He wanted some reaction from me, and he wasn't getting it.

Time to change the subject. "There was something else I wanted to talk to you about, actually. I think we can use the truck of drugs we stole from the Steel Knights to our advantage. It might be the key to taking them down for good—and in a way that won't require tying ourselves to some other gang."

Dad's eyebrows arched. "Intriguing. What exactly are you suggesting we do?"

I spoke with all the confidence I had in me. "We set things up so Colt Bryant and many of the other prominent players in the Steel Knights get caught by the cops on major charges."

I could tell at once from Dad's expression that I was on shaky ground. His lip curled with a hint of disgust. "You want us to take help from the police?"

"Not exactly," I said quickly. "We'd be using them like the dogs they are. Sic them on our enemies, and let them fight it out with each other while we laugh from the sidelines."

That framing toned down his initial reaction enough that he didn't yell at me to get out, anyway. He eyed me narrowly. "Continue."

I didn't have much time to convince him. I sucked in a breath. "We *have* a huge batch of the drug—a brand new drug that the cops must be aware of and eager to crack down on. I know you don't have any interest in distributing it ourselves. Rather than just toss it in the trash, we can use it as bait. We put out word on the street that we *are* going to start selling it and take over distribution from the Steel Knights."

"That would certainly piss them off," Dad said dryly.

"And that's what we want," I said, warming to the pitch. "We'll make sure just enough detail gets out for them to determine that we're storing and distributing the drug out of a building we've chosen specifically for our plan. Bryant and his men will come to take revenge for our theft and to try to show they can overpower us. But we'll also have to give a few tips to the cops that the Steel Knights are about to make a big move."

Dad's expression still hadn't budged. "This all sounds very precarious, Wylder."

"It doesn't have to be. Once they've stormed the building, we'll make sure they're trapped inside, and we'll have left nothing to incriminate the Nobles. We could even set up recording equipment that's supposedly surveillance cameras and turn them on then so there'll be video evidence of the Steel Knights with the truck. Then we send the cops in after them, they'll find the drugs and Bryant and the rest, and they all get arrested. We can leverage the dirty cops we have on the payroll to make sure the case isn't dropped or settled out of court. They go to jail, we have no more problems, and we keep our hands clean of the whole mess."

Dad started to laugh. The sound was so mocking, my stomach clenched. He always made me feel like I was still a thumb-sucking child, incapable of making decisions for myself.

"Are you done yet?" he asked.

I'd thought what I'd already said should be enough. I frowned at him. "Well—"

His tone turned outright icy. "The attack on our territory has already put a dent in our reputation. The last thing I need on top of that is to look so weak we'd turn to the police for help. It's nothing short of pathetic."

The back of my neck burned. "It wouldn't be weak —it'd be playing things *smart*. Why should we put our men at risk when we can—"

"That's enough," Dad interrupted. "I listened, and I've told you what I think of your 'plan.'" His voice dripped with derision. "Think of a better one next time, or don't bother wasting my time."

He swiveled his chair away from me, a clear dismissal. Anger and shame seared through my chest, but what else could I say to him? Maybe it'd been a losing battle trying to get him to consider *any* idea I came up with. He still only saw me as his second choice.

As I got up, Dad's phone rang. When he looked down at the caller ID, he frowned before lifting the phone to his ear. "Jasper, how nice to hear from you. I assume your evening went well?"

I stopped in my tracks, my pulse stuttering despite my best efforts at keeping my emotions under wraps.

After a pause, Dad went on. "I hope the girl met your expectations?"

I waited with bated breath, watching what I could see of my father's face carefully. All my nerves were clanging for a fight.

If the bastard had so much as laid a finger on Mercy I was going to fucking kill him. Even if that meant moving against my father and raising hell, I wasn't sure I could stop myself. Because Mercy was worth it... and that was the whole damn problem.

Jasper talked for a little longer, and Dad's lips pressed together. Definitely not a good sign. My body tensed.

"I see," Dad said. "I look forward to enjoying the results of our arrangement. Good night, my new friend."

He cut the call and turned to me. "Well, that was an interesting chat."

"And?" I said, swallowing the question I really wanted to ask. "Is the deal on?"

"It appears so. He liked Mercy very much. He seemed quite impressed with her."

I found his tone even harder to decipher than usual. Was he just keeping his delight at the news that the deal had gone as planned subdued, or had something else gone wrong that he wasn't mentioning?

"That's a good thing, right?" I said.

"Yes," he said, without a hint of enthusiasm. He paused and eyed me so shrewdly the hairs rose on the back of my neck. I did my best to mirror his impassive expression. After a moment, he looked away. "We have a powerful ally on our side. No need to rely on agents of the law. Is there a reason you're still here?"

"I just wondered whether the alliance had gone through. Good night." *You prick*, I added mentally as I pushed past the door.

He'd barely considered my plan. He'd started shooting it down from the very beginning of my explanation. When I was out of hearing range of the study, I slammed my fist against my palm in annoyance.

How the hell was I supposed to step up and prove myself the way he supposedly wanted when he decided every thought I had was worthless before he gave me a chance?

"Wylder?"

I looked up to see Gideon walking down the hall toward me. He looked almost as wound-up as I felt. What was he so on edge about?

"What's up?" I asked.

He tipped his head toward Dad's study. "I saw you coming out. You looked pretty pissed. What's going on?"

My jaw worked. If Gideon thought the plan was stupid too, then at least I'd know it wasn't just my dad dismissing me out of hand. "Let's go to my office, and I'll tell you."

In the room where I spent more waking hours than anywhere else, my eyes caught on the broken glass I'd left on the side table. Gideon's gaze slid over it too, but he made no remark. He was smart enough not to poke a dragon—at least, not unless he thought he really needed to.

I dropped into my usual chair, and he sat down across from me. As I laid out my idea the same way I'd explained it to Dad, he nodded here and there. After I finished, he set his chin in his hand, staring toward the wall with a distant expression.

It couldn't be *that* stupid if he hadn't dismissed it yet. He was actually considering the plan.

"It's high risk, of course, but whatever move we make against the Steel Knights will have to be," he said eventually. "I'd imagine that if we can control most of the parameters, it just might work. Which location were you thinking of?"

"I haven't thought it through that far yet," I said. "But it doesn't matter. Dad shot it down."

Gideon shrugged. "Why does that have to stop you? You've acted without his permission before."

"But never directly against his orders." I grimaced. "This is bigger than me. It affects all of the Nobles. I can't mess it up."

"That's true." His fingers drummed against his thigh, and I was struck again by the sense that he was agitated—in a way I'd rarely seen him unless he had some difficult problem in front of him. "Has there been any news about Mercy?" he asked abruptly. "How late are we expecting her to get back?"

I hesitated, studying him more closely. Was he worked up about the situation with her and Jasper? I mean, I was, but I had a reason to be. I'd never seen Gideon care much about what happened with the few women he'd spent time with over the years. Hell, I'd never seen him look this anxious over Kaige's or Rowan's safety, for that matter.

"Apparently she's fine," I said. "She's done with her meeting with Jasper and on her way home. It seems like she managed to please Jasper incredibly well."

Gideon's fingers twitched and his jaw tightened in a way that made me suddenly sure he was just as uncomfortable with the thought of what Jasper had expected from Mercy as I was.

How the fuck had that happened? *When* the fuck had that happened?

A flare of possessiveness shot through me, as if I should be the only one allowed to care, but at the same time... My best friend had finally found a woman who could get under his skin. Maybe I should be congratulating him. It was kind of nice to know he was human enough under his often robotic exterior to fall for someone.

"Just how bad have you got it for her?" I asked.

Gideon tensed even more than before, his gaze jerking to me. "What are you talking about?"

Was that a *blush* turning his cheeks faintly pink? I'd have laughed if I hadn't felt so heartsick at the same time. "Come on, Gideon. I've known you since we were nine years old. You think I wouldn't pick up on it when you finally had your first crush?" We'd leave aside however long it had actually taken me to notice.

Gideon sputtered. "I don't have a crush on Mercy."

I rolled my eyes. "With that reaction, I know for sure you do. Some things make more sense to me now."

He gave me a side-eye. "What?"

"Well, for starters, you've started tolerating her company, and you don't complain about her when she's not around like you do with just about everyone else." I kicked his shin lightly. "It's okay, man. It's *normal*. I was getting a little worried something in there was out of whack for you."

Gideon let out a frustrated sound. "Maybe I find her more... compelling than I'd have expected. It doesn't matter. My focus is still completely on my job, and I obviously wouldn't interfere with anything you have going on with her."

I forced myself to snort. "If you didn't get the memo, *I* don't like her much."

This time he rolled his eyes at me. "I've known you for thirteen years too, remember? I know what you're doing. I don't think she deserves it, but I'm not going to argue with you about it when you have... the reasons you have."

"Good," I said, abruptly grouchy. "Then let's stop talking about it."

Silence hung between us, but it didn't feel as comfortable as it usually did. My throat constricted. There was more I should say. More that *Gideon* deserved. If Mercy would have him, why should he have to go without just because I was forcing myself to?

"Gideon," I said finally, "just to be clear, if anything happens between you and Mercy while she's insisting on staying here, I swear to you it'll never cause a conflict between us. You're free to pursue anything you want with her."

Gideon chuckled disbelievingly. "Are you giving me your blessing?"

"Call it whatever you want. You've never liked a girl before, so it'd be very shitty of me if I cock-blocked you the one time you really wanted one."

Gideon opened his mouth, but the sound of smashing glass cut him off. Shouts rang out downstairs. We glanced at each other and leapt to our feet in unison, dashing for the door to find out what fresh hell was going on.

Mercy

I KNEW SOMETHING WAS WRONG THE MOMENT THE car pulled up at the Noble mansion. The outside security lights appeared to have been turned up to twice their usual glare. There were about a dozen men in view spread out across both sides of the lawn, fanning out as they scanned the terrain around them.

I frowned. I'd been gone for only a few hours. What the fuck had happened here?

A guy I only vaguely recognized was standing by the front steps. He wheeled his arm to direct me inside. "Go straight to your room and wait there."

I glared at him. "What? Who gave you permission to order me around?"

"I did." Wylder appeared in the doorway, his expression both fierce and so grim it made my stomach drop. Whatever was going on, it was *bad*.

I marched past him inside, annoyance prickling

through me. After the night I'd just had, the last thing I needed was this new hostility of his.

More men were hustling around inside. A few of them were dumping plastic bags in a small heap in the middle of the foyer. As I watched, one hit the floor with a disturbing squelching sound that sent a twinge of nausea through me.

"What happened?" I demanded. "What's in the bags?"

"Don't worry about it, Princess," Wylder snapped. "Just go to your bedroom and stay there until someone tells you it's safe to leave."

I whirled toward him, my fancy dress rustling around my legs. "Are you fucking kidding me? There's obviously something huge going on, and I want to know what we're dealing with. So can you cut the shitty attitude for one hot minute, please? I've dealt with enough assholes for one night."

Something flashed behind his eyes, and for just a second the unfeeling mask cracked. "Why? What kind of crap did Jasper pull on you?"

I rolled my eyes. "Like you care."

To my surprise, he caught me by my shoulder, his grip unexpectedly insistent. "Tell me."

I shook him off, and he yanked his hand back as if I'd burned him. "I'm fine. He barely even touched me. Not that you'd be worried about my innocence anyway."

"Right," Wylder said, his jaw flexing. But he got over it—whatever it was—in a few seconds, his demeanor becoming frosty again. "You shouldn't be out here. Move, now, or I'll find Kaige to carry you up there."

"For fuck's sake." I turned away from him and strode over to the pile of bags to find out for myself.

Most of them were tied off, but a couple gaped open. A pungent smell that was far too familiar hit me in the nose, putrid and sour. It reminded me... of the mangled cat corpse we'd found on the lawn.

Holding back a surge of horror, I yanked open the nearest bag just as Wylder caught up with me.

The smell hit me even harder. I gagged, both at the stench and the sight of the rotting, eye-less face staring up at me from the bag.

It was a severed head, the skin patchy with gray and green, maggots squirming in the empty eye sockets and the ragged flesh at the base of its neck... and it was also somehow familiar.

As I dropped the bag, the sense of recognition clicked into place. That face had been imprinted in my memory nearly two weeks ago when *I* had severed that head from its body. After I'd already chopped the guy's limbs up for easy transport as part of one of Wylder's tests.

Rowan and I had buried the cut-up pieces in the forest hours from here. What the hell were they doing at the Noble mansion? Was this some kind of sick joke?

My head swam, bile rising in my throat. I took a step back, and Wylder clamped his hand around my elbow.

"I told you to go upstairs," he said in a taut voice.

I shook my head, but my thoughts kept spinning. It took a few seconds before I trusted myself not to vomit the moment I opened my mouth. "I've seen it now. I can't forget what's down here. You have to tell me what happened."

Wylder sighed, but I guessed I'd made a good enough point. "I can tell you recognized him. Someone must have dug up the corpse from wherever you buried him and hauled the pieces back here. About a half an hour ago, they smashed the living room window and hurled everything into the room from outside."

"Why—did anyone see who did it? Did you catch the guy?"

"No." There was enough fury in that single syllable to tell me just how pissed off that fact made Wylder. "Whoever did it was gone by the time the nearest men got to the spot. Gideon's been scanning the footage for any clue, but he hasn't reported back yet, so I'm assuming he hasn't found anything useful. We're dealing with a sick bastard and a fucking sly one."

I spun so I couldn't see the pile of bags at all, but the image of the rotting head floated behind my eyes. "It's a threat," I said. A threat meant for me. It wasn't any old corpse but the one I'd chopped up and buried. This had to have come from the same psycho who'd left me the disturbing sketch and the dead cat.

And the incidents were escalating... What would it be next?

Would Colt really have done all this just to get back at me? He'd been angry and some of his talk had made him seem kind of unhinged, but this was a totally other level. I had trouble picturing him coming up with a scheme this deranged.

Of course, I'd misjudged him before.

Another thought occurred to me with a sudden chill. "How did they even know? I cut up the guy right here in your basement—Rowan and I made sure no one was around when we buried the bags. I'm sure we didn't leave any evidence."

Wylder's mouth flattened. "Whoever it is must be watching you very closely. And your stalker is obviously well-versed in stealth. I'm starting to get the impression this is some kind of game to them."

Who else might hate my guts that much? For a second, my mind darted to Ezra, but the drawing and the cat tail had turned up before he'd even known I was in his house, let alone met me. And would he really have set things up so his own home looked so unsecured to his underlings? That didn't feel right either.

The longer I stood here with the body right behind me, the queasier I felt. But I sure as hell wasn't going to hide away in my room just to make the Noble heir happy.

"I'm going to talk to Gideon and see what's going on with the cameras," I said.

Wylder scowled, but before he could argue with me any more, I walked off. He needed to learn someday that he couldn't just order me around and expect me to jump at his command.

My legs wobbled with my first few steps, but by the time I reached the stairs, my stride had steadied. I hurried up, leaving the scene below and all the memories it'd stirred up as far behind as I could.

What a fuck-up of a night.

I didn't bother knocking, just walked right into

Gideon's office. He was in almost the same pose as when I'd come to talk to him about the dead cat. His shoulders were rigid, his body tipped toward the array of screens.

He startled a bit as I swept in and spun to face me. He looked as exhausted as I felt—and almost pained.

"You're back," he said, his gaze sweeping over me. "You look okay. You handled Jasper, then?"

He sounded tense, but there wasn't a trace of doubt in his tone. *He'd* believed I could handle myself.

For just an instant, our brief but panty-meltingly hot kiss came back to me. I swallowed hard, the heat of the memory merging strangely with the much less pleasant sensations already roiling inside me.

"That's one way of putting it," I said. "He didn't take anything from me I couldn't stand to give. Of course, things don't seem much less dangerous here. You haven't found anything from the surveillance cameras?"

He winced. "You saw what happened downstairs?"

"I saw enough." I flopped into the chair next to him and frowned at the screens, which were all showing different feeds from the security system. "How could none of the cameras have caught anything? I know this asshole has that trick with disrupting the Wi-Fi, but didn't Ezra put those new hardwired cameras in?"

Gideon nodded with no shift in his uneasy expression. "He understood the problem and approved the installation as soon as I explained. But there's only one that has a view of the right part of the lawn, and your stalker appears to have found a way to disrupt that too."

He clicked a few keys, and one of the streams of

footage zoomed into rewind mode. I squinted at it, wondering why it looked blurrier than the others. Men bustled about on the lawn in reverse, then vanished, and then—

A dark blotch filled the screen so suddenly I flinched. "What's *that*?"

"Oil or paint is my best guess," Gideon said. A rasp was creeping into his voice. "The men are too busy searching the grounds for me to ask anyone to take a closer look yet. It's not like it'll help us find the prick. He must have shot at it with something like a paintball gun. It dripped off after a few minutes, but that was all the time he needed."

My spirits sank. This guy was too fucking smart. He probably could have killed me already if he'd wanted to. But no, he must be enjoying terrorizing me.

It *had* to be Colt, right? Who else would revel in my distress that much?

"There *is* something," Gideon muttered, flicking through the footage. "Right—"

He nodded to the screen. Just as the liquid that had splattered the lens started to separate, I caught a flicker of movement in one of the gaps. But from the look of it, it wasn't more than someone's heel.

"If I could just pick up one identifying feature..." Gideon leaned close to the screen again, the glow reflecting off his pale face, his brow knit. He played that scrap of footage over and over, but the shape never revealed more than that dark flicker.

"Gideon," I said after a few minutes. "I don't think you're going to get anything from that. Even if we could see it clearly, the back of someone's leg isn't going to narrow things down much."

"It'd be something. Fuck!" He slammed his hand against the desk in frustration, a gesture so unexpected from the guy who was usually so coolly analytical that my skin jumped.

"It's not your fault," I said. "He obviously had it all planned out, and—"

"And I should have anticipated it," Gideon cut in, his rasp becoming more pronounced. "This fucker strolled onto our property and tossed a goddamned *corpse* through the living room window, and I can't even tell you for sure it's a *he*. What the fuck good am I if I can't even stop shit like this from happening? My one fucking job—all this fucking tech and I can't even protect you—or Wylder—or anyone here that much—"

He lowered his head and raked his fingers into his blue hair. "I can't go out there and start shoving our enemies around. I'm a liability in the field. But this, this is my kingdom. This is what I do. And I'm failing miserably."

I had no idea how to deal with a Gideon this distraught when I'd rarely seen him even mildly upset before. Tentatively, I eased my chair close enough to touch his arm. "You're doing more than anyone else could."

"But not enough. I can't afford to fail like this, not when sickos like this are lurking around just outside our doors. I can't be the weakness that allows them to come inside."

"You're not, Gideon," I said, my heart wrenching.

"And there are so many ways you've helped. You're the reason we could grab the truck of drugs from Colt's territory."

But Gideon wasn't listening to me. His hands had balled on either side of his head, and his chest was hitching, the rasp filling even his breath now as if he couldn't get enough air inside him.

My pulse hiccupped. Were his lungs acting up? He was pushing himself so hard mentally, maybe he'd put his body into overload.

Like when I had my panic attacks. The fear of enclosed darkness could squeeze the breath from my lungs and turn my blood to ice in an instant.

"Gideon," I said, as soft and steady as I could manage. The way Rowan had talked to me way back when after he'd found me in the museum. "Listen to me. Just focus on my voice. Whether you want to believe it right now or not, you're the smartest person I know. Whoever is pulling this shit is just really fucking smart too. But you're figuring out his strategies, and the rest of us will do whatever we can to find clues our own way, and we'll work it out."

I squeezed his arm and then reached to rub his back with slow strokes. His breaths gradually evened out, the rasp fading. He pressed the heels of his hands over his eyes, bowing his head even more.

"Thank you," he said raggedly. "Sorry. Sometimes I can't— You must think I'm pathetic."

Every particle in my body flared in rejection of that statement. "No fucking way. You saw me freak out in the freezer the other day. I know what it's like to not be able to control your body's reactions. I'm sure as hell not going to judge someone else. You've got even more excuse than I do. There's nothing medically wrong with me."

He finally looked at me, his gray eyes clear and intense. Having all his analytical focus directed at me sent a tingle over my skin that I didn't really mind.

"What happened to you to give you a trigger like that?" he asked. "With a reaction that strong, I'm guessing it didn't just start out of the blue."

I shook my head, my throat tightening. But he'd just shown himself to me at his most vulnerable, whether he'd liked it or not. I could talk about my history if it made him feel better about that. I'd already told Kaige, after all.

"It started when I was a little kid," I said. "One of my father's favorite ways to punish me."

As I explained about the pit in the basement and the hours-long sessions I'd spend trapped in there, Gideon's eyes narrowed. "That bastard," he spat out when I was finished.

I gave him a crooked smile. "Well, he's dead now. I hope he's enjoying his stay in Hell."

"No fucking doubt." Gideon sighed and swiped his hand through his hair again. He looked at the screens for a moment before dragging his gaze back to me. "I know what it's like to have family that treats you worse than even strangers should be expected to. My lungs weren't always this bad, you know."

I hesitated and then asked quietly, "What happened to you?"

"It started out as just asthma—a pretty bad case, but I was okay as long as I had my inhaler. But the kids in the neighborhood saw me as an easy target because I couldn't defend myself that easily. I got beat up a lot, and my older brother and sister just thought it was funny. They'd even egg people on..."

He trailed off, and I thought he might stop there. But then he cleared his throat.

"One day, when I was eight, my brother stole my inhaler off me and then started shoving me around, calling over the other kids to join in. My lungs started to seize up, and I tried to grab the inhaler back from him, but I didn't stand a chance and the effort just made everything worse. I ended up collapsing on the sidewalk, and they just stood over me laughing. That's what kids do, right? Everything is a joke to them."

"Psychotic kids," I muttered. "That's awful."

"The attack got bad enough that it did permanent lung damage because I didn't get treatment soon enough. I passed out, and when I woke up, I was in the hospital. They had to perform emergency lung surgery to get me breathing again. It stabilized me, but my lungs were twice as messed up as before. Nothing's ever going to fix them." He shrugged as if it wasn't that big a deal, but I could see the anguish that passed through his eyes.

"Oh, Gideon." I didn't know what else to say. I couldn't even imagine that happening to an eight-year-old boy. His skinny body lying on the cold concrete, betrayed by his own family. "You didn't deserve that."

"It is what it is," he said, back to his usual matter-of-fact tone. "And maybe it wasn't completely a bad thing, because somehow it brought me and Wylder together. He was in my class the next year, and I saw some of the other kids hassling him in the schoolyard for some stupid reason, and it reminded me of what happened to me so much I kind of blanked with rage. Ran in there with fists flailing even though he could have defended himself just fine."

That I could imagine. My lips twitched with a smile. "Was he just as big a jackass back then?"

Gideon made a face at me. "Probably, but he also recognized loyalty just as well as he does now. I ended up wheezing in the nurse's office for my efforts, but from that day forward, he had *my* back no matter who came at me. He's supported everything I've wanted to do, taken me in when I couldn't stand to live with my family any longer. So the least I can do is make sure homicidal maniacs aren't breaking down his front door." He shot another glare at the surveillance footage.

The vulnerability he'd offered with the things he'd revealed squeezed my heart. I had the urge to lean in and steal another kiss—to keep kissing him until I'd melted all the doubt out of him. He was gorgeous and stoic and strong in ways he didn't even seem willing to admit to himself.

And he was Wylder's best friend.

Gideon probably wouldn't have kissed me earlier if I hadn't caught him by surprise. I wasn't going to throw a wrench into their long-standing friendship. It was bad enough having Wylder treating me like a second-class citizen without me making Gideon a target by association. If he'd even want to be associated with me that way.

"I have full faith in your abilities," I told him. I had to smother a yawn. "Don't beat yourself up over this. I know I don't have any authority around here, but that's an order."

There was something softer than usual in Gideon's eyes as he gazed back at me. "Thank you for listening and not treating me like something pitiful afterward. With whatever authority *I* have, I'm saying I think you should get some sleep."

"You might be right about that." Reluctantly, I got to my feet. "Make sure you get a little rest in there somewhere too."

I walked to the door, but I couldn't quite bring myself to open it without saying *something*. I turned back to look at Gideon, finding him still watching me. Something in his gaze sent a fresh flicker of heat through my chest.

"Since we're being honest," I said, "I wanted to kiss you again just now. But I can tell how important your friendship with Wylder is, and you've obviously seen how he feels about me these days, and I don't want to cause any tension between the two of you by going for it. What happened this evening won't happen again. Just—just so you know."

Gideon stared at me for the space of a few heartbeats. His silence said enough. Before I totally humiliated myself, I ducked out of the room and hurried down the hall to mine.

Gideon

I PACED FROM ONE END OF MY OFFICE TO THE OTHER, too keyed up to even sit down. The rhythmic hiss of the aquarium filter should have soothed my nerves, but at the moment it only sounded like an irritating thrum. What I really wanted to do was punch a hole through the wall, but I knew that chances were I'd break at least one finger in the process.

"Jesus fucking Christ, Gideon," I muttered. "Get a grip on yourself."

I was almost certainly the sharpest mind in this building, but I was also an idiot. Mercy had all but spelled out in neon lights that she wanted me. And I'd just sat there like it was nothing to me, when the truth was the total opposite.

If I was being honest, something about her had grabbed my attention from the first instant I'd met her, and she'd only become more fascinating since. The moment this evening when her lips had locked with mine—fuck, I'd never felt anything like that rush of fiery hunger in my life. But just now, I'd been out of sorts after spilling my guts, trying to pull myself back together, and then she'd tossed out that comment out of nowhere—

No, there was no excuse for gaping at her like a dimwit. She'd talked me down from the start of an attack. She'd listened to me confess the ugliest parts of my past and treated me as no less human, no less whole, than she had before. She understood the kind of darkness I faced, and she didn't shy away from it.

She was everything I could have asked for in any kind of companion, and I'd given her the absolutely wrong impression.

I stopped in front of the espresso machine, but caffeine wasn't what I needed. I needed that hot mouth under mine, that soft yet powerful body against me...

I'd just go and talk to her. Set the record straight. And she could make of it what she would. That was the only logical approach.

Of course, logical didn't mean easy. I took several deep breaths and then marched out into the hall, my whole body jittering with anticipation. Unfortunately, the second I'd locked my office door and turned around, I found myself faced with Ezra Noble.

"Gideon," he said in his typical smooth, assured voice. "Just the man I wanted to see."

Really? Oh, shit, he probably wanted to know what I'd turned up from the surveillance footage, and I'd have to spell out my failure all over again. I held myself stiffly straight, bracing for it. "What can I do for you, Mr. Noble?"

He wagged his finger at me as if I were a petulant child. "I've told you several times, Gideon, you may call me Ezra."

"Yes... Ezra," I said.

Ezra smiled at me. It wasn't a smile I trusted. He might have looked like an older version of my best friend, but Wylder had a number of qualities I appreciated that his father lacked. A willingness to think outside the box and see the strengths in those many would consider weak, for example. Ezra had only grudgingly allowed me to move into the mansion and barely acknowledged my presence until I'd worked out a solid enough setup to start delivering useful intel regularly.

This was a man who only cared about using everyone around him as thoroughly and brutally as possible. Yes, he did what had to be done, but he could also be unnecessarily cruel at times. Especially to Wylder.

He was the one person I'd never be able to protect my best friend from, not as well as I'd have liked to, and some part of me hated him for that.

But tonight he surprised me, though not in a good way. Instead of asking about the footage, he folded his arms over his chest and said, "What do you think of Mercy?"

I blinked. "I'm sorry?" Had he seen her leaving the office—did he have some idea that I'd been heading to her right now?

A flush started to creep up under my skin, but Ezra

chuckled lightly and made a dismissive gesture. "Let me be more specific. What do you make of the recent activities on our property that appear to be targeting her?"

Interesting. I had the sense he was fishing for some kind of information. "I would agree that the perpetrator appears to be focused on her," I said carefully. "All of the incidents have been tied to her in some way." Did he know about the cat tail and the drawing as well as the more recent intrusions? If not, I wasn't going to be the one to inform him.

Ezra nodded. "Have you uncovered any evidence pointing to who might be responsible?"

Something in the way he spoke put me even more on the alert. "Not yet," I admitted. "But the available facts all point to Colt Bryant or someone acting under his direction. The nature of the incidents suggests someone with a deep personal vendetta."

"Agreed." Ezra tsked to himself. "She's being targeted on our property to the point that somebody breached our home to get to her. I can't help thinking that makes her a liability."

My hackles came up. If he expected me to agree with that statement, he had no idea who he was talking to. Apparently he didn't have much idea about Mercy either. But I couldn't tell him he was an idiot to his face.

"I think we'd have to weigh both sides of the equation," I said evenly. "We've faced some unpleasantness from this intruder, but no one has been harmed. On the other hand, Mercy has already provided valuable intel on multiple occasions and otherwise aided with the success of important operations. I believe her skills and experience will continue to benefit us in many ways."

"Perhaps not enough to offset the damage if this unstable party continues to escalate their hostilities."

"I don't think we have enough data to make predictions about that yet," I said, which wasn't actually true. "Besides, you sent her to meet Jasper today, and her presence helped solidify that alliance as well, didn't it?"

Something in my words made his expression harden. Wylder had told me that Jasper had called up Ezra to tell him something. Now I wondered what it was.

When he didn't speak, I continued. "It's my opinion that her value to the Nobles far exceeds any misdirection that an unknown enemy might be trying to create."

Ezra cocked his head. "So, you think the goal is misdirection?"

I shrugged. "As the former heir to the Claws, she's in a strategic position to help us greatly. Maybe someone doesn't want that to happen. Which is all the more reason we shouldn't throw away a resource before discovering its full potential."

"An interesting take, Gideon," Ezra said, his expression thoughtful. I could tell from his tone that he wasn't convinced, but he gave me a pat on the shoulder and walked off—in the opposite direction from where I'd been headed, thankfully.

I stood there for a moment, letting the conversation settle in my head. The fact that he'd insisted on sending Mercy on a date with a known predator hadn't sat right with me in the first place. It almost seemed like he hadn't wanted her to succeed. And now that she had, he was finding other excuses to question her place here... I didn't like it at all.

I might not have any clue how to protect Mercy from her unnervingly capable stalker, but I could certainly keep an eye on Ezra's reactions to her. There was something brewing in his devious mind, and it meant nothing good.

Right now, though, the only person I wanted my eyes on was Mercy herself. The interruption had rattled me, but as I strode down the hall toward the new guest bedroom Mercy had taken over, my heart fell back into a steady—if slightly accelerated—rhythm. Anticipation and anxiety twined together in my chest.

I stood in front of the bedroom door for several seconds before the fear that someone—like Ezra—would catch me there chased off the fear that she'd laugh in my face. It wasn't as if I could imagine the Mercy I knew doing that anyway. I knocked, keeping the sound quiet enough that it wouldn't travel down the hall.

For a moment, there was no response. I was on the verge of convincing myself that she was already asleep and I should walk away when there was a click, and the door opened.

Mercy looked alert enough that I didn't think I'd woken her up, but her dark brown hair was rumpled from lying down and she'd washed off the heavy makeup Anthea had painted all over her face. She'd changed from the satin gown into a thin tank top and pajama shorts.

She'd looked gorgeous all done up in her dress, but

in one glance, I knew I preferred her like this: practical and straightforward and still pretty as hell.

"Hey," she said, peering out at me. "Did something else happen? Did you find something in the footage?"

Of course she'd think that's why I was here. Somehow faced with the reality of her, I lost my grip on my tongue. "I—no. I'm sorry. I didn't mean to disturb you. You're obviously headed to bed." My gaze fixed on the front of her tank top, and I noticed the faint splatter of an oil stain before I yanked my eyes away from what was also the swell of her breasts. "You should buy new clothes."

"Thanks for the advice," Mercy said dryly. "Is *that* what you came over to tell me?"

I'd obviously messed up here. Was there any chance of retrieving my foot from my mouth? "No, not that either."

She crossed her arms in front of her chest. "So, what exactly did you want to talk about, then?"

I opened my mouth and closed it again, managing to think through my next words before I said them out loud. "Can I come inside?"

The implication of inviting myself into her bedroom at night wasn't lost on me, and it probably wasn't on her either. She gave me a more evaluating look. "Sure. The hall isn't a great place for a conversation anyway."

She stepped back, and I followed her into the room. The door thumped shut behind me, and I was abruptly struck by the gravity of what I was hoping to do here.

I'd slept with women before, sure, but it'd only been for the physical release. It'd never mattered even a fraction as much as the mere expression on Mercy's face meant to me now.

She needed to know that our kiss hadn't been a mistake, that I hadn't meant to reject her just now.

I caught myself worrying at my lip ring with the tip of my tongue and shook myself. Mercy sank down on the edge of the bed. It was a basic double in an utterly basic room, like the other few guest rooms in the mansion: just a bed, a side table, and a chair in the corner. A couple of Mercy's origami figures were posed on the table. She'd only switched rooms a few nights ago, but she'd already made this one her own.

Mercy was watching me. Right. Because I was supposed to be explaining why the hell I was here. I inhaled slowly and decided that talking wasn't getting me very far. Maybe I was better off just showing her.

Ignoring the nerves jumping in my stomach, I bent down, slid my fingers along her cheek, and kissed her the way I'd been imagining since her lips had first touched mine hours ago.

A perfect little gasp slipped from her mouth, and then she was kissing me back, and every other thought swept from my mind. I felt like I was standing in the middle of a storm, and I wanted—no, *needed* more.

Before I could make good on that urge, Mercy eased back and stared up at me. Her cheeks were flushed in a way that brought out her natural beauty even more, and exhilaration flooded me at the thought that I'd made her look that happy.

"Gideon," she said, "I thought—"

I sat down on the bed next to her, tracing my hand

along her cheek and down the side of her neck, reveling in the silky smoothness of her skin and in the flutter of her eyelids at the caress. Her pulse beat against my fingertips at the base of her throat.

"I gave you the wrong idea back in my office," I said. "I—I'm not used to feeling this way about someone. I want you. A lot. And you don't have to worry about affecting my friendship with Wylder. He and I already talked about it. It isn't a problem."

She blinked. "You and Wylder discussed the fact that—"

"It was a short discussion," I broke in, before she got the wrong idea all over again. "Covering only the most essential points. But it was enough. And talking isn't what I want to do now. Unless... if there's something you think we need to—"

"No," Mercy said, her voice going rough, and yanked me to her.

That kiss was even better than the first. Our breaths mingled hot between our mouths, and her tongue twined with mine. I kissed her until I felt like I'd drown in her.

Her hands traveled over my chest, and I was suddenly giddy with the thought of all the places I wanted to touch *her*, all the things I wanted to do to her—things it seemed she was just as eager for as I was. I had no idea how that had come to be, but I wasn't going to question it, not in this moment.

I tipped her down on the bed as gently as I could and then climbed atop her. Her hair fanned over the white pillowcase. As I kissed her again, I looped a strand around my finger and tugged on it. Her moan echoed into my mouth. That was all the encouragement I needed to repeat the gesture.

Her tongue came out to play against mine again. I explored the delicious cavern of her mouth, thrusting in and out with my own tongue as if I was fucking her with it. Mercy gripped me hard, her fingers digging into my shoulders like she couldn't bear to let me go. My cock that had only been half-mast went rigid, straining against my fly.

I resisted touching her entire body as I pressed more kisses along her jaw. Mercy let out little noises of encouragement with each one. She was a tempestuous being, and yet here she lay beneath me as I laid siege to her body, ready and willing to open herself up to me. It was such a fucking turn-on.

I pushed my fingers into hers as I let her feel more of my weight, her warm body cushioning me. Some part of me wanted to stay here forever.

We had all night, at least, and I wasn't going anywhere.

I continued my trail of kisses down her neck, taking in each of her reactions until I found a particularly sweet spot just above her collar bone. At the brush of my lips there, her chest hitched. Ah ha. I'd seen her touch this spot before when she was nervous.

I stopped and kissed her there again, this time using my mouth to suck softly before letting my wet tongue bring some relief to her inflamed skin. Mercy moaned, the sound deeper this time.

Oh, yes, I'd just discovered a gold mine. But I was

determined to seek out every spot that could set her on fire.

I eagerly continued my explorations, this time moving up to her ears. I nibbled on her earlobe before flicking my tongue around it. Her hips pushed into me in answer with a growl that practically made me come in my pants.

I brushed her hair away from her face and looked down into her blue eyes that had darkened in lust. "I haven't even gotten to the best part yet."

Mercy grinned. Her voice came out breathless. "I think you're doing a pretty good job so far."

I teased my hand down her body and placed the heel of my hand against her sex. "Fuck," Mercy mumbled, pressing into my touch. She was so fucking wet it'd dampened the crotch of her pajama shorts. I wanted to pull them down and feel her gushing for me, let my fingers glide through the slickness. But I was enjoying this too much, charting the little pieces of her that brought her the most intense pleasure, which in turn made me hornier than I'd ever been before.

My hands brushed against her breasts. She breathed out, as if she was waiting for me to go farther. Instead, I kissed her until she was arching against me. When I let the full press of my weight meet her body, her legs rose alongside my hips as if urging me even closer to her.

I pushed against her and watched her eyes roll back as she felt my rigid cock. I did it again, this time a little urgently. A slight burn entered my lungs at the exertion, but not so much that I couldn't ignore it.

I bent down to taste one of her nipples through the

fabric of her top. She wasn't wearing a bra underneath, and I felt the nub harden through the flimsy cotton. I suckled a little before biting down, making her squirm under me.

Then, all of a sudden, Mercy set her hand on my chest and nudged me back. "Wait."

My lust-hazed thoughts jumbled. Was she having second thoughts? I pulled back, braced for the rejection that might have been inevitable.

Mercy

THE DELICIOUS PRESS OF GIDEON'S WEIGHT ON ME was turning everything around me hazy. All I could see and feel was him and his wicked, wicked tongue. He had managed to discover a few spots that made me go almost insane, and he wasn't even inside of me yet... Heck, we hadn't even taken our clothes off.

He swiped his tongue over my nipple, setting off an electric jolt through my nerves. But the intensity in his expression when he glanced up at me, a thin but pleased smile playing with his lips, made something in me twist.

I didn't know what this meant to him. I didn't know what I'd want it to mean to me beyond this moment. And there were a whole lot of things *he* didn't know that maybe he should.

He lowered his head again, and I caught him with a hand on his chest. "Wait."

He stopped, braced over me, and I regretted the loss

of his touch almost immediately. Something shuttered behind his gray eyes that had gleamed with so much passion a second ago. "What's wrong?" he asked.

"Nothing," I said quickly. Gideon had said he hadn't really wanted anyone like this before, and having seen his normal behavior, it didn't surprise me to know he hadn't exactly been a ladies man in the past. I didn't want him to think I wasn't enjoying every second of this. "I just—I want to make sure we're on the same page."

He cocked an eyebrow. "How so?"

"I..." His analytical gaze made me want to look away, but I didn't let myself. "This is good. *Really* good. Just so we're clear. But—I'm not sure how much you've realized—I've been with Kaige and Wylder. And with Rowan, a long time ago. I might want one... or more... of them again. I'm not sure where we're going with this, but I'm not ready to tie myself down to anyone. I just thought I should say that before we go any further."

Maybe he'd think it was weird that I'd found myself drawn to all four of them. Maybe it *was* weird. I didn't know how I'd come to feel so connected to this tight-knit group, but I did. However weird it might seem, I didn't want to give them up. I belonged with them now, no matter what Wylder said or did to try to convince me otherwise.

Gideon blinked at me. There was a moment when I thought he might pull back and end the whole thing. But then his smile came back, curving wider this time. He brushed his fingers over my cheek in an unexpectedly tender gesture.

"That's why I like you," he said. "You say what you feel and what you mean, you don't mince words about it, but you've got your principles too. I'm not sure where we're going either. I don't think I'd want to tie you down. Well, not that way." The sly gleam that came into his eyes made me instantly twice as wet. "All I'm sure about is that I want to keep going right now."

A slightly giddy giggle tumbled out of me. "Well, full speed ahead, then."

He reached for me, and I pushed myself upward to meet him halfway with a kiss. I sucked on his lower lip, taking the metal ring in my mouth before I swirled my tongue around it.

Gideon's breath hitched. He grabbed the back of my hair urgently as he fused his lips back on mine. He might not have the overt physical power the other guys did, but he sure knew how to take what he wanted, and it was hot as hell.

He broke from the kiss to pull off my top. My nipples puckered in the air conditioned coolness of the room, stiffening more under Gideon's hungry gaze. Little thrills went down my body as he rolled one nipple between his fingers before bending down to take the other in his mouth. He sucked on my tits softly at first before biting down hard enough to provoke a gasp.

His other hand dipped inside my pajama shorts, stroking over my pussy and taking it from hot to scorching. My elbows wobbled, and Gideon took the opportunity to press me back down into the mattress. He put his legs on either side of me to hold me there firmly.

"Stop squirming," he murmured. "Let me worship you."

How could I say no when he was so good at it? He seemed to know which spots would make me keen and which ones would make me whimper.

He kissed a trail down the valley of my breasts, squeezing my tits together and offering equal attention to both sides, before continuing his path down to my belly. When he flicked his tongue inside my belly button, I almost arched right off the bed. He chuckled, his hot breath sending another flare through my torso.

His fingers slipped beneath my shorts again, and he let out a sound that was strained but approving. "You're so wet for me." His low voice and something in his expression, so awed and pleased, just made me gush even more.

He pushed his middle finger inside me, exploring me with the same certainty as when he'd been kissing me all over. "Don't move," he warned me again.

"Ummm," I said, unable to come up with anything more coherent.

As his finger curled into my sex, another wordless noise of approval tumbled out of me. He eased a second finger in and flicked his thumb against my swollen clit. While he continued to fuck me with his fingers, my body rocked against him to bring myself more relief.

Then he withdrew farther down the bed, yanking my pajama shorts off in one swift motion. He eyed my throbbing sex hungrily. His tongue flicked over his lip ring, and I quivered at the thought of it brushing against my clit.

As if sensing that thought, he dove down. In an instant, his tongue was ravaging my clit before finding its way to my slit and sucking on it. I groaned as pleasure built inside me, clutching at the bedsheets to hold myself in place.

Gideon was eager—urgent even—in his ministrations. His tongue dipped right inside my cunt. He swirled it around the top of my slit right to my bottom, almost brushing against my asshole. The slight chill of the metal lip ring against my wet pussy ignited a friction that left me gasping, heightening all the sensations in me.

The pressure was slowly rising through me, pushing me to the edge of a precipice that made my toes curl up. Gideon didn't stop—he didn't slow down one bit as his tongue continued to work on my cunt, fucking it fast before twirling around and then repeating the motion. My body buckled as the wave of pleasure crested, threatening to drown me.

I looked down hazily to see Gideon's stark blue hair bobbing as he feasted on my cunt. The sight made me moan. He looked up and met my gaze even as he continued to loll his tongue around, making little sounds of approval as he did so. Lust shone in his eyes.

I couldn't have stopped myself if I'd wanted to. Just as he dipped his tongue in again, I climaxed hard, gushing in his face. My legs shook at the force of the orgasm.

Gideon was on top of me in seconds, not leaving a moment for me to recover. His hard cock aligned at my pussy, the head pressing against my clit. Oh, fuck, I wanted that too, so badly, even though I'd just come.

I sucked in a ragged breath and noticed that Gideon was panting too, a rasp creeping into his breath. I doubted he'd want to admit it, but sex took a lot out of a person physically. It must be hard on his lungs. The final act would be even more so. He didn't look like he had any intention of slowing down, though, no matter what it did to him.

I wasn't going to remind him of his one weakness, but I could give him an excuse to recover a bit. I tugged at his shirt. When Gideon hesitated, I pouted at him. "Isn't it a little unfair that I'm completely naked while not a single piece of clothing has come off you?"

Gideon's eyes heated before he chuckled. "I like seeing you this way. You're perfect." He ran his hands along the sides of my body, which made my pussy clench again. Just his simple touch seemed to ignite every one of my nerve endings. "I, however, am not."

I tipped my head to the side against the pillow. "What are you talking about?"

He hesitated again and then put his hands under his shirt to pull it off, revealing a slim but leanly muscled chest marked with a dark tattoo that covered him from collarbone to belly.

My eyes widened as I took it in, tracing the tendrils that rose from the top of the menacing shape and the dark eyes that peered into mine from the shadowy figure's face. A few of the whirling lines followed ridges in his skin—the raised lines of scars. They blended into the strokes of the tattoo, but it didn't hide them completely.

Tension gripped Gideon's body as he watched me. I grazed my fingers down the center of his chest, avoiding the scars. "What is it?"

"The darkest god there is, ruler of death and destruction." His mouth twisted. "If the scars from the surgery were never going to go away, I figured I should do my best to turn them into something powerful."

"It's stunning," I said honestly.

A hint of a smile came back to Gideon's lips. "Hades seemed particularly appropriate. He too was shunned by his siblings and cast out of his own home. He always fascinated me with his shadowy prowess. And besides, I've looked him in the eye and survived him—several times now."

"Can I..." I trailed off, letting the question hang in the air between us. This was an important moment between him and me, and in some ways even more intimate then when he was fucking me with his tongue just moments ago.

Gideon nodded. I ran my hand farther across the expanse of his chest, admiring the taut planes of muscle that defined his slender frame. I could feel the strength running through his body, even when I gently traced the scars. I stopped, fingers splayed, right where his heart thundered in his ribcage against my palm.

"I'm not fragile," Gideon said. "I know physical strength isn't my forte, but I won't break apart under your fingers."

"I know that," I said. "You're not fragile in any way."

I thought of how little Gideon had protected Wylder in school all those years ago, how he was still protecting him all these years later. "You're brave and strong—and powerful."

He gazed at me until I couldn't bear it any longer. I pulled him down to me and kissed him hard. Then I pushed us onto our sides and sat up next to him, fumbling with the button of his fly. Gideon helped, yanking off his slacks and his boxers. He grabbed a foil packet from his pocket before kicking them off the mattress onto the floor.

"You came prepared," I said, delighted and amused.

Gideon shot me a rare grin. "I try to anticipate every possible situation."

I admired his cock, my mouth watering. Thick veins ran down its substantial length, and the bob of its head practically called out to me. I snatched the condom from him and nudged him down on his back as I straddled his legs.

Gideon stared up at me. "Mercy, what—"

"No arguments," I said, tapping my finger to his lips and then rolling the condom over his length. His breath stuttered, and his cock pulsed against my fingers. Fuck, I couldn't wait to feel it inside me.

I positioned myself over him and stroked my fingers over his tattooed chest again, holding his gaze. The sultry seductress role had never felt all that natural to me, but right now, it was as if some kind of goddess had taken me over. This position would be easier on Gideon's lungs, but that didn't mean he had to give up the control he'd obviously been enjoying so much.

"I want to ride my dark god and do his bidding," I purred. "What would you have me do first?"

Desire flared in Gideon's eyes. He gripped my thighs. "Take me," he ordered. "All of me."

I was more than happy to fulfill that desire. I plunged down over him, and he thrust up to meet me. Pleasure crackled through me as my pussy stretched to accommodate him. When he was completely inside me, I gasped at the feeling of fullness. Looking down, I took in our joined bodies, licking my lips at the erotic sight.

"Ride me," Gideon commanded. "Hard and fast like I know you'll like it."

Hell, yes. The authority in his voice turned me even slicker around him.

I raised myself up and lowered myself again, gaining speed as I found my rhythm, and Gideon matched me stroke for stroke. He thrust slow and deep and then faster, with a rolling motion I realized was mimicking the strokes that had gotten me off so well with his tongue. The man was a fast learner.

Sweat rolled down my chest and glazed his. As we rocked together, I leaned down to reclaim his mouth. He kissed me back hungrily, tugging my hair in the way he'd discovered that sent sparks shivering from my scalp all the way to my sex. Then he raised his hips beneath me to press his cock against just the right spot inside me to make me shatter apart again.

Gideon wasn't done yet. He continued to guide me up and down his shaft, our motions becoming more erratic with every thrust. I set my hands on his chest to steady myself as I jerked against him, chasing one more release alongside his. My hair swayed around me with our wild bucking.

A sensation like lightning shot through my body. I ground my hips into his, he swiveled to meet me, and a curse stuttered from his lips.

His expression of pure, unadulterated lust as his release rocked his body was too much for me to handle. I came right alongside him, moaning as our orgasms simultaneously battered our bodies.

It took me a few minutes to catch my breath. Finally, I slid myself off his cock and lay down beside him on the bed. Gideon pulled me closer, his own breath rough but not concerningly so.

"Wow," I said. It seemed to be the only word I had left in my brain.

His arm tightened around me. "That was amazing."

"Maybe even godly," I said, and earned a chuckle. To my surprise, he kissed me on my cheek. Something in that sweet gesture warmed my heart.

There had been, however, nothing sweet in the way that he had fucked me. Even when I had been on the top and he had let me lead it, he'd been right there, working his hips into mine, every step of the way.

I didn't think I could give him up now either, even if I'd wanted to.

Mercy

"I HAVE A MISSION FOR YOU," EZRA SAID, LEANING back in his throne-chair.

I gazed steadily back at him, trying not to show the tremor of apprehension that'd run through me at his words—only a little smaller than the one that'd hit me when Axel had summoned me to the Noble leader's audience room a few minutes ago. The last mission Ezra had sent me on had nearly ended with me bloodied and raped.

But I'd survived it, and he'd see that I could survive whatever else he threw at me, just like I'd proven to his son. He hadn't said a word about my sealing the deal with Jasper in the past two days. Not that I needed the credit, but it would have shown he had a little more faith in me now.

"Great," I said. "What is it?"

"Now that we have the Demon's Wings willing to

send support"—he eyed me for a second as if checking for a reaction to that vague reference to my "date" with Jasper—"it's time to proceed with the next part of our plan against Colt Bryant. We need to destroy the foothold the Steel Knights have gained in the Bend."

Well, I was a hell of a lot more for that than entertaining sleazy gang bosses. I let a little more enthusiasm enter my tone. "I'm ready to do whatever it takes. What's the plan?"

"It's come to my attention that Colt has been storing a large quantity of weapons in one of the warehouses in the industrial district of the Bend."

I nodded. "I'm aware. I saw them."

Ezra gave me a narrow look and then continued, "He hasn't been too subtle about it either. He seems to be sending a message to those who haven't joined him yet or are on the fence that they'll be able to defend themselves and no longer need our protection. We're going to show how wrong he is about that and effectively disarm him."

"Sounds good to me," I said, hoping plain old agreement would go over better.

It did get me a mild smile. "Wylder is going to run you through the details, but the primary objective is to take out the warehouse with all its weapons. Naturally, the place will be heavily guarded, so he'll be taking a large force, including both our men and some of Jasper's. But I felt it was important you joined in with your inside knowledge of the Bend and the aptitude for fighting you've already shown."

The words sounded way more generous than I

expected Ezra to be. I considered him warily even as I kept a smile pasted on my face. "I appreciate that. I'll help any way I can. There's nothing I want more than to see Colt Bryant broken and bleeding and the bastards who helped him slaughter my family right there alongside him."

"Excellent." Ezra stood up and motioned to the door. "Then there's nothing further we need to discuss. Check in with Wylder, and he'll give you your marching orders."

Chances were Wylder's first orders would be to march in the opposite direction as far as I could go, but he couldn't put me off for long when his father had directly instructed me to come along. I was almost looking forward to throwing that fact in his face. Although something about the conversation with Ezra still didn't feel quite right to me.

As I left to figure out where the Noble heir was right now, I caught sight of Gideon down the hall. He stopped in his tracks, no doubt taking note of what room I'd come out of. There was something hesitant in his expression, but it didn't interfere with the new hint of warmth in his gaze.

Things had been a little awkward between us since the other night when we'd come together so passionately, but I guessed that wasn't surprising considering Gideon's lack of experience with any kind of relationship. Half the time he wasn't friendly to his own friends, other than Wylder. I actually found the tentative awkwardness combined with the undeniable signs of attraction kind of adorable in an unexpected way.

It was a heck of a lot better than how his best friend had reacted after our earlier hook-up.

"Hey," I said, walking over to him. "Did Ezra want to fill you in on the new plan too?"

His gaze flicked over my face, settling for a longer moment on my lips before returning to my eyes. But there was an odd note in his voice when he spoke. "He had a couple of files he wanted to pass on to me. What were you doing in there?"

Hadn't I basically just explained that? "He called me in to tell me he wanted me on the upcoming mission."

"Just that?"

"Yeah." I frowned. "Would you have expected something else?"

Gideon's gaze had gone distant again. Somewhere behind those cool gray eyes, a whole lot of gears were turning.

I didn't like how serious he looked, but then he shrugged it off. "No, I only wondered." He offered me a quick, tight smile. "I'd better get those files so I can watch over the rest of you properly while you're out there kicking Colt's ass."

I smiled back even though his demeanor had left me uneasy. Was something bothering him that he wasn't telling me? But we weren't exactly close enough that it seemed right to try to badger him about it. The one thing I was sure of with Gideon was that if he'd consider logically whether I was better off knowing and tell me if he determined I was.

"We'll be counting on you," I said, and set off in search of his asshole best friend.

———

Several hours later, I was crouched by a car down the street from the old warehouse building where Colt was storing his weapons. The summer humidity had already turned my shirt sticky against my skin even in the darkness of the early morning hour, well before dawn. The smell of gasoline and hot asphalt prickled in my nose. And Wylder was scowling at me.

Nothing so new about that. I ignored him, which I hoped just pissed him off more.

A shiny black sedan entered through the main gates of the warehouse. Could Colt be in it? I'd love for him to be inside when we blew it up. But we couldn't move from our place. We had to wait.

Finally, a man showed up a few blocks down the street in the opposite direction from the warehouse. I didn't know this guy who looked to be in his early to mid-twenties with shaggy brown hair. The sleeves of his shirt were rolled up, and I caught the tattoo of the demon skull over his right wrist.

He nodded in our direction even though I was pretty sure he couldn't make us out in the darkness.

"I still kind of feel iffy working with Jasper's men," Wylder admitted under his breath.

"Maybe you should have thought of that before I went to him," I said sarcastically.

He looked at me, his eyes narrowing. "Wouldn't want your efforts to go to waste now, would we?"

"Oh, fuck you," I muttered as I turned back to face

the Demon's Wings man who was slowly making his way towards us.

"You already have," Wylder said in a matter of fact voice. I had the intense urge to hit him, but I wasn't going to compromise the mission over his dickishness.

The man stopped when he reached the car. Wylder motioned him closer. "Did you bring everything?"

He ducked down across from us and nodded. "Enough explosives to take this whole thing down twice over. Everything's in our truck. But how are you going to take it inside?"

I met Wylder's eyes before we stepped out of the darkness. I wore a sleeveless hoodie with the hood up to cover my hair and a red bandana on my arm. Wylder was dressed in a similar way.

We were going in as the Steel Knights ourselves—or at least the underlings pledged to them. We were counting on there being so many new recruits that any regulars we couldn't stealthily kill would be used to unfamiliar faces. The bandanas weren't even official Steel Knights ones, just mocked up to look that way with red fabric and black sharpie.

Wylder made a signal, and the rest of the Noble people on the job moved toward the Demon's Wings truck, slipping through the night's shadows. Then he and I parted ways.

I followed the Demon's Wings guy back to the truck, and he ushered the last few men into the back. I was bringing in very dangerous cargo tonight, but it would only be deadly to the Steel Knights. A slight smirk played across my lips at the thought.

I got into the driver's seat. A few moments later, Wylder appeared at the passenger side of the cab. "All clear."

I drove around to the side entrance, a narrow passageway that led out to the large compound around the warehouse. Wylder had disposed of the two guards he'd dispatched there. As we got out to lay down the first set of explosives, I spotted one of the bodies, which he'd dragged behind a storage container.

After we were done, we slunk toward the main building and hid behind a couple of old steel drums to observe our surroundings. A few Steel Knights men were patrolling around the building, with more no doubt inside. The black sedan was parked out in front. I wondered again who'd come inside it.

Wylder checked his watch. "Where the hell are they?" he murmured. "They were supposed to be here a minute ago."

As if on cue, the front gates to the warehouse burst open, and a shiny blue Range Rover Kaige had picked out for the mission roared inside. It crashed into the sedan, which sent the other car's tail spinning away to smash into the boundary wall.

Shouts carried from inside the building. As planned, the crash had caught the Steel Knights' attention, which meant the guards wouldn't notice the rest of us just yet.

Wylder tugged on the side of my shirt. "Come on, we don't have much time."

I nodded. We had several key strategic places we needed to plant the explosives if we were going to blow this place to the ground, all plotted out by Gideon using old blueprints of the warehouse he'd managed to dig up online.

At the end of this mission, there'd be nothing left but cinders.

Wylder sent a quick text on his phone. A swarm of people—both Nobles and Demon's Wings—poured out of the back of the truck. A handful of them ran to join us, while most came around the building to pick off the guards as they raced out to confront Kaige.

Axel was in the bunch who came to a stop beside us, his expression grim. I wouldn't be surprised if he'd insisted on being part of this group just so he could grumble to Ezra afterward about all the issues he had with Wylder.

I sent a worried glance toward the Range Rover, where Kaige was just climbing out, semi-automatic rifle in hand, ready to meet the enemy. But I had to keep moving. That was the last thing I saw before we slipped past the warehouse door.

Inside, we found ourselves in thicker darkness. Only the faintest light from the city streetlamps seeped through the grimy windows. Wylder shone a small flashlight ahead of us as we hustled past the crates between us and our destination. He motioned to the men carrying some of the homemade bombs to plant them in various nooks and crannies.

There was a dull roar outside and the sound of running footsteps. Wylder yanked me down behind one of the crates, flicking off his flashlight. His hot breath ruffled the hair on the back of my neck, and an unwelcome tingle shot through my nerves at his closeness.

It didn't last long. The hallway outside quieted, and we could hear the distant blare of guns firing. I itched to be in on the action, but this was more important. And chances were we'd be doing at least a little fighting before we were out of here.

"Clear," Wylder called out softly. We walked down the hallway as quickly as we could before it widened to lead us to a rusted staircase. We planted another bomb at the foot of the stairs before walking into the old, out of order furnace in the center of the building.

The place was rotting away with time. There were obvious signs of the Steel Knights' presence, Wylder's light catching on their mark on the blotchy walls and printed on the huge crates. I had no doubt what was inside those. I'd seen the heaps of guns mixed in with straw just a few weeks ago.

Sudden footsteps brought us whipping around. "What the fuck?" a man shouted from a nearby doorway. Shit—we'd been discovered.

In the split second that it took for Wylder to shoot the man in the forehead, he'd already raised an alarm with a shrill cry. Five more Steel Knights came racing down the metal staircase, their footsteps clanging. They rushed towards us. The sound of bullets hitting the metal pipes echoed around us.

We all leapt behind the crates for shelter. Wylder and the other guys fired off shots around the wooden edges. I peeked out, gripping my gun, trying to get a clear enough view to shoot someone I was sure was on the opposite side.

One of the Demon's Wings men with us gave a shout, and my head jerked around. More Steel Knights were coming at us from the other direction. As I whirled, the nearest one leapt right at Wylder, who was in the middle of firing at someone on the other side of the room. A knife flashed in the attacker's hand.

No. Despite all my frustration with the Noble heir, every nerve in me resisted the idea of seeing him wounded—or worse, dead. I leapt forward with a cry of warning. Instinctively, I groped for the knife Wylder had given me, knowing I could use it better in hand-to-hand combat than a pistol.

I'd thrown myself between the attacking man and Wylder, so he slammed into me instead, tackling me to the ground. He grabbed my shirt and tried to pin me. I jabbed my knife right between his ribs. With a groan, he slumped on top of me, all dead weight.

Then Wylder was there, heaving him off me. "You okay?" he asked, his face oddly pale in the eerie dimness. His flashlight had fallen somewhere. The other men were silhouettes lunging back and forth through the fractured shadows—and then there was another Steel Knight barreling straight toward Wylder as he bent to help me up.

I grabbed Wylder's hand, yanked him to the side, and slashed my knife at the incoming attacker. I wasn't quite fast enough. The guy got off a shot as I bashed his arm to the side, the bullet carving a gouge through the flesh of my shoulder. I bit back a cry and stabbed again, this time managing to plunge the knife into his throat.

He fell with a gurgle. My ear drums rattled with two shots as Wylder dispatched a couple more Steel Knights men. Then he turned to stare at me, his eyes fixing on the blood streaming down my shoulder. "He was coming for me," he said.

"No kidding, jackass," I retorted. "So was the first one. You might wish *I* was dead and buried so you didn't have to put up with me, but for some crazy reason, I happen to want you to stay alive."

He blinked, and something shifted in his expression. A dark chuckle fell from his lips. "Maybe you really are merciful."

Before I could figure out how to respond to that, Axel let out a yell from deeper in the room. "The last one's placed. We've got to get out of here and blow this place to smithereens."

Wylder's jaw clenched at his dad's right-hand man taking over the orders. "Kill anyone who stands between us and the door," he added, sweeping his arm for everyone to go.

We took off running towards the exit, the two of us bringing up the rear so we could cover the others. I clutched my gun in one hand and my now-bloody knife in the other. But we'd only made it a few paces when another yell rang out behind us.

We swung around, Wylder cocking his gun. The others were already firing. Rather than shooting, Wylder hauled me out of the way behind one of the crates. He bobbed up over the top of it and fired back. I peered around the edge of the crate, gun ready, but our attackers had taken their own shelter.

"Whatever you think you're going to do here, you're never going to get away with it," a voice called out. Did it sound a little familiar? I watched closely as one of the men rose up to take a shot at us. It was Jenner. My pulse stuttered.

He saw me too. "What the fuck are you doing here, Mercy?" he snapped.

So he was acknowledging my presence now. "I should ask you the same question," I said. "Didn't take you long to change sides, huh?"

"Everyone looks out for themselves. You ran off to find new company too, obviously."

I scoffed. "At least I didn't go running to the traitor who killed my dad and wiped out the rest of his family and inner circle in one single night. Who needs *that* kind of loyalty?"

Shock flared across Jenner's features. He ducked down again, but his voice had roughened. "What are you talking about?"

Wylder let out an incredulous laugh. "As if you don't know that Colt Bryant assassinated Tyrell Katz and his family in cold blood."

"You mean Colt killed Tyrell because Tyrell wanted to have him assassinated. Nobody but your father is responsible for the demise of the Claws."

"Is that the cock and bull story Colt's been feeding you?" I made a face at the ceiling. "Do you really think my dad would spend a year making plans for my marriage and his alliance just to assassinate his future son-in-law a day before the wedding? If Tyrell Katz had wanted Colt dead, he'd be six feet under already."

"He was biding his time," one of the others said, but I thought I caught a trace of doubt in his voice.

"Look, I was *there*. It was my rehearsal dinner, remember? Colt attacked us when we were unprepared and had given him our trust. He even tried to kill me, and I sure as hell hadn't been plotting against him. Deep down, you have to know what I'm saying is true. Unless you sold your brains along with your dignity."

"Bitch," another of the guys spat out. I caught a glimpse of him around the crate—he wasn't anyone I recognized, probably from a different gang. "Stop spewing garbage. Come on, let's take them."

Tires screeched outside, followed by a volley of angry shouts. That didn't sound good.

Axel and a few of the other men had come hurrying back to defend the Noble heir—I doubted they cared about me. "Their back-up's arrived," Axel hollered. "Let's get going, now."

Wylder tugged my shoulder. I thought of how Ezra had so easily dismissed my idea that I appeal to the former Claws members, and resolve gripped my chest.

"If my father—and the Claws—ever meant anything to you," I called out to Jenner, "give me a little faith too. Colt should be destroyed for what he did to my family and our people. I want you to help me take him down, once and for all."

Wylder pulled me away, Axel and the others training their guns past us in case the other men showed their faces.

"Get them!" Jenner ordered in a cold voice. "Don't let any of them escape."

I flinched inwardly, but my body knew enough to start running. Wylder cursed under his breath, keeping half his attention behind us as we sprinted toward the door. He fired a few shots, and I heard a body thump. Some ridiculous part of me hoped it hadn't been the former Claws men, even after all that.

Axel and the others came charging after us, sidestepping so they could return the fire that was aimed our way. We reached the door, I rammed my shoulder into it, and just like that we were stumbling out into the humid summer night.

Fighting had broken out all across the courtyard. More cars had pulled in through the front entrance; the concrete yard was a mess of brawling bodies. Kaige and Rowan were right in the thick of it, landing punches and kicks between pulling their triggers at opponents farther away.

We had to get back to the truck so we could get out of here. There were so many men and guns between us and it. I gritted my teeth, wiped the blood off my wound, and dashed into the heart of the fight, Wylder right beside me. My pulse thrummed with a weird sort of eagerness I didn't look at too closely.

I concentrated on the attackers in front of us, kicking the legs out from under one of the Steel Knights and aiming my gun at another who was firing at one of the Demon's Wings guys. My bullets caught him in the chest, but too late—our ally was already crumpling to the ground, blood gushing from his neck and shoulder.

Damn it. I swung around at a rush of movement nearby, and found myself careening to the side as a burly form shoved past me. Before I could catch my balance, I'd collided with someone's back.

My shoulder screamed in protest at the impact against my wound. Our feet tangled, and we both tumbled over.

It was another of the Demon's Wings guys I'd stumbled into—the one with the shaggy hair who'd brought the truck. He glared at me as we scrambled to our feet. Pain seared all through my arm.

Axel reached down and yanked me the rest of the way up, ignoring the gasp of pain I couldn't hold back. "Didn't see you there," he said with a sneer. I guessed he was the one who'd bumped into me. I barely held back a glare as I steadied myself on my feet.

The Demon's Wings guy snarled at me. "Do you want me to get killed, bitch?"

My jaw twitched, but I reined in my temper. "It was an accident. I apologize."

"Stay in your lane." He pulled out another gun and started shooting at the men coming at us. Axel raised his hands as if in surrender. I didn't have time to waste my breath on him, so I hurried onward, my gun raised.

Up ahead, Kaige had already jumped into the driver's seat of the truck. It looked like I wasn't the getaway driver this time.

Wylder had made it to the truck too. "Everyone with me, get over here, away from the building," he yelled, holding up the device that would detonate the explosives.

He was going to set them off. That would definitely turn the tide in our favor—as long as we were out of the way.

I rushed toward them alongside our other allies, getting in a few more shots to help clear the path. I was just five feet from the truck when Wylder pressed the button.

The first explosion held enough power to shake the ground. I staggered, and Rowan was there, grabbing my arm to stop me from falling again.

The structure of the factory rattled, bricks shaking loose from the spire and a terrible rattling sound reverberating from inside. Debris rained down on the Steel Knights who were still closer to the warehouse.

The booms thundered louder and louder as the chain reaction sped up. Flames burst through the shattering windows, and smoke gushed up. With one final bursting sound, the roof collapsed in like it was a house of cards. The walls shuddered and toppled in on each other, the fire devouring everything in the mess of the broken warehouse.

Pandemonium had broken out across the yard. The Steel Knights who'd been too close were now just scalded bodies in the midst of the rubble. Others wove back and forth looking dazed, bleeding and dusted with soot.

The rest of the Nobles and the Demon's Wings gathered close around the truck, staring but ready with their weapons all the same. This might have been a little more destruction than we'd pictured. My eyes watered with the wafts of smoke and dust that reached us.

"Everyone into the truck," Wylder shouted.

Rowan started to guide me by the arm, but my gaze snagged on a figure swaying out of the wreckage. Jenner. He looked to be in bad shape, blood pouring from his forehead. The factory behind him burned brightly, the flames of it so hot that I could only take a few steps toward him before it became too much. But that's where I held my ground.

Rowan tugged on my arm. "Let's go, Mercy." He followed my gaze to see Jenner, whose foot caught in the rubble and tripped him to his knees. "He'd have killed you if he had the chance."

He had no idea just how true that was. But just then, the fire must have reached one of the crates of ammunition. Another explosion went off, sending a fresh burst of flames and flying rubble almost to Jenner's heels. Something in me balked at turning my back on him.

I couldn't just leave Jenner like that. He'd ordered my death moments ago, but he'd been misled by Colt... just like I'd been for nearly a year. If I could be tricked by the man for that long, if Dad could have been, did I really have any place blaming someone else for believing his lies?

I couldn't see one of our men lose his life because of one stupid mistake.

Ignoring the heat, I took off running towards him. Behind me, Rowan yelled my name. I hefted Jenner to his feet and started dragging him on his unsteady feet. He was heavier than I expected.

Both Rowan and Wylder ran over to me with tense expressions. "I'm not leaving him here," I said before they could get on my case. "Help me or get out of my way."

"For fuck's sake," Wylder muttered, blowing out his breath in frustration, but they both stepped in and pulled the guy away from me. Before I had to protest, they jogged with him over to the edge of the compound where at least there was no chance of the fire or any new explosions reaching him.

That was all I'd wanted. I dove into the back of the truck. The two guys followed me. We crouched there with the rest of the men as the engine roared. Kaige turned us toward the street, and I tossed one last look toward Jenner before we tore around the corner and away.

Mercy

FRANK FINISHED THE LAST OF THE STITCHES ON MY shoulder and dabbed the wound with an amber liquid. It stung enough to make me hiss through my teeth. He shook his head at me. "You're making this into a habit."

"Yes, she is." Anthea swept into the kitchen where Frank had been cleaning me up, her heels rapping on the floor. "Is she reasonably in one piece?"

"For now," Frank said dryly. He taped a bandage over the wound and patted me on the back. "No push-ups or pull-ups for at least a few days."

"And here I was so looking forward to busting open my stitches in the gym," I muttered sarcastically at his retreating back.

Anthea clucked her tongue and propped herself against the counter across from me. She looked me over. Frank had gotten my arm clean while he'd been treating the wound, but my clothes and the rest of my body were still smudged with soot and dappled with dried blood, and I stunk of smoke.

Anthea might have liked me now, but she still wrinkled her nose, which I guessed was warranted. "Come on," she said. "Clearly the boys aren't the only ones who need 'Auntie Anthea' looking after them."

She led me back to what I realized on stepping inside was her bedroom. It was twice the size of the guest rooms I'd stayed in, with a sliding glass door that led out to a small sundeck I'd noticed before from outside. The frame of her sleigh bed gleamed with dark mahogany, and I caught a peek inside a walk-in closet that held more clothes than I'd seen in one place anywhere outside of a shopping mall. The whole space smelled of the same crisply delicate perfume Anthea always wore.

"This isn't my permanent home, but Ezra makes it clear I'm always welcome here," she said in a voice that didn't sound totally happy about that fact. I hadn't pried into her relationship with her brother, but it was obviously complicated.

She shooed me toward the en-suite bathroom. "Wash yourself up, and I'll pick out something acceptable for you to wear. If you won't take me up on my offer to *buy* new clothes for you, then you can at least make sure my cast-offs go to good use."

I doubted that anything Anthea owned was in poor enough condition to be a cast-off, but when she had that many clothes, it seemed silly to argue. "Nothing too frilly or fancy," I called over my shoulder, and heard her snort.

I didn't want to get my bandage wet in the shower, so I scrubbed myself down as well as I could sitting on the edge of the jacuzzi bathtub—now *that* was a perk I could get behind—until I was sure I wasn't going to stain the ivory towels when I dried myself off. Anthea bustled in with a pair of yoga pants and a casual blouse that were still dressier than my typical wear but comfortable enough I could thank her genuinely.

When I was dressed and feeling more like a human being and not a walking dumpster, she brought me out onto the deck. The sun was just peeking over the horizon, casting a rosy golden glow over the lawn. We sank into the two lounge chairs there.

As soon as my back hit the cushions, my muscles relaxed. I hadn't slept much before we'd left for the mission. I wouldn't mind a little doze right here, but that seemed insulting to my host.

"You're putting yourself through a lot for that man," she said.

"Who?" I said, startling. The first place my mind went was Wylder—all his snark and his ordering me around, the way I'd jumped in front of him a few hours ago despite how he'd been treating me.

Anthea raised an eyebrow at me. "Your ex-fiancé. All this fighting and risking your life to get your revenge."

Oh. Of course that's what she meant. I grimaced and sagged back into the padded chair. "Someone needs to see justice done for my family. It wouldn't be the same if I let someone else handle it. I don't trust anyone else to make sure it gets done right."

"Fair enough. But I'm glad you did make it back in one piece today—and that you did from Jasper as well."

That reminded me. "Do you need your hair pin back? I didn't have to use it, but with the kind of jobs Ezra's already given me, it seems like it might come in handy again."

She waved the question off. "Please keep it. I have a few on hand, and I can always make more."

That didn't surprise me at all. But it did trigger a prickle of curiosity. "How did you get started on the whole poisons and subtle murders thing anyway? Was it just a way to pitch in with the family business?"

"Oh, no." Anthea's laugh held no humor. She tipped her face to the brightening sunlight. "My and Ezra's father didn't believe in women having *any* role in the business other than as a bargaining chip. He didn't even bother to have me trained as your father clearly did for you, although I still managed to pick up plenty by watching. It's hard to live in a house like this without absorbing some knowledge."

"I know what you mean," I said. At least half of the things I'd learned over the years had been in spite of Dad, not because of him.

"In more ways than one, I'm sure. As soon as I was eighteen, he married me off—to a man nearly three times my age, who was looking as much for a punching bag and slave as a wife."

I winced, able to picture the type of man she was talking about far too easily. A fragment of memory came back to me from an earlier conversation. "You got rid of him. As he obviously deserved."

The corner of Anthea's mouth quirked upward. "I did, and he did. There was nowhere to go when my father would have tracked me down and punished me even worse if I'd tried to run. So I kept myself sane by researching every possible way I might be able to off the bastard without it being obvious I'd done it. The internet is a wonderful thing, isn't it?"

I couldn't help grinning, thinking of all the parkour moves I'd learned that way. "It sure is."

"Well, dear old Dad took a bullet in a bad way during a deal gone sour, and my brother stepped up to lead. Ezra can be harsh and unyielding, but he'd never liked the man who'd been picked for me. He'd argued against the marriage. And at that time I'd gathered plenty of knowledge. My husband had a shocking accident that of course I had *nothing* to do with, and Ezra welcomed me back into the fold."

She shrugged. "I have my own apartment in Manhattan now and my own business connections there, but I help out the family whenever I can. I enjoy seeing justice served as well."

"Then I'm sure you can understand why I won't let this go."

"I do. That doesn't mean I like seeing you bleeding over it." She turned to look at me. "You thought I meant someone else when I first mentioned what you're putting yourself through. I find that very interesting."

I put on my most innocent face. "I just wasn't sure what you meant."

"Hmm. You're good at many things, Mercy, but you're not a skilled enough liar to get away with it around me." She considered me shrewdly. "I have picked up on some tensions, both good and bad, between you and Wylder's inner circle. Is there something going on there?"

A flush crept over my face. Would it be an appropriate time to bring up the fact that I had slept with all of them at some point? How weird would she think that was?

"I have a history with Rowan," I admitted. "And Wylder... Wylder has been acting like a dick, but I guess that's not exactly news. The others... it's complicated."

"*They're* complicated—each in their own ways. If you ask me, there's way too much testosterone around."

I grinned. "I'll agree with that."

Anthea drew in a breath. "Well, look. I'll say this. They can *all* be dicks. That's what men in this kind of life are like. If you want to make something of it with any of them, you have to be firm. Demand the answers and the actions you need from them. Hold them accountable. I've known those boys for quite a while now, and I think they've all got a lot worth admiring in them—if you insist on them showing it."

"It's not like I'm perfect either," I had to acknowledge.

"Maybe not, but we women need to have our acts more together than they do, because the second we slip up, it's suddenly a judgment on our entire existence." She grimaced. "If you can make honest men out of them, I'll be more than happy."

I looked at her suspiciously. Was she implying what

it sounded like she was? Could she possibly know what was actually up with me and the guys?

"We'll see about that," I said noncommittally. "Thanks for the tip." Then I couldn't restrain a yawn.

Anthea tutted and sat up straighter. "*You* obviously need to go back to bed. Come on. I'm not going to be responsible for you ending up sleep-deprived."

———————

After a few more hours of sleep, my stomach started grumbling too loud for my still-groggy mind to ignore it. A little more refreshed than before, I headed down to the kitchen to scrounge up some breakfast, lunch, or whatever meal it theoretically was at this time of day.

I'd just popped some bread in the toaster when Rowan walked in. He came right over to me, stopping just a couple of feet away. "Are you doing okay? How's your shoulder?"

I reached toward the bandaged spot instinctively and caught myself. "It's fine," I said shortly. "I've been through worse." *Like, oh, that time when you left me in the lurch with a broken heart.*

Rowan didn't take the hint. He kept hovering by me as I got out the peanut butter and jam. Nothing wrong with a little PB and J as a pick-me-up no matter how old you get.

"You should make sure to get plenty of fluids into you too," he said. "An intense mission like last night, it drains you more than you realize."

My old irritation flared inside me. Rowan had told

me before that he wasn't going to fight about me joining forces with the Nobles or get in my way. He'd helped me during the operation last night. He was trying to look out for me now. But none of it could really matter when he still hadn't explained the horrible way he'd hurt me years ago.

My first impulse was to shut him out like I had before, but Anthea's advice came back to me. Maybe I could get the answers I wanted. Maybe I just hadn't demanded them firmly enough

I spun toward him. "Why are you acting like you care about me and my well-being anyway?"

He blinked. "I'm not just acting. I do care about what happens to you." His gaze darted to my injured shoulder as if that somehow proved his point.

"Really? How am I supposed to believe that when you completely screwed me over back when you suppos-edly *loved* me? You've never even bothered to explain why you totally abandoned me." I waved the knife I'd picked up to spread the peanut butter, annoyed at myself for the raw emotion that'd crept into my voice.

I shouldn't care anymore. He shouldn't have any power over me at all.

But, fuck it, he did. And he still would until I under-stood what he'd done five years ago.

Rowan closed his eyes, looking pained. "It wasn't like that. I swear it, Mer, I wanted to be there. I meant to be there."

"Then why the hell weren't you? If you really want to make things right, then own up to what actually happened. If we're even going to work together properly, I have to know who I'm dealing with. Unless I'm dealing with a coward."

He winced, and I knew I'd stung his pride. His jaw worked. For a second, I thought he'd refuse like he had before. But then a sigh rushed out of him.

"You're right. I just—I thought it'd be easier not to talk about it, and somehow I'd let myself be angry at you too when none of it was really your fault. At the same time, I didn't want you to have to feel guilty over it the way I have for so long..."

He rubbed his hand over his face in frustration, so much anguish showing in his expression that my heart skipped a beat. Rowan had always been so good at holding up a cheerful front. I wasn't sure I'd ever seen him look so upset.

My voice softened of its own accord. "What happened, Rowan? *What* wasn't my fault—what would I feel guilty about?"

I could tell it took an effort for him to meet my gaze. "That night... I meant to come, right up to the end. I had my bag packed, everything ready. I was just waiting the last few minutes until it was time to go, and then—then I heard the gunshot."

My heart outright stopped. "Gunshot?"

"From Carina's room."

"Someone shot your sister?" I burst out. I'd never gotten to meet any of Rowan's family, but I'd seen pictures of them. I'd heard him talk about his little sister, who was only six then and the total baby of the family. The affection had always been so clear in his voice, I'd felt almost like she was my kid sister too.

"No," Rowan said raggedly. "They tried to. She was —she was having a sleepover, and she let her friend have her bed while she took the sleeping bag on the floor. Someone shot the girl in the bed through the window— they must have assumed it was her."

Abruptly, I remembered. I'd caught a few shocked murmurs in the halls at school about some little kid who'd gotten shot in their sleep. But the name hadn't been familiar, so in my confusion over Rowan's disap-pearance, it hadn't even occurred to me that the two events were connected.

It still didn't make sense to me. "But—why would anyone—"

"Because of me." Rowan's hand clenched against the countertop. "Because... your father found out that I was seeing you. A week before, after we'd already finalized our plan, he stopped me in the street and warned me to stay away from you. He told me I'd regret it if I didn't stay out of your life. But I thought we were already so close to getting away, he didn't seem to know about that part, if we just hung in there..."

"And he sent one of his men to kill your sister as punishment for ignoring him." My voice sounded hollow to my ears. Oh my God. Just when I thought I'd discovered the limits of the horrors my father had been capable of, he proved me wrong. "Why didn't you tell me—about the warning, or about Carina?"

He swallowed hard. "I was a stupid, over-confident teenager who didn't really understand just how bad things could get. I knew how much of a hold he had over you. I was worried that if I told you he knew about us, you'd give up the chance we worked so hard for. You'd insist that we couldn't see each other again. I *loved* you, Mer, so much that I forgot all the other things that should have been important to me, I didn't see how much danger I was dragging my whole family into..."

His head drooped. For the first time since I'd seen him here, I recognized the weight he was carrying. "Rowan..."

"I was afraid to say anything to you afterward," he went on. "What if he came after Carina again when he realized he'd gotten the wrong girl? It killed me to know you had no idea why I hadn't shown up, but it could have literally killed her if I'd kept any contact with you. And my parents were so shaken they decided it was time to get out of the Bend. They couldn't stand to stay in the house. They let us skip a few weeks of school while they arranged a new place in the city and then moved us there. Not that the change of scenery helped all that much."

That last statement constricted my throat even more. "What happened after?"

His shoulders rose and fell in a hopeless motion. "Carina never totally got over seeing her friend murdered. My parents kept arguing, and finally they split up. Mom took Carina with her out west where her parents live, and I stayed with Dad because I'd gotten in with Wylder by then and I didn't want to start over yet again. And Dad, well... let's just say that these days he prefers vodka to me."

Tears pricked at my eyes for the man in front of me

—and the boy who'd been broken so badly before becoming that man. If I'd known…

But that might have been even worse. He was right —if Dad had caught us communicating again, who knew what he might have done? Everything that'd happened to Rowan and his family and that poor little girl who'd been in the wrong place at the wrong time, it was because of me and *my* rotten family.

"I'm sorry," I said, knowing the words were too small to address the damage done.

Rowan cracked a soft, sad smile. "I might have been angry with you sometimes, but it wasn't fair of me. You never lied about what kind of man your father was or how scary he could be. I insisted on being a part of your life anyway. I fell in love with you and embraced it. None of that is on you. Besides, you're not responsible for your father's actions."

I wasn't—and neither was Rowan. All these years I'd blamed him and cursed his name over something that hadn't been his fault either. What could I say he should have done differently? Everything I'd thought about the past had been wrong.

I'd been so hard on him since I'd gotten here. Now I had no idea what to say to him. My emotions were one big jumble.

Wylder poked his head into the kitchen. He opened his mouth as his gaze fixed on me as if he meant to say something, but my expression seemed to stop him. He caught himself as if he'd thought better of it. Then his attention shifted to Rowan.

"My father wants to speak with you as soon as possible."

Rowan tensed. As I watched, he straightened up, and the anguish smoothed from his face. He'd gotten so good at burying the trauma of his past, this golden boy who'd once been mine. So good I'd never so much as suspected it.

"I'll see him now," he said, and gave me one last look. "I'm sorry it took me so long to tell you."

Then he walked out of the room at Wylder's heels, leaving me shaken to the core.

Kaige

I couldn't sleep, again. No surprises there. I stretched out in the hammock and took a big bite of the spicy taquito I'd grabbed on my late-night snack run.

The pot brownie in my pocket was going to make the perfect dessert. If I couldn't rest, I could at least have a good time.

I was just popping the last bite of the taquito into my mouth when faint voices reached me. It was three in the morning—who the hell else would be wandering around at this time? Unless one of the guys on patrol was talking to himself.

Tipping my head to the side and squinting in the thin moonlight, I made out two figures coming to a stop under a tree several feet away from me. The thicker shadows there obscured their faces, but they were close enough for me to make out their low voices clearly now, and the one who spoke next was none other than the big boss himself.

"Is everything in place as we discussed?" Ezra asked.

I froze, holding my massive body as still as I could. What was the head of the Nobles doing having a chat out here in the middle of the night? Nothing good, I had to guess. Whatever was going on, Wylder would want to know about it, since there was no guarantee his dad would fill him in.

The other man's head turned to scan the surroundings, and I stopped breathing, but he didn't pause when his gaze skimmed past the hammock. Here between the two trees that held it up, it must have looked like nothing more than a vague blob in the darkness.

When he spoke, I recognized his voice as Axel's. "I snagged the phone during the fight. The guy never had a clue. He'll definitely remember her slamming into him, though. I gave her a good shove. He was pretty pissed."

My nerves prickled. Was he talking about Mercy? I'd seen her collide with one of the Demon's Wings men in the middle of the fighting yesterday. I hadn't realized Axel had set that up, though. What the fuck was he playing at?

"And the rest?" The understated menace in Ezra's tone made my blood run cold.

"It all went smoothly. I used Jasper's contact details in the phone to arrange for him to be at a specific restaurant expecting to make a deal tonight. I just heard his men fended off the mercenary, and now he's rightfully pissed that someone tried to take him out. He's eager for blood for sure."

"Perfect," Ezra said. "Let me have the phone. I've already put out a request to speak with Jasper here this morning. I doubt he'll take much convincing. I'll say I caught her with the phone, and he'll put the rest of the pieces together from there. Easy to encourage him to believe she was acting on wounded pride after the date she was forced into."

I could hear the smirk in Axel's voice. "And then you hand her over?"

"Naturally. We wouldn't harbor some stray who'd commit an offense like that against an ally of ours."

Axel chuckled, and my hands clenched. "Two bucks says that she doesn't live past sundown."

There was a rustle as Ezra must have pocketed the phone. "That's my expectation, Axel. We get her out of the way while solidifying our alliance with a show of good faith. I look forward to seeing it through."

Every muscle in my body tensed, my vision hazing with rage. I was going to kill *them* for talking about Mercy that way—for setting her up for some kind to attempted murder—they wanted to see her *dead*. After all Ezra's talk about taking her into the Nobles—

A snarl caught in the back of my throat, and I was a split-second from flinging myself off the hammock and charging at them, fists swinging. I shifted my weight— and then closed my eyes.

No. No running in half-cocked. As satisfying as the idea was right now, pummeling Ezra Noble and his right-hand man wasn't going to fix anything, was it? They'd probably kill *me*.

And then there'd be no one left who knew and could defend Mercy from their sick scheme.

For once, I needed to think. I had to be like Gideon, sharp and strategic.

Oh, who was I kidding? Better plan—I needed to get Gideon and let him do the thinking. And Wylder and Rowan, maybe Anthea too. I didn't care how many people Ezra ruled over or how brutal he could be. We were not letting him destroy Mercy.

I waited several minutes, the thumps of my pulse almost deafening in the quiet of the night, until I was sure Ezra and Axel had gone back inside. Then I eased off the hammock and hurried to the house, all thought of anything other than protecting Mercy gone from my mind.

Everyone else was asleep, as you'd reasonably expect at this hour. I went to Wylder's room first. It was his dad—he'd have the best idea how we should handle this.

On my way down the hall, I tapped in the emergency text code we'd decided on that would provoke an obnoxious ringtone to wake him up. I could tell it'd worked because I heard him muttering swear words under his breath through the door before I even rapped lightly on it.

As Wylder opened the door, he swiped his hand over his weary face and glowered at me. "The emergency had better not be that you're out of Red Bull."

"I wouldn't use the code over something like that," I

said under my breath. "This is important. Mercy's in trouble."

Wylder snapped to alertness in an instant. No matter how much of a dick he'd been toward her, he clearly didn't like the idea of anyone else causing her problems. He motioned me into his room and shut the door behind me. "Tell me everything."

Half an hour later, we'd gathered with Gideon, Rowan, and Anthea in Wylder's office, and I was just wrapping up explaining what I'd overheard again.

"Ezra said he's called Jasper in for a meeting this morning," I finished, my gaze darting to the window to check for any sign of dawning sunlight. That morning was creeping closer way too fast for comfort. "He's going to 'expose' Mercy then. We've got to figure out some way to stop it, fast."

Gideon rubbed his eyes, but when he dropped his hand, his face was set in an expression so coolly determined I wouldn't have wanted to face off with him, lung condition or not. "I didn't think he'd make a move this quickly. I might have caught on otherwise."

I stared at him. "You *knew* Ezra was going to turn on Mercy?"

He shrugged as if anyone with half a brain cell would have known. "He talked to me briefly the other night after the... corpse incident. Whoever's been targeting Mercy here, it's made him see her as a liability."

"He wasn't convinced she was more useful to him than trouble to begin with," Wylder grumbled. "He doesn't think much of the gangs in the Bend or of women." He cut his gaze toward his aunt with a slightly apologetic grimace.

Anthea just shook her head. "Oh, you're not saying anything I don't know. I wondered when he insisted on sending her to Jasper—whether it was really because he thought she'd handle him best and not because he was hoping she wouldn't and it'd be an easy way to take her out of the picture."

"He didn't seem all that happy about her success." Wylder sighed. "She's a wild card. He prefers to only work with people he can fully control and anticipate. The way she handled Jasper and came back unfazed probably made her seem like not just a liability but a potential threat to his authority too."

Silence descended on the room. We knew what happened to those who had earned the wrath of Ezra.

"Jasper *did* like Mercy, whatever happened that night," I ventured. "Would he definitely believe this story?"

"I can't imagine she won him over enough that he'd forgive a murder attempt," Anthea said. "She has a reasonable motive, and with the phone and the way Axel set her up to look as if she'd had an opportunity to steal it from his man, the circumstantial evidence is awfully convincing. And think about it—if Jasper wants to say it wasn't Mercy, he'd be accusing Ezra of lying. Whose favor do you think he cares more about?"

Even I knew the answer to that question without needing to think about it. I scowled at the wall. "There's got to be something we can do."

"Everything revolves around the phone, doesn't it?"

Rowan said. "If we can get rid of the phone, then there's only a motive, no evidence of any kind."

Wylder nodded slowly. "He'd have it in his office, most likely. Possibly the audience room if he's planning on meeting Jasper there. But either way the room will be locked, and he'll have tucked it away somewhere secure inside. And he's an early riser no matter how late he was up. We can only count on an hour or two before there's a good chance of us getting caught."

Shit. My nerves jangled with apprehension and a prickle of what might have been panic. "So let's get moving, then!"

"Hold on," Gideon said evenly. "If we barge in without planning carefully, we'll only get caught. We need to take a few minutes to decide our best possible approach. Starting with, how are we going to get past those locked doors?"

A small smile curved Anthea's lips. "I think I can help with that."

After a brief, intense discussion, Wylder and I ended up being the ones to tackle Ezra's office, while Rowan and Gideon headed to the audience room. Anthea's bedroom was near her brother's, so she was playing look-out, ready to alert us the second he got up for the morning. But she'd lent us some tools.

I shifted my weight from foot to foot as Wylder fiddled with the lock picks from his aunt's personal kit. "Do you figure she's done a lot of breaking and entering before?" I whispered.

Wylder let out a low chuckle. "I'd be surprised if she hasn't done at least a little. There's a reason my dad takes good care of her, and it's not just because she's family. He protects his valuable assets." There was a trace of bitterness in his voice.

"Mercy's fucking valuable," I muttered.

"But she's too much of an unknown. And—" Wylder shut his mouth, and the door clicked open.

We slipped into the office. Not wanting to risk one of the sentries noticing the light under the door, Wylder set his phone facing away from it to cast a thin glow over the elegant room. "I'll take the desk," he said. "You check the bookshelves first."

I went to the built-in shelves and ran my hands over the rows of books there, making sure the pages moved under my fingers and that none were secret containers. Then I felt the backs of the shelves for loose spots that might have held a hidden compartment.

No such luck, and no phones just lying around either. Wylder rummaged through the desk drawers. He stepped away with a frustrated sound.

We started nudging and tugging at every other object in the room, careful not to shift anything so much that it'd be clear it'd been moved. My heart had started to sink when Wylder let out a soft cry of victory. He'd raised the top of the ottoman by Ezra's wing chair in the corner and was now lifting a phone out of the storage box inside.

I pulled the vial of clear liquid that Anthea had given us out of my pocket, some kind of concoction she'd had just lying around that would erode the metal and destroy the phone. Wylder set the device in the sturdy box she'd given us for that purpose, and I poured the stuff over it.

With a sizzling hiss, the screen melted, the metal warping, until nothing was left but a solid gray lump that could just as easily have once been a pair of fancy sunglasses or something.

A surge of relief swept through me. The phone was destroyed; there was no way Ezra could use it now. But we also needed to make sure he didn't find out who'd taken it.

We ducked out of the room, Wylder resetting the lock behind us, and hustled back to his office. Wylder texted the others on the way to let them know the first part was done. "Might as well let them get a little more sleep if they can," he said.

"What are we going to do with that?" I asked as we stepped into his office, tipping my head to the box he was still clutching.

He considered it. "I don't think we want it on our property, even if it's practically unidentifiable. You go for morning runs pretty often. Suit up when it's not too early, and chuck the phone in one of the trash cans farther down the street when you're well out of view of the house."

I glanced at the window. Just the faintest hint of light was touching the sky. "I could probably get away with going in a half hour or so."

"Perfect." He dropped into his chair and rubbed his forehead. His face looked unusually drawn, and I didn't think it was just fatigue.

"Are you okay?" I asked.

"I can't believe Dad would pull something like this on Mercy—and without even telling me. No, that's not even right. I *can*, and it pisses me off that I didn't see it coming soon enough. It pisses me off that he's such a piece of shit to begin with." He sighed. "And this won't end it. He isn't going to stop until he's gotten what he wants."

Which was Mercy gone.

"We'll think about that when we get there. At least she's safe for now." I paused. I must have been amped up from the precarious mission we'd just completed, because then I dared to say, "One of these days you're going to have to admit that she's tough enough to stand her ground."

Wylder raised his eyes. "What's that supposed to mean?"

"Oh, come on. I may not have Gideon's brains, but the tension between you two is obvious. You're crazy about her, aren't you?"

I wasn't going to tell him Mercy had outright admitted they'd had sex. He wouldn't have let himself go that far unless either he hadn't cared about her at all, which obviously wasn't true... or he was so caught up in her he hadn't been able to help himself.

He frowned. "Maybe you're talking about yourself."

I raised my hands. "Hey, *I* won't deny it. She's fucking amazing. Hell yeah, I'm crazy about her." I hesitated. "Is that going to be a problem?"

There was a pause before he spoke again. "No," he said. "Why would it? Mercy doesn't owe me anything."

"That's not what I'm asking. We're both into her. If she's going to pursue something with both of us—"

"No need to worry about that. I'm sure she hates me by now."

Having seen the way they'd interacted over the past week, I wasn't so sure about that. "I think she's just pissed off at the way you're treating her. Because you *are* being an ass. I get why you're pushing her away, but she's nothing like Laurel. She knows what she's gotten into. She's tough enough to face it."

"It doesn't matter," Wylder snapped. "The story always ends the same way. Isn't today proof of that? Dad will keep coming after her."

"And what good does constantly going off on her do when she's proven she isn't leaving no matter what you say? You're just putting yourself in a position where she won't even come to you for help if she realizes she needs it."

Wylder was silent for a long moment. He didn't appear to have an argument for that. Lowering his head, he pinched the bridge of his nose as if he had a headache. Then he said, quietly, "*She* protected me, you know. In the warehouse. A guy was coming at me, and she jumped in the way and started fighting him off. That's how she got shot. I've been a total asshole to her, and she still risked her life for mine."

"She cares about you, you dumbass." If he'd been anyone else, I might have smacked him across the head to drive the point home. "She's obviously seen enough of the not-so-asshole parts of you to think your life is worth something. Give her a chance."

"It has been harder keeping my distance after that." He sighed and glanced up at me, his eyes narrowing. "Wouldn't you mind if I went after her?"

I shrugged. "She told me straight to my face that she isn't currently a one-guy kind of girl. If she's playing the field, I'd rather she stuck to people I actually respect. And there aren't a whole lot of those."

Something strange crossed Wylder's face. Then he motioned to the door. "You'd better get ready for your run. We don't want that phone on any of us for any longer than necessary."

I didn't feel like the conversation was exactly done, but I wasn't going to push him any more than I already had. I wasn't that much of an idiot.

I tucked the phone-blob into the pocket of my sweatpants before I set off, and found a bin near the front of one of the properties at the end of the block. No one else was around that early. With a flick of my wrist, I sent it sailing into a half-open garbage bag.

Mission accomplished. There was nothing left to do but wait.

After breakfast, we purposefully decided to hang out in the sitting room that had a window overlooking the front drive and a doorway that opened to the foyer. Around ten, Jasper showed up. As one of Ezra's men ushered him to meet the boss, he glanced around with a displeased expression. One look at his porky face and those lips he must have tried to plant on Mercy made me want to kick his ass right back out the door, but I stayed where I was.

It was only a few minutes later that Jasper marched

back to the front door, this time in a real huff. Whatever had happened in there had pissed him off.

As the head of the Demon's Wings drove off, Ezra emerged into the foyer, his face tight and his eyes so dark a shiver ran down my spine. When he sauntered over to our room, we acted busy with our phones, only looking up when he stopped in the doorway.

"Everything all right, Dad?" Wylder asked evenly, a picture of innocence.

Ezra smiled thinly. "I'm determining that." He scanned the room, his gaze lingering on each of us in turn, and I knew he was wondering about us. We were the only guys in the house who'd shown Mercy any support so far, after all. Of course he'd suspect us.

But if he had no proof we'd been involved, he couldn't do anything about it... right?

25

Mercy

IT STARTED AT BREAKFAST. OR RATHER, ON MY WAY TO breakfast.

The second I stepped out of my room, Kaige was there, ambling down the hall as if he'd just happened to be coming my way at the exact same time. Which maybe he had been.

"I heard Anthea's making bacon," he said, slinging his arm around my waist. "Can't be late for that!"

The other guys were already in the kitchen when we got there, along with Anthea, a sizzling pan, and a meaty smell in the air that made my mouth water. Wylder didn't scowl or make any snarky remarks about my arrival, though. And I could have sworn some kind of look passed between all of the guys as if they were confirming something with each other.

Weird.

"Is something up?" I asked, and Kaige just laughed

and guided me to the table. Then Gideon started showing me a major shopping website he'd hacked into for kicks a few months ago—"They still haven't noticed," he said, pointing out the little puke emoji icons he'd programmed into the product pages, with a gleeful chuckle I'd never heard from him before but found both disturbing and sexy—and I got distracted.

After we'd eaten, Anthea ushered me to her deck even though I'd been planning on working out—abs and legs only, of course, considering the wound on my shoulder. She kept me there for at least an hour, chatting about random things and topping up my glass of lemonade whenever it got slightly low.

Then all of a sudden Kaige was back, dressed in his work-out clothes and suddenly eager to join me in the mansion's home gym. That was when I really started getting suspicious. It all felt weirdly coordinated.

We passed Ezra in the hall, and I thought his gaze lingered on me more intently than usual. Maybe he was just making sure my injury wasn't noticeably slowing me down. But Kaige drew a little closer to me without a word, and that set warning bells jangling in my head too.

I waited to see if he'd tell me something once we were alone in the gym, but instead he challenged me to a crunch competition and then a kicking one. Once we were thoroughly sweaty, he escorted me all the way to the shower. By that point, I was surprised he didn't follow me inside, though he probably would have if I'd invited him.

I washed and changed quickly and headed out only

to notice Rowan meandering along several feet behind me. He appeared to be absorbed in whatever he was looking at on his phone, but when I went into one of the lounge rooms to watch some TV, he followed me, settling into a chair on the other side of the room.

I still didn't know what to say to him after his confession the other day. He didn't seem to want to talk to me anyway, staying focused on his phone. He'd just... happened to want to be in the same room?

No, there was definitely something more than that going on.

To test that theory, I got up again after just ten minutes and marched out. Rowan stayed where he was, but lo and behold, Wylder came around the staircase, looking as if he'd hustled to make it there, just as I reached the foyer. I pretended not to see him and headed for the front door, totally at random.

"Where are you going, Princess?" Wylder asked. Okay, so he hadn't completely lost the snark.

"For a walk," I replied. "That's still allowed around here, right?"

Something flickered in his eyes. "The last time you went strolling on your own, it didn't work out so well. I could use some fresh air."

And then I'd have to endure his glowers and grumbles for the next hour? No, thank you.

I tapped my pocket and the bulge at the back of my jeans where I'd stuck my pistol. "I'm much better prepared this time. I don't need babysitting."

A crooked smile twisted his lips, one I'd used to find irritatingly gorgeous. And maybe still did, just a little. "What if I do? You can take care of me, Kitty Cat."

The smile and the fonder nickname sent a flare of heat through me that only left me uneasy. What the hell was happening here?

"What are you going to do if I say forget it?" I asked. "Chase me down?"

I stalked outside, and Wylder didn't follow. But I'd only made it to the edge of the Noble property when Gideon came trotting across the lawn with his tablet under his arm. He stopped and looked as if he was taking pictures of a couple of things near the wall, but as soon as I walked past it, he followed.

I spun on him. "What is going on with all of you today?"

Gideon blinked at me. His jaw ticked, and I knew for sure I was on to something.

"I don't know what you're talking about," he said. "I happen to find that stretching my legs now and then is an excellent way to clear—"

"Bullshit," I interrupted. "The only time I've seen you set foot outside the house before now is to go from the house straight to a car. What. Is. Going. On?"

He got a bit of a deer-in-the-headlights look, but his mouth clamped shut.

"Fine." I strode past him back to the mansion. "I know who'll have put you all up to this, so I'll just ask him."

If Wylder was involved, then he was the one giving the orders. And there he was, standing idle in the foyer as if he had nothing else to do with his time.

He cocked his head when he saw me. "That was a short walk."

"Fuck you." I marched right up to him and jabbed my finger at his chest. "Why are you all refusing to let me out of your sight? Did something happen? Was there another corpse left for me on the lawn—or right inside here?"

Wylder's gaze twitched away from me as if he was checking the room around us for anyone who might overhear his answer. That didn't bode well. "Can you keep your voice down?" he muttered.

"No," I said, deliberately raising it. "I want you to tell me—"

He caught my arm, his grip firm but not painfully so. Heat flooded my skin where he touched me. "Fine," he said under his breath. "You want to know? I'll tell you. But we're not talking about it here."

I yanked my arm back. "Then feel free to show me where we *can* talk."

He set his hand on the small of my back and escorted me up the stairs toward his area of the house, moving aggressively enough that my panties might have been soaked by the time we reached the top. Not that I'd ever have admitted that to him. He was still being a total douche. My brain knew that even if my body didn't.

Wylder stayed silent until we were in his office with the door shut. He moved away from me to the small liquor cabinet and poured himself a glass of the brandy he liked so much.

"Well?" I prodded.

He took a sip, grimaced, and turned to fully face me. "Did you hear that Jasper stopped by this morning?"

A chill washed over me. This had to do with Jasper? Had he "liked" me enough that he'd decided he wanted more? Shit.

But then, no one had told me, let alone come to get me, so maybe not.

"No," I said. "Why was he here?"

"Because my dad invited him, because he planned to frame you for Jasper's attempted murder."

For a second, I just stared at him. Most parts of that sentence didn't make sense to me even in isolation, let alone all together. "Wait—what with the who now?"

Wylder's bright green eyes bored into mine. "He set you up. Axel lifted a phone from the guy he made you crash into at the warehouse the night before last. They used it to arrange an attempted assassination. When Jasper came, my father was going to turn over the phone, saying he'd caught you with it, and then turn *you* over to the Demon's Wings for punishment."

I was still having trouble processing all of this. I sank into the nearest chair. "But—why? How did you find out? Why didn't he go through with it?"

"Thankfully, Kaige the insomniac happened to over-hear my dad and Axel talking late last night," Wylder said, his tone dry yet humorless. "We took care of it before the meeting happened. The phone is long gone and irretrievable."

So I wasn't in immediate danger. But... I pressed my hand to my forehead. "I don't understand—why would

Ezra set me up like that? If Jasper thought I'd tried to order a hit on him, he'd want me dead."

"Yeah. Which means my dad wants you dead." Wylder threw back a larger gulp of brandy. "He doesn't like the disturbances your presence here seems to have provoked, and he doesn't like that you were strong and smart enough to handle Jasper. You're a wild card, and a capable one, and that makes you a threat. The only way Ezra Noble deals with threats is by crushing them."

"Oh, fuck." Through my rising horror, the pieces clicked together in my head. I raised my eyes to meet Wylder's stark gaze again. "That's why you all have been on my ass no matter where I go. You don't want to leave me alone in case he tries something else."

Wylder offered a tiny shrug. "It isn't something we can sustain long-term without getting noticed, but we haven't had much time to come up with a better strategy yet."

A flicker of anger seared up through my horror at the situation. I sat up straighter. "And it never occurred to you that the most obvious part of any strategy would be *telling me* the man whose house I'm living in wants me dead?"

"I'm sure we'd have gotten to that eventually," Wylder said, but his tone wasn't exactly convincing.

I stood up, my jaw clenching. "It should have been the first thing you did. It's my life on the line. How the hell am I supposed to look out for myself if I have no idea what I'm dealing with?"

The stubborn bastard just glowered at me. "*We* were looking out for you."

"That's not good enough! What, did you think I'd give away that I knew and screw things up for you? Say the wrong thing to Ezra—as if that's *more* likely to happen when I know to be cautious, not less likely? For God's sake, Wylder, it's fine if you don't want to fuck me again, but I thought by now I'd earned a little more trust than that from all of you."

I swallowed hard, a jabbing sensation running through my chest. I wasn't just angry—I was hurt. From the second I'd walked into this house, I'd been running myself ragged proving how much I could handle, and they still thought I was safer in the dark about something like this.

As Wylder gazed back at me, something fell away in his expression. For a second, he looked almost haunted. I hesitated, expecting the rare show of emotion to vanish behind his walls as quickly as it emerged, but he didn't shake it off. He glanced at the floor and then back at me. "No matter what I say to you or how I treat you, you're not going to leave, are you?"

I folded my arms over my chest. "You only just figured that out?"

"No. Well—I don't know." He lowered himself into his own chair, looking so conflicted that my heart tugged to go to him despite everything. "I'm sorry. You *have* earned that trust, more than earned it. I just—I was trying to protect you."

The great Wylder Noble was apologizing to me? I was stunned, but not so much that I couldn't sputter a laugh at the last thing he'd said. "By treating me like dirt not even worthy of sticking to the soles of your shoes?

Like I was a fucking piece of *tissue* you jerked off into and then wanted to toss in the trash?"

He actually winced. My voice might have come out pretty harsh. I'd told myself I didn't care, but I was angry about a whole lot of things from the past several days here, and it was all bubbling to the surface.

"I know it sounds stupid," he said. "But I didn't feel like I had a whole lot of choice."

"Of course you did. You had a choice not to be an asshole to me. You had a choice to let me in on the missions without fighting me every step of the way. You just didn't make those choices."

"Not because I don't trust you," he insisted. "Because I don't trust my dad. I didn't *want* to treat you like that, but I thought if I could just come down on you hard enough to force you to go before he could do even worse... I know it sounds awful, but you have no idea how far he'll go to hurt you—or me."

Hurt *him*? I found myself staring again and forced myself to sit back down. "I don't understand."

Wylder considered what was left of his brandy. Then he tossed it all down like a shot. He set the glass on a side table hard and frowned at the wall.

"When I was fifteen, I started hooking up with a girl from school. Laurel. She was... sweet and bubbly and totally separate from everything here. When I was with her, all the violence and the expectations didn't seem to matter that much. It became more than just hooking up. I fell for her. I was seeing her more and more—and then Dad found out."

A lump formed at the bottom of my throat. I knew

how this kind of story ended. Rowan had told me one version of it yesterday.

"What did he do?" I asked. My voice came out quiet. Some part of me didn't really want to know.

Wylder's tone stayed flat, but he couldn't quite wring the emotion out of it. "He didn't want his heir getting distracted. Especially not by a girl. I was supposed to pump and dump them, not get attached. He saw it as a weakness and a threat to our security—if I cared too much, then our enemies could use her to manipulate me. So he decided the problem needed to be eliminated. He had her grabbed off the street, put a gun in my hand, and told me to shoot her."

I flinched. "Did you do it?"

"*No*," Wylder said savagely. "I told him he was fucking insane. He told me I was a shameful excuse for a Noble. Then he took the gun from me and did it himself. Axel and Titus were there—Titus had to hold me back from throwing myself at him, and even then I might have broken free if Axel hadn't punched me hard enough to break my nose." He rubbed the slightly uneven slant of it, the imperfection I'd noticed the first time we'd met. "And then it was already over."

My throat constricted even more. "I'm so sorry." It'd been bad enough losing Rowan and not knowing why, feeling he'd betrayed me. If I'd had to watch my father kill him in front of me...

Wylder finally looked at me again. "Ever since that day, I've been fighting my way back into his good graces. He's never forgotten that I wouldn't follow that one order. That I picked her life over his authority. If he had *any* reason to think I was at all invested in another woman now..."

Ah. It all made a bizarre kind of sense now. A humorless laugh tumbled out of me. "So what you're saying is you treated me like shit not because of how little you care about me, but because of how much you do."

Wylder's eyes narrowed. "I wouldn't put it exactly that way."

"Of course you wouldn't." God forbid he spell out anything about his feelings for me even now. But that was okay. I wasn't composing any sonnets in his honor either.

His story had doused the flames of my anger. All I had left in me was achy ashes. How could I be mad at him when he'd been trying so hard to keep me safe, even if it'd been in the most frustrating possible way?

But then he surprised me. "I *am* sorry," he said. "I meant that. You didn't deserve any of the crap I've thrown at you since we—since that morning in the kitchen. I didn't mean any of it. And I should have known it wasn't the right way. With Laurel—I kept her as far from the gang part of my life as I could. Whatever bits she did figure out, she assumed I'd protect her, because she sure as hell wasn't equipped to."

"But I can," I said. "At least if I know what I need to be on guard against."

"Yeah, you can. I don't know whether to be glad about that or pissed off that it means I can't get you away from my dad completely." He offered me a pained-looking smile. "Make no mistake, Ezra is going to keep coming after you. He doesn't react well to failure. You're not safe now even if he has no idea that I'd want you to be. But we still have to do something."

"Any suggestions?" I asked.

Wylder leaned forward. "You know, if this is the kind of crap my dad's going to pull, I don't see why I should trust his judgment in general. We can still carry out the plan *I* wanted to put in motion. If we can crush Bryant and the Steel Knights' influence all on our own, he won't be able to dismiss it. We're going to earn his respect and end this once and for all."

26

Rowan

ONCE WYLDER SET HIS MIND TO SOMETHING, THERE really was no stopping him. That was part of the reason I admired the guy.

Just a few hours after he'd pulled us together to say we were going rogue with a plan of our own to take down the Steel Knights, we were cruising through the streets where Paradise City started to bleed into the Bend, checking out possible locations for our scheme.

"How exactly is this supposed to work again?" Mercy asked from where she was sitting in the back of my Toyota. This time she'd made Gideon take the middle, perched between her and Kaige. "How can we make sure the crime actually gets pinned on Colt and the others?"

"If the cops find them in the building with that amount of product, it shouldn't be hard to get the charges to stick," Wylder said. "With a new drug on the streets, they'll have been itching for someone to blame. And the Nobles have a few cops in their pocket to ensure everything gets filed and processed as it should."

"The trick is going to be making sure we can keep them in the building until we bring the police down on them, right?" Kaige said. "We need a place without too many potential exits."

Gideon nodded. "Anthea suggested some impressive techniques for subtly rigging the doors so we can make it very difficult for them to force their way out once we blockade them in. And I'll have the cameras set up as well so that there's footage of the Steel Knights with the truck."

Mercy's brow knit. "But how can we be sure Colt will show up?"

Wylder smiled grimly. "He came when we started kicking butt in the Bend before. I think he'll want direct payback for the theft and what we did to his warehouse."

"He'll have lost a lot of face and want to prove he can stand up for the people supporting him," I agreed. "We just have to be careful not to do anything that might raise his suspicions that it's a trap. I've already started spreading the word about the Nobles gearing up to sell this Glory stuff through a few channels. It's probably already gotten back to him."

"He just doesn't know where." Kaige glanced out the window. "Of course, neither do we."

"We're getting there." Wylder tilted his head toward the window. "What're we looking at, Gideon?"

Gideon swiped through his tablet and pointed out a

few buildings we passed on the winding route he'd given me before we'd left. We all just looked and considered until we came up on a red brick building with a large, steel garage-style door that filled about half of the front of the place.

"I like that one," Kaige announced. "We could drive the truck right in there no problem."

"Assuming there isn't much garbage or equipment inside," Gideon said. "It's an abandoned auto-repair shop, went bankrupt about a decade ago, no one's ever bothered to take it over. But it does seem like a good bet on paper. Two entrances at the front and one at the back, all of them sturdy doors. The windows are barred so no one's breaking out that way. And, like you said, it *should* be easy to drive the truck in."

Wylder drummed his hands on the dashboard. "What are we waiting for, then? Let's take a closer look."

The lock on the back door turned out to be broken. We walked inside to a musty smell that made me wrinkle my nose. Wylder and Kaige turned on the flashlights on their phones and held them up.

Teenagers had clearly been partying in here—there were beer bottles gathering dust in the corners, chip bags and fast-food wrappers scattered around, and random, artless graffiti tags on the walls. I studied the spray-painted lines automatically, my fingers itching for a chance to put something more skilled up over them.

But I didn't draw pretty pictures, not anymore.

The main work bay in front of the garage door was otherwise empty. The shop equipment must have been sold off to cover the debts. I dragged in a breath, my sensitivity to the mustiness fading, and had to conclude: "This is the place."

"I agree," Wylder said. "Let's figure out where we'll set everything up."

"How soon do we want to bring the truck in?" Kaige asked.

"I'll have to spread a few more rumors, make sure we'll have some eyes in the wider area when we bring it in so word about the general location can get passed on," I said. "And we want to keep the timeline tight so they don't crash the party before we're ready."

"Makes sense."

Gideon pointed to a couple of concrete beams down the middle of the wide room. "I can mount cameras up there and there. With the angles of the shadows, I don't think anyone will notice, and it'll capture most of the activity down here."

Wylder clapped him on the back. "There we go. It's all coming together just like that."

We were all coming together. A sense of purpose— no, not just purpose, of *community*—gripped me like I didn't think it had since Mercy had walked into the mansion. When we all put our strengths to a task, we could be nearly unstoppable. I'd seen it in the past, and I could feel the same energy coming together now as we studied the room around us.

Only Mercy herself still looked doubtful. Kaige shouldered her playfully. "What's the matter, Kitty Cat? You don't like the plan?"

She swatted at him, but his teasing provoked a smile

with undeniable affection. "I didn't say that. I just—"
She looked around again and sighed. "Getting arrested,
even getting sent off to jail for however many years,
doesn't feel like enough punishment for what Colt did."

Wylder guffawed. "Bloodthirsty to the end, Kitten.
Don't you worry. We'll still take care of him exactly as
he deserves." He'd seemed more at ease with Mercy
since yesterday, and as he spoke, his eyes focused on her
with a gleam that held both amusement and admiration.

Mercy raised her eyebrows at him, still smiling.
"What do you mean?"

To my surprise, Gideon returned her smile as he
answered, as if he was relishing the idea of offering her
revenge instead of just stating the facts. "The Nobles
have plenty of contacts in the prison system, as you'd
expect. It's *very* easy to arrange a painful death during a
seemingly random brawl or shanking."

Mercy didn't appear to be convinced. She might
have had some kind of a vibe going on with all the other
guys—and it might have provoked a weird sense of jealousy mingled with pleasure inside me, wanting to keep
her to myself while also enjoying seeing her become
part of our harmony—but I'd known her so much
longer. I could read her expression even if I'd never seen
one quite like it on her face before.

"You were hoping to do it yourself," I said quietly.

She grimaced, but she didn't deny it. "He shot my
father himself. I meant to return the favor—you know,
just times about ten or so."

Wylder gave her ponytail a light tug. "Let me think
on it, and I'll see if there's some way we can get you

your moment." He turned to me. "Have you dropped the first tip to the cops yet?"

I shook my head, reaching for my phone. "I was waiting until we had our plans more solid. I can do it now."

As I walked out back where the phone wouldn't pick up the others' voices, I realized I'd grabbed the wrong one. I had my usual phone on me and a burner I'd meant to use for the tip, in case anyone tried to trace it. I was holding my regular phone. An alert for a missed message flashed on the screen. I should check that first.

I tapped through to voice mail and raised the phone to my ear. When my mother's voice carried through the speaker, my heart stuttered.

"Hi Rowan. It's been so long since we last talked, honey. Too long. Anyway, you know your sister's birthday is coming up this weekend. Carina would love it if you could make it down here for the weekend. I know it's a long way and last-minute, and you have a lot going on, but I'd pay for the ticket. Let me know soon. And either way, give me a call when we can catch up a bit, please? I love you."

My hand kept pressing the phone to my ear after the dial tone kicked in. I closed my eyes and forced myself to end the call. A burning sensation seared through my chest.

I couldn't go. I didn't even need to think about it. There was too much happening here in Paradise Bend right now, too many people counting on me to help hold things together, too many threats looming far too close on the horizon.

I'd gotten into this life at least in part to make sure I'd be stronger, readier, deadlier if anyone ever came for my family again, especially for Carina. And now my little sister was barely in my life at all. I hadn't seen her or even spoken to her since half a year ago at Christmas. I'd already ordered a couple of birthday presents to be delivered, things I was pretty sure she'd be excited about, but it wasn't the same as being there. I knew that from the look in her eyes every time I stepped away from those rare family get-togethers.

But she *was* safe, and I'd made other commitments since then.

I stuffed my regular phone in my pocket and dug out the burner. When the cop manning the line picked up, I had my voice go a bit hoarse and let a thread of confusion creep into it, doing my best impression of a nervous bystander on the street. The guy I might have been twenty years from now if I'd never known Mercy Katz.

"Hi, yeah," I said, with a little cough. "I was just walking past Firkin Street on Carlton, and I saw a bunch of young guys who looked pretty... shady, you know? Hoodies and these red bandanas and all that. They were saying something about how they'd be moving in soon and taking over. I didn't like the sound of it at all. Anyway, it seemed like something the police might want to know about."

The officer asked me a few questions and then thanked me for my call, and I hung up with a sense of satisfaction melting a little of my regret. I'd picked an intersection far enough away that investigations there wouldn't stop us from bringing in the truck, but close enough that I could easily lay a few more breadcrumbs to bring the cops right here. And I'd also primed them to assume it'd be the Steel Knights setting up shop in this neighborhood.

I stayed out in the fresh air for a minute longer, waiting for my emotions to completely settle. As I turned to head back inside, the door swung open and Mercy stepped out.

"Are you all done?" she asked. "I was just going to grab the cameras for Gideon."

"Yeah. I made the call." I found I couldn't tear my gaze away from her. There was nothing extraordinary about her appearance today, just her typical ponytail, T-shirt, and jeans, but... she was kind of extraordinary just as herself, wasn't she? What a fucking force of nature she'd become, even more so than when I'd known her and loved her way back when.

An ache squeezed around my heart. It was no wonder the other guys were all drawn to her. I couldn't blame them for that, and I couldn't blame her for however much she wanted all of them.

But that didn't mean I had to roll over and pretend I didn't care.

She was the one part of my old life I'd somehow found my way back to. I had to hold onto her this time.

"Mercy," I said as she started to walk away.

She stopped and glanced at me. "What's up?"

I swallowed thickly and stepped toward her to grasp her hand. When I'd explained to her what'd happened the night I'd been supposed to meet her and after, I'd seen the anger fading from her eyes. It'd been obvious from her response that she'd forgiven me. She could understand the awful position I'd been in and why I'd made the decisions I had, and that was more than I'd dared to hope for. But I still had to say this.

"I don't think I ever properly apologized for what I put you through five years ago. I had my reasons, but still—you didn't know, and I abandoned you to that asshole. I made you feel like you hadn't meant anything to me after all... I wish I could have found a way to stay with you, to fight back—"

Mercy's fingers squeezed mine. "It's okay. There's no way you could have gone up against my dad. *I* could barely go up against him, and I knew him better than anyone."

"I still wish I could have." I held her gaze, willing her to recognize how much I meant this. "I'm glad you're here with us, Mer. I know I said a lot of crap when you first showed up that suggested otherwise, but I was just startled and, well, scared, and I acted like an idiot. I'm sorry about that too, and for not clearing the air sooner. Having you back in my life is the best thing I could have asked for."

Her eyes widened, and something glimmered in them—were those *tears*? Before I could wrap my head around that, she tugged me to her, reaching to grip the collar of my shirt with her other hand. Then she rose up to press her lips to mine.

I kissed her back, lost in an instant in the sensations that were both so familiar and so new. It felt like coming home after a long trip away. She smelled like she always had, like hot summer days and violets, and her lips were just as soft, but there was a confidence to the kiss beyond what she'd had before. It spoke of experience, yeah, but it also said that she was going to take what she wanted, and right now what she wanted was to be kissing me.

How could I take that as anything but a total honor?

Mercy pulled back much sooner than I was ready for. Her eyes were shining with no hint of tears now, but a bittersweet smile tugged at the corners of her mouth.

"No hard feelings," she said. "I get it, all of it. It isn't like we can pick up where we left off, but—I'm glad I'm here with you too." She dropped my hand to head toward the car. "Now let's take these fuckers down once and for all."

Mercy

ONE OF THE OTHER FEATURES THAT'D MADE THE derelict auto shop an ideal location for Wylder's plan was the also long-abandoned restaurant next door. After Gideon set up all his gear, he and Rowan headed off to take care of work elsewhere, leaving me, Wylder, and Kaige at the old restaurant to keep an eye on things.

There wasn't much to keep an eye on, though. It was a pretty boring stretch of town, which meant it'd make sense as a place to keep a secret stash of drugs. But I wanted to see some action *now*, and there was too much left to prepare for us to set the plan in motion until tomorrow night.

We spent a couple of hours sitting on the rooftop terrace in chairs we'd dragged up from the mess of discarded furniture below. The breeze kept the muggy evening much more bearable than in the sweltering rooms below. The laptop Gideon had left behind played footage from four different cameras inside the auto shop—footage of the vacant space with its scraps of trash and nothing else. We were keeping well back from the brick wall that surrounded the terrace, not wanting any of the neighbors to spot us, which meant I couldn't see anything below.

As the evening crept on toward night, I got so restless I couldn't sit still. Leaving Wylder and Kaige discussing the ideal time to lure the Steel Knights here, I wandered back down into the vacant restaurant. My hand slipped into my pocket to brush my fingers over my childhood bracelet, but it didn't offer much comfort.

My exploring was pretty dull until I opened a cabinet near the overturned hostess podium and discovered a bottle of whiskey had been forgotten there. I grabbed it and decided it was time to head back up to the terrace.

Wylder and Kaige had gone from strategy discussion to debating the ideal spot to hit someone if you wanted to break his jaw. They fell silent when I walked over waggling the whiskey bottle.

"Hello, boys," I said. "Look what I found."

Wylder eyed me. "Are you drunk?"

"Nope. I haven't even started yet. I should probably get on that."

Kaige made an uncertain sound as I twisted off the lid. "Do you really think it's a good idea to get drunk on the job?"

I took a small swig. The alcohol burned going down, sending a woozy rush through my veins. Oh, that was strong. But it was good. It smoothed the edges off the tension that'd been itching at me.

"Who says we're getting drunk?" I said, and allowed myself another gulp. "We're twenty-four hours or so away from shattering the Steel Knights. I think we can celebrate—in moderation, of course."

Wylder snorted, but he snatched the bottle from me and tipped it to his lips with a bob of his throat I couldn't help ogling. He glanced at the label before handing it to Kaige. "It's pretty old. Nice stuff."

Kaige took a swig and shook himself. "No kidding. That's strong shit."

"You know what they say, the older the whiskey the better," I said in a singsong voice, pulling my chair around so we were sitting in a sort-of circle. I made a grabby gesture with my hand. "Don't be greedy with it."

Kaige frowned, holding onto the bottle. "What's gotten into you?"

"Nothing," I said. Everything. *Maybe* we were going to shatter the Steel Knights tomorrow. Maybe it wouldn't actually be this easy. After all the anguish I'd been through since Colt had slaughtered my family, it was hard to believe I could be almost at the end.

Was it just like Rowan said, that I'd wanted to look Colt in the eyes while I sliced him open from throat to gut? Wouldn't it be enough to see him realize how he'd been outwitted and overcome by us?

What kind of person was I if I'd rather blow off an easy plan that didn't require much violence just for the chance to splatter his blood across a room?

I didn't want to look at any of those questions too

closely. There wasn't anything else we could really do tonight anyway, so why did we have to think about it at all? Part of me did want to get drunk, to let the buzz wash everything else away.

But Kaige kept the bottle close, raising it to his lips again. A wicked impulse gripped me. There were other ways to get a buzz, ones that wouldn't give me a hangover tomorrow.

When he lowered his hand, I pushed myself out of my chair and leaned over him. "Fine, I'll just get a taste this way."

I grasped his jaw and kissed him. Kaige froze for just a second, no doubt as aware as I was of Wylder stiffening in the other chair, but then he set down the bottle with a thump and pulled me closer to him. His mouth opened, and the silk fire of the whiskey's flavor swept from him to me with the heat of the kiss. Delicious in every possible way.

Even more delicious because of my sense of Wylder watching us. I eased right down onto Kaige's lap. When I tipped my head back, Kaige couldn't resist moving his lips to my neck. I hummed encouragingly before glancing sideways, straight at Wylder.

His brows had come together, and his hands were fisted at his sides. But there was something other than anger in his expression. His eyes had darkened to the color of a sea caught in a storm, and I could see the lust written there clear as day. The sight turned me on even more.

I turned back to Kaige and kissed him even harder,

giving in to the urge to grind my hips into him. His dick pressed rigid and wanting against me.

With a growl, Kaige grabbed one of my tits through my shirt and squeezed. He brought his teeth to the sensitive column of my throat, shifting under me. Even though we still had layers of clothes separating us, I could feel his pulsing cock at my core as he rubbed up and down my pussy. I hissed in pleasure.

Wylder's gaze was transfixed on us, but he was looking only at me. I opened my eyes just a fraction before I slid down over Kaige's dick again. Then I tore at his T-shirt. Kaige's muscles tensed for a second as if he objected to me taking the lead. He yanked the shirt the rest of the way off and gripped the sides of my face in a gesture of control, but then he looked at Wylder.

I followed his gaze. Wylder didn't look away, his eyes burning into mine. I was burning all over, but it could be so much more than this. If the guys could handle taking things that far.

Looking back at Kaige, I gave him one more kiss, this one softer though still passionate. In a way it was a question. The tenderness with which he kissed me back, even though I could still feel the tension running through his body, seemed like enough of an answer.

I'd make sure he didn't regret it.

I eased out of his embrace and stepped over to Wylder's chair, running my fingers along the Noble heir's shoulder. He stared up at me, not quite a glower. His jaw was tight, his hands still clenched, but he couldn't seem to look away. The humid air practically thrummed with tension and heat. Still, he didn't move.

He was pissed. I wanted him to do something about it.

The whiskey had loosened my tongue. "Are you just going to sit there and watch him fuck me?"

Something snapped in Wylder. He reached for me with a snarl and yanked me to him with his fingers tangled in my hair. The shot of pain that ran over my scalp brought a wave of pleasure with it.

Wylder kissed me furiously, his fingers knotting deeper in my hair as his hot tongue invaded my mouth. As I kissed him back, I ran my hands down the flexing muscles of his chest. Our teeth knocked against each other, our tongues dueling. Then he was pushing me down to the ground with him braced over me, careful of my bandaged shoulder.

Kaige got up, his breathing uneven as he walked over to us. My limbs tangled in Wylder's as he kissed a path down to my collarbone, his hands skimming under my top. In one swift motion, he pulled the shirt off me so all that was left was my bra.

I gazed up at them, their faces framed by the night sky with its studding of stars. The collective hunger in their eyes made my stomach lurch with anticipation. I'd never done something like this before, never been with more than one guy at once, but it felt right. Necessary. Like if we didn't fulfill the promise of this moment, we'd never get it back again.

Kaige had brought the whiskey bottle with him. He took a gulp as he sat down beside us but made no move to reach for me. Wylder's scorching mouth traveled down the valley of my breasts, stopping to swirl his tongue around my nipples through the soft cotton of my bra. As his teeth bit down on me, the feeling teetering between pain and pleasure, I moaned.

I squirmed under him as he marked a trail of kisses to the edge of my jeans and popped open the button. As he tugged them off, Kaige knelt down, his expression as hungry as a predator waiting to pounce on its prey. With a flick of his thumb, he opened the front clasp on my bra. The cups fell away, leaving me in nothing but panties.

Kaige's eyes roved my bare skin like a caress. Wylder leaned back on his heels to take me in too. As the combined heat of their attention washed over me, Kaige upturned the bottle of whiskey so that the amber fluid trickled onto my chest. The liquid warmth flowed over the curve of my tits before forming a rivulet down my bare stomach. My breath hitched in anticipation.

Wylder and Kaige glanced at each other. Even though they didn't speak, I could tell they'd communicated with each other silently.

Wylder settled over one of my breasts and slicked his tongue up the mound to the peak. Kaige descended over the other. His hot mouth sucked hungrily as if he wanted to drink in every last drop of the whiskey on my body.

I writhed under them as their solid bodies encompassed me. Their combined weight felt delicious. Our increasingly ragged breaths mixed together as they cocooned me between their muscular chests.

I looked at them with my eyelids at half-mast. My pussy convulsed at the sight of their heads bobbing up and down, lapping up every trace of whiskey and spreading heady bliss in their wake.

"Oh, fuck," I murmured.

Kaige traced his tongue down to my stomach. He poured more of the whiskey into my belly button and began to lap at it hungrily. I rubbed my legs together, my panties completely soaked now, chasing the climbing pleasure.

Wylder saw what I wanted. His fingers slipped over my throbbing pussy. He rubbed up and down the slit with the heel of his hand against my clit. My breath caught, and I let out a moan when two of his wicked fingers rose to my clit and flicked at it.

Wylder observed my face before he did it again, more urgently. "That's right, Kitten. Let's hear you mew."

"Time to get these off," Kaige announced, jerking my panties down my legs so fast a few of the threads at the seams snapped. He gazed down at my cunt, looking like his mouth was watering. "So fucking gorgeous."

Wylder hooked his fingers right inside me, making me arch off the ground. He pumped them until I was bucking against him and then held them to my lips. "Take a taste."

His gaze was so bright and avid I opened my mouth and lightly sucked on his fingers. Wylder's eyes turned hooded. He pinched my nipple as if in reward and bent down to kiss me at the same time Kaige lowered his mouth to my pussy.

I groaned against Wylder's lips. He drank up every sound I made as he ravished my mouth and Kaige licked my pussy like it was an ice cream cone in his favorite flavor. I was just climbing to the edge of the precipice when Kaige stopped and grasped my waist to flip me over.

I shifted onto my hands and knees, favoring my wounded shoulder, and squealed as Kaige pulled me back by the hips. He positioned me in front of him, and there was the sound of foil ripping open. I only ached with the lack of attention for a few seconds before his hard cock rubbed against my slit.

It slipped inside my pussy, which was so wet he met no resistance. My inner walls expanded to accommodate his girth. His dick hit an angle so deep inside me that my eyes rolled up and I nearly forgot to breathe.

Kaige drew himself out before rolling his hips right back into me, not giving me time to recover. I growled in answer as I thrust my hips back to match his rhythm. My shoulder prickled, but every other part of me felt so good I didn't give a shit.

Wylder unzipped his jeans. He freed his cock, his hand moving up and down its engorged length as he watched his friend fuck me from behind. The piercing at the tip gleamed faintly in the twilight.

I licked my lips. I'd wanted to feel that ring against my tongue since the first moment I'd seen it. "I need a taste of that too," I said, my voice coming out husky.

Wylder grinned. "Oh yes, you do." He wound his fingers into my hair again and tugged me toward him. I reached for his cock eagerly.

The shaft twitched as my lips closed around it. I swiveled my tongue around the piercing, and Wylder groaned. The force of Kaige's thrusts propelled Wylder deeper. The feeling of fullness both in my mouth and my pussy threatened to overwhelm me.

I bobbed my head up and down, sucking hard at the tip. Wylder began to grunt, his hips pumping toward me with increasing urgency. Kaige gripped my hips and pounded into me with equal vigor. Our moans mingled together as all three of us raced our way to our orgasms.

Kaige reached between my legs and flicked at my clit. I came apart around him, my pussy convulsing violently as it milked his cock. "That's right," he muttered. "Just like—*fuck*."

As he came, my mouth tightened around Wylder. The Noble heir came with a sudden spurt of hot, salty cum across my tongue. I lapped and swallowed as he rocked to a halt. His breath was harsh, but his hand was suddenly, startlingly gentle as he teased his fingers through my hair.

When he slid out of me, Wylder trailed his fingers down the side of my face to my jaw. He tipped my chin up so I'd look him in the eyes.

"You belong with us," he said vehemently, repeating the words he'd given me weeks ago that he'd seemed to go back on. "*All* of us. And if anyone tries to say there's a problem with that, we'll make it their problem instead."

Like his father. Would dealing with Ezra's disapproval really be that simple? But in that moment, my body wrung out with pleasure, I couldn't say I cared.

Mercy

KAIGE GAVE THE DOOR OF THE TRUCK ONE LAST SWIPE
with his rag and turned with a big smile on his face. I
wasn't sure he'd stopped smiling since our spur of the
moment threesome last night. When his eyes caught
mine, a tendril of heat unfurled through me despite the
jangling of my nerves over the operation we were
setting in motion.

"All clean," he announced.

"Good." Wylder set a somewhat possessive hand on
my shoulder, but he grinned back at his friend without
any noticeable animosity. "I think that's the last of it.
Rowan?"

"Just finished the doors," Rowan replied, emerging
from the back. "There shouldn't be any sign left that we
were ever here."

A smirk curled my own lips. "But the Steel Knights
will leave their fingerprints all over the place coming in.

Let's see them try to explain away that." I was starting to warm to the idea of getting my revenge by siccing the cops on those bastards. Colt would hate being behind bars, losing control over his budding empire while he slowly rotted away in prison.

Wylder motioned for us to follow him. "Let's get back to our lookout spot and kick off the last few pieces."

We slipped out the back using gloved hands and headed into the restaurant next door. It was cooler today, especially now that evening was falling, a slightly damp breeze wafting against my face. We'd just driven the truck into the old auto-repair shop an hour ago and spent the rest of the time wiping the place down of any trace of our presence.

Once we were inside, I stuffed the gloves in my pocket and touched the outline of my bracelet through the fabric there, then the smooth pearl on Anthea's hair pin, which I'd worn today as another lucky charm. I'd gotten through one dangerous situation in an unusual way wearing it. Maybe as long as I had it on me, it'd somehow protect me from actually needing it.

Okay, that was silly superstition, but I liked the idea even if I didn't totally believe it.

We rejoined Gideon on the rooftop terrace. He nodded to us and tapped a few keys on the laptop balanced on his knees. "Cameras now sending their footage to the hard drive in the front office." He'd set up the surveillance system so that the cops could find the recordings we wanted them to have, but he could still keep an eye on them from his computer. I doubted he'd sever that connection until he absolutely had to.

Kaige prowled over to the narrow notch we'd carved into the terrace wall from the top edge to halfway down. It allowed us to watch the street below without anyone catching a glimpse of us. "Nothing strange going on out there right now. What do we have left to do?"

Rowan pulled out his phone. "I'll have a couple of connections drop our last rumors about the exact location of the drug shipment."

Wylder nodded. "Gideon will keep an eye on the traffic cams to see when the Steel Knights start heading our way. Mercy, Kaige, and I will head down so we're ready to spring the jams on the doors once the Steel Knights have stormed the place. Then Rowan will give the cops their final tip to bring them down here ASAP. And we get the fuck out before all hell breaks loose."

Everything was taken care of. I dragged in a breath and froze when I saw Kaige stiffen.

"Hold up," he said. Rowan lowered the phone he hadn't yet placed a call on. "There's a guy outside. He just drove up in front of the restaurant, and now he's rapping on the door like he's trying to get someone's attention."

"What the fuck?" Wylder stalked over to the wall.

I hurried after him. Once he'd gotten a look, I peered out. In the hazy evening light, the face I saw below us made my pulse hiccup.

I pulled back, speaking under my breath. "It's one of the Claws members—well, former Claws. I've seen him with Jenner helping out the Steel Knights."

Rowan frowned. "That's not good. No one should have figured out the exact location yet. But why would he come alone if he knows what's up?"

"Maybe he doesn't?" Kaige said doubtfully. "Maybe someone spotted one of us around here, but they don't know the whole thing."

"That still doesn't explain what he's up to," Wylder said, and paused. "He isn't wearing one of the bandanas."

The guy's voice reached us then, rough—almost frantic sounding. "Mercy! I know you've got to be around here. I have to talk to you."

A shiver ran down my spine. Had *I* screwed up somehow, and the Steel Knights had tracked me here?

Gideon had ambled over to take a look. He rubbed his jaw. "It doesn't make sense. He poses no threat. You could take him even with that bullet wound in your shoulder. Why would he think you'd come out?"

"Because I know him, and he isn't actually here to hurt me?" I suggested.

Wylder jerked around, giving me an incredulous look, but I was remembering the appeal I'd made to Jenner in the warehouse the other night. This guy had been there too—he'd heard me.

Had one person actually listened?

"Is there any sign of any other Steel Knights or their allies around?" I asked.

Kaige shook his head, and Gideon went back to his laptop. He flipped through several feeds of street footage. "He does appear to be alone."

I wavered for a second and then turned toward the

stairs. "I'll go talk to him. Like you said, I can take him on my own if I have to."

Wylder was at my side in an instant. He grabbed my arm to stop me. "I don't think that's a good idea."

I stared back at him, matching the intensity of his gaze. "Even if he made the stupid decision to side with Colt without knowing the whole story, he's still one of my dad's people. One of *my* people. What if he knows something important?" I pulled out my gun. "I'll be careful. And if you're so concerned, you can come along for backup."

Wylder's mouth flattened, but he let me go, following close at my heels as we descended through the two floors of the restaurant. When I reached the front door, he hung back to stay out of view unless he was needed.

I eased the door open a crack. "Back up a couple of steps," I said, pitching my voice just loud enough to reach the guy outside. "I'm here. And I've got a gun on you, so keep your hands where I can see them. What do you want?"

The guy held his hands out at his sides as he followed my order. His skin looked jaundiced in the yellow light of the streetlamps, but that couldn't explain the tension and, I thought, fear etched all over his face.

"I came to warn you," he said. "Colt found out what you're planning, I don't even know how, and he's rallying the Steel Knights right now to charge over here in full force."

So our plan had just gotten off to an early start?

"They're coming to recover the truck?" I said, feeling like there had to be more to it.

The guy grimaced. "No. Well, maybe that too, but he knows you're planning to ambush them. He knows you'll be staked out here, and he's planning to catch you with his own ambush. Unless you've got a whole army in there with you, you've got to take off before they get here."

A chill washed through me.

"How the fuck are we supposed to believe you?" Wylder asked, coming up beside me. He released the safety on his gun with an audible click.

The guy outside blanched. "I swear," he said, raising his hands higher, "I'm just trying to do the right thing. I shouldn't have listened to Colt—I didn't know what went down with Tyrell—but I should have realized it wasn't like him to plan to stab someone in the back. The Claws were like family to me. I'm not doing some snake's dirty work. Just hurry."

"Stay there," I told him, and yanked the door shut. I turned to face Wylder and realized the other guys had come downstairs to listen too, Gideon with his laptop balanced against his hip so he could keep an eye on the footage at the same time.

"It's got to be another of Colt's plans to fuck with us," Kaige said. "He wants us to leave so he can grab the stash without us getting in the way."

Gideon was frowning. "If he already knows that we're not actually using the truck ourselves, that it's bait and we're waiting here for them to come, then we *can't* get in the way. They're not falling for the trap in the first place—he's made us. The question is, how?"

"I'm not sure that matters right now," Rowan put in. "If that guy is telling the truth, we don't have time to figure it out. The five of us can't fight off Colt's entire force if he's decided he doesn't care about pissing off Ezra anymore."

Wylder exhaled roughly. "The Steel Knights have already tried to kill me once. I think it's safe to say that ship has sailed." He looked at me. "This was one of your father's men. Do you believe him?"

I swallowed hard. Was the decision really going to come down to my judgment? I got a little giddy knowing that he trusted me enough to ask, but I was also nervous as hell to be making the call for all of us.

All I could say was the truth. "I do. If Colt knows we're here, he'd have a much easier time killing us if he took us by surprise. I can't see how he'd benefit from getting us to run, expecting his men to arrive at any second. Rowan's right—we wouldn't stand a chance against a whole horde of them anyway."

Kaige swore. "We can't just leave the truck. I'm not letting them put that garbage on the street after all."

Gideon cleared his throat. "We might not have a choice." He jabbed at his laptop's touch pad, leaping from feed to feed. "There *are* a hell of a lot of cars heading this way in a big group—from a bunch of different directions. They're ready to box us in. We'll have a better chance getting out of here unnoticed in the smaller car."

"But the drugs—"

"Let's go!" Wylder snapped. "Run upstairs, grab anything you might have left that'd point to us being here in case the cops come after all, and let's get out of here."

I hadn't brought anything with me that I didn't already have on me. My heart thudding, I cracked open the door again. The former Claws guy was shuffling his feet nervously. He jerked to attention when I peeked out.

"Thank you," I said. "Now you get going too. If Colt finds out you tipped us off—"

He shuddered. "I know. You did a good thing for Jenner, Mercy. The Claws live on as long as you're still with us." Then he darted off into the night.

The guys were pounding up and down the stairs, shouting questions and orders at each other. I hustled to the back and peered out into the alley. We'd parked Rowan's car down by the end of it, a few buildings away. The alley was completely silent, but the air felt heavy like the hour before a storm.

"Go, go," Wylder shouted from behind me. We burst out into the alley—

And then tires screeched to a halt all around us, including at both ends of the alleyway.

Men with red bandanas around their arms poured out of their vehicles to charge down the alley toward us. I backpedaled. Wylder grabbed my elbow to spin me around, and we all raced back into the shelter of the restaurant.

Kaige slammed the deadbolt into place. I ran for the front of the building to make sure the other entrance was secure, but before I'd even made it halfway, the wide front window shattered with the bash of a baseball bat. I skidded to a halt with the guys behind me.

Cars and jeeps filled the street outside. A swarm of men had gathered on the sidewalk in front of the restaurant. I gripped my gun tightly, my palm sweating against the metal. They hadn't taken us by surprise, but we were still in an awful situation.

Wylder and Kaige fired a few shots through the window, and the men there fell back to the sides or behind the cars, but they didn't look all that scared. Someone was already battering the back door. How long would those hinges hold?

Then a familiar figure stepped out of the shadows. The light from the streetlamps glanced off Colt's golden hair. He held a semi-automatic in one hand, and its muzzle was pointed at the forehead of the Claws member who'd warned us. He shivered in Colt's grasp, his eyes wide and panicked, as the asshole used him as a human shield.

"Too late," he sneered at us. "Your stupid little trick failed, and now it's all over."

"Get out of here before you regret it," Wylder said, as if he were in any position to make threats. "This is Noble territory."

"I wouldn't be so sure about that, Mr. Noble. If my friend is right that there are only the five of you working this operation, I have twenty men for each of you. You're at my mercy."

His friend?

Before I could wonder more about that, Colt's gaze

fixed on me. "Speaking of which—did you miss me, Mercy? This time there won't be any crazy stunts and quick escapes. Every avenue is cut off to you. And soon I'll be cutting you down."

"Not if I get to you first." I spat on the ground in front of me.

A couple of the Steel Knights laughed. Colt simply wrenched back the head of the guy he was clutching. "Why don't you all come out peacefully, and at least a few of you can survive. I'll even promise that Mercy and the Noble heir will get much less painful deaths than if I have to send my men in there after you."

"I'd rather shoot myself in the head," Wylder said.

Colt's face turned grim. "You chose this."

He made a motion with his hand, and a hail of gunfire shattered the last chunks of glass clinging to the window frame. Kaige and I dove behind the hostess podium, the other guys ducking behind overturned tables. The furnishings rattled with the impact of the bullets, but at least they were solid enough to catch them.

When the men outside moved toward the window again, we all shot at them. My wounded shoulder was already aching from the tension in my stance. Wylder managed to hit one guy in the forehead, Rowan one in the chest.

They pulled back again, but two out of a hundred hardly evened the odds. And the back door was still thumping and groaning. We couldn't defend ourselves from both sides.

"What now?" Gideon asked in a low voice from

where he was hunched over his laptop. "We could put a call out for back-up."

"It'll take anyone we can reach too long to get here to really help. And then my dad will curse my memory even more than he will anyway." Wylder reloaded his gun and cocked it. He caught my eye across the shadowy space. "No, we're doing this ourselves, and we're going to take down as many of those fuckers as we possibly can. We won't let Bryant win. Forget clever plans. It's time to go at them guns blazing, just like he came at Mercy's family."

29

Mercy

MORE BULLETS CAREENED THROUGH THE BROKEN restaurant window. We fired back, trying to pick off anyone who showed a vulnerable area, but the best I managed was a hit to one guy's arm. There were too many of them, moving too quickly in the dark.

And the banging on the back door was getting louder. I thought I heard the wood of the frame starting to splinter.

"Careful with your shots," Gideon said, his voice low but urgent. "We don't want to run out of ammo too soon."

Oh, shit, I hadn't even thought of that. I only had one spare clip on me. The other guys might have been carrying a few more, but I'd already seen each of them reload at least once. Did we have enough between us to take out every one of our enemies out there even if they'd lined up for clear shots?

My stomach sank, dread filling me despite Wylder's determined words. We were going to go at them guns blazing, sure, but it was becoming more and more obvious that we'd just be mowing down as many of them as we could before they took us out.

I just hoped I could put Colt in a lot of pain before I kicked the bucket. That wasn't too much to ask, was it?

As that question passed through my mind, someone flung an object like a large can through the window. It hit the floor a few feet inside with a clatter, and thick smoke burst out of it.

Oh, no. "Smoke bomb!" I yelled, scrambling farther backward.

The smoke followed us toward the kitchen, forming a giant impenetrable haze. It moved faster than we could. In seconds, the guys disappeared somewhere within the blanket of smog. My eyes watered. I ducked low, coughing as I tried to squint through the worst of it.

Footsteps thundered toward us. The Steel Knights had used the cover of the smoke to storm the building through the window. I fired at the blurred figures that came into view through the gray fog, praying that the guys were still beside and behind me, not out there in that mess.

The shots blaring on either side of me seemed to confirm that. Several of the figures dropped. But more kept coming. I pulled the trigger on my gun and realized I'd emptied my second clip. The gun was useless now.

The smoke was clearing now, revealing dozens of men barging toward us amid the toppled furniture, using it for cover just like we had minutes before. I dropped my gun just as three Steel Knights converged on me. Throwing myself backward, I banged my ass against the wall. I'd been cornered.

One of the guys leered, brandishing a gun in one hand and an axe in the other. "Colt wants to be the one to kill her, but that doesn't mean we can't carve her up a little first."

Adrenaline blared through my veins. They expected me to cringe in the corner while they descended on me. Yet another bunch of assholes assuming I was a pussy just because I had one.

"You can try," I retorted, and launched myself at them, whipping out my knife at the same time.

Shoving between two of the men, I jabbed the blade into one's side. As he screamed in pain, I yanked it out and swung it in the other direction. It sliced across another attacker's chest just as he snatched at me. I kicked him hard, sending him stumbling backward into the third guy. A searing pain spread from my wounded shoulder, but I focused on the thudding of my heartbeat instead.

More men were crowding in on us. Kaige shot one point blank in the head and then ducked down next to me. He yanked me toward the kitchen, and I dashed there with him, staying low.

He got off a couple more shots at guys who came too close, but one managed to slam a baseball bat across his back. He staggered, groaning, but swung his powerful fist to clock the prick in the temple. As the other guy reeled backward, Kaige shot him too.

We were seconds from the kitchen door when I heard the back door finally give out with a crackling of broken wood. Kaige jerked me in another direction. I spotted the other three guys crouched behind a long banquet table that'd once stood at the back of the room. Our last bit of shelter in the chaos.

As we ran toward it, a man lunged at me and hauled on my knife hand. Another two guys tackled Kaige. At the twist of my wrist, my fingers spasmed and the knife fell from my grasp.

Wylder let out a shout, and both he and Rowan threw themselves toward me to help. Rowan's shot caught my attacker in the throat. The guy sagged with a gush of blood, but more shots rattled my eardrums from farther away.

Wylder stumbled as a bullet clipped his thigh. Another caught Rowan in the side of his chest. He staggered into me, a red blotch spreading across his shirt just below his armpit.

"No!" The word burst from my lips, and I was dropping with him, trying to cushion his fall. He twisted with a grimace of pain and pointed his gun at the men closing in on us, but nothing happened when he pulled the trigger. He'd used his last bullet defending me.

Wylder got off two more shots, and then there was nothing but a hollow clicking sound from his pistol too. He sank down next to us, his other hand pressed to the bleeding wound on his thigh.

Gideon stared at us from behind the table, his jaw

tight, his hands empty. Either he'd run out of ammo earlier or he'd given his to the other guys who were more practiced fighters.

Kaige was now flailing under the combined weight of three guys trying to wrestle his gun away from him. When he shot one, another leapt in to take that guy's place, stomping on Kaige's elbow. A groan reverberated past Kaige's clenched teeth.

"Hold them for Colt," someone said, and understanding hit me like a punch to the gut. We were done. It was over.

But as the men loomed on us, yells rose up from farther away. Gunfire blasted outside, which didn't make much sense considering the Steel Knights had no one to shoot at but us, and we were way back here.

Several figures burst through the crowd. "Claws!" one of them shouted, punching his fist in the air. It was Jenner.

Even as I gaped at him, he and the men he was leading opened fire on the Steel Knights around us. Dozens of the men with red bandanas crumpled, too startled to shoot back in time.

My appeal had worked. Not just on the one guy who'd warned us, but on Jenner and whoever else he'd spoken to as well.

Just for a second, my spirits soared. We could get out of this—get Rowan to a hospital, get Wylder patched up—

Then someone behind me grasped my hair and wrenched me away from the guys. Pain exploded through my scalp. When I lashed out with my fists, the muzzle of a gun jammed against my temple.

On my knees, I stared up to see Colt standing over me, one hand still clutching my hair, the other pressing the gun to my face. He sneered down at me before raising his gaze toward Jenner and the others, who'd stopped in their tracks at the sight.

"Drop your weapons," Colt said in a voice so vicious it was almost a hiss. "Or your princess dies right here."

Their gun hands wobbled, and panic shot up my throat. I might not be able to make it out of this alive, but the guys would still have a chance. If the Claws gave up, we were all dead.

"Don't listen to him!" I said, my gaze darting around me for anything I could use as a weapon. "He's going to kill me either way."

"Bitch." Colt wrenched my head back and forth so violently I saw stars. "I'm going to have my men shoot yours now, and you can watch them die in front of you, knowing you brought this on them."

No. Wylder had refused to give up, and I wouldn't stop either. I swung my hand toward my hair where Colt was gripping me, clawing at the strands—and my fingers brushed against something small and cool that came loose at their touch. Something I'd almost forgotten.

"No more surprises," Colt said with a cold smile, and slammed my head against the wall.

Agony spiked through my skull. I fought against the wave of pain and caught his wrist with my other hand. As he twisted to the side to dodge the blow, probably thinking I was aiming to strike at his chest or gut, I stabbed Anthea's pearl hair pin straight into his forearm where his artery would be.

Colt swore and kneed me in my belly, knocking the breath right out of me. I collapsed to the floor. His gun still trained on me, he glared down at the pin lodged in his arm. "Did you really think that would hurt me? Surely you—"

His voice cut out with a sway of his legs. His whole body lurched as he tried to regain control and failed. His knees gave, and he fell forward onto his hands, his gun smacking the floor.

Anthea's poison had worked its magic.

"What the fuck did you do to me?" Colt rasped, but he was shaking all over, unable to catch his balance enough to spin on me. Anthea had said the stuff wouldn't kill a man, just slow him down a lot. And that was all I needed.

"Get them!" Colt snapped out, but Jenner and his men were no longer so worried for my safety. The second any of the Steel Knights moved, they shot them, walking toward me and the guys to form a protective barrier around us.

Us and Colt. I heaved myself to my feet, ignoring the pain in my head and the spinning of my thoughts. I could still focus enough to finish the job I'd been waiting to carry out for so long.

"You, Colt Bryant, are a dead man walking." I slammed my heel into his ribs, and he sagged to the floor. His fingers twitched around the gun before Gideon stepped in, kicking it away.

Gideon knelt beside Wylder and Rowan, pressing his hands to their wounds. "I figured it was reasonable to call for back-up *now*," he murmured. "Your father's men will be here within twenty minutes. Try not to bleed too much before then."

As Wylder muttered something about disobedient underlings, I crouched with my knees on Colt's back to hold him in place and then jerked down, slamming his head against the tiled floor with my elbow. I punched him once, twice, three times for good measure, until his nose crunched against the tiles and his eye was purpling.

And still he laughed, sputtering blood from his mouth. "You don't get to win, Mercy. You've already lost everything."

Rage unlike anything I had ever felt before turned my vision red. My hand found my fallen knife on the floor and raised it. The smile vanished from Colt's face.

"No," I said. "You tried, but I found everything I really needed. And now you're *never* going to have the chance to take another person from me."

I shoved him onto his back and slammed the blade into his chest. Blood welled up around the wound, and Colt's expression stuttered.

I yanked out the knife and stabbed him again and again—for Grandma, for Aunt Renee, for every person in my family that he'd slaughtered. For Wylder and Rowan and Kaige and Gideon, who he'd tried to do the same to. More blood spurted up, hot against my skin, but I kept going, tears burning behind my eyes.

When my hand finally fell to my side, the handle

slick against my palm, solid arms wrapped around me. They brought Kaige's musky scent.

"You're done, Mercy," he said in a low voice. "He's dead. Colt is dead."

I blinked and stared down at the body before me. Colt's head had lolled to the side, splattered with blood from the multiple wounds in his chest. His unblinking eyes shone glassily. Not a hint of life remained in his pallid skin.

He was dead. I'd killed him. It was over.

A broken laugh spilled from my lips. As I grasped Kaige's arm, hugging him back as well as I could in that moment, the remaining Steel Knights fell back and fled the building. They had no fight left in them faced with the Claws members' guns and the dead body of their leader.

"Thank you," I said to Jenner when he glanced back at me.

He dipped his head. "I should thank you for reminding me of my proper priorities. We'll stay with you until the Nobles arrive. And when you're ready to raise up the Claws again, we'll be waiting."

I couldn't wrap my head around those words right now. I turned toward the guys, groping for Rowan. His face had paled, and half of his shirt was stained red, but he met my gaze steadily enough to reassure me that he wasn't on the verge of death himself. "Don't worry about me," he said raggedly. "I can hang in there."

"He'd better," Wylder muttered, wincing when Gideon balled a new rag against his thigh to replace the blood-soaked one. "Knowing my father, if I lose even *one* man in this goddamned fight against ridiculous odds, he'll still call it a loss."

Kaige let out a raw, wild laugh, and then the others laughed too, and I knew that as bloody and damaged as we were, we were going to be all right.

Mercy

THE GATHERING CONSISTED SOLELY OF EZRA, THREE men from his inner circle, Wylder and his closest associates, Anthea, and me. I had to assume the only reason the head Noble was holding it in his audience room instead of his office was my presence. Apparently I still hadn't earned enough clout with him to be trusted in that space, which I suspected meant he was also still plotting my doom.

I didn't let that vague threat dim too much of my enjoyment of the wine and hors d'oeuvres he'd offered up, though. There was a celebratory vibe in the air. Colt was six feet under, along with a substantial number of the Steel Knights. His other lackeys had backed off from the corners they'd previously claimed. And after a week to recover from their wounds, Wylder and Rowan were both on their feet, standing near me.

Ezra held up his wine glass. "To my son, for eliminating the greatest threat we've faced in years on his own initiative and with no lives lost on our side. And to a Paradise free from any challenges to our authority!"

"To Mercy too," Kaige piped up with a rebellious glint in his eyes, "for being the one to put that bastard Colt Bryant in the ground."

Ezra's lips thinned slightly, but he still drank with the rest of us. His gaze slid over me, pausing to offer only the palest of smiles.

Yeah, the guy definitely wasn't ready to exchange friendship bracelets just yet.

Axel brushed past me to the side table, not quite touching me but making my body tense at how close he'd come. I hadn't forgotten the role *he'd* played in framing me. The less time I spent in his presence, the better.

"Now that the Steel Knights have been crushed, we have new questions to consider," Ezra said. "I hope we can all put our minds together. While we rule over all of Paradise Bend, we've always managed the areas outside the city proper through our associations with and dominance over the lesser gangs there. The destruction of both the Claws and the Steel Knights will create a power vacuum there."

Anthea nodded. "Which means we need to keep an eye on who steps in to fill it."

I kept my mouth carefully shut. The guys and I had decided not to mention the assistance we'd gotten from Jenner and the other former Claws members during the last fight. Knowing there were men loyal to me in the Bend, even if it was only a handful, would only increase any worries Ezra had about me. And understandably, Wylder had also preferred not to mention that we'd have been slaughtered without the sudden arrival of help we couldn't have counted on.

There were all the smaller gangs that Colt had caught up in his push for power... and the mysterious group we'd never been able to find out any details about. The memory of the strange, silent men standing behind Colt that one time sent a prickle down my spine.

Maybe they'd gone back to wherever they'd come from now that he was gone, and that was that. But I'd have liked to know for sure.

"Exactly," Ezra said, picking up from Anthea's remark. "Over the next few days, we'll reach out to the small bases of power in the Bend and feel out what their intentions are and how much loyalty we can count on from them. We may need to dole out some... consequences to those who aligned themselves with Bryant. But the greatest challenge is behind us."

His men drew closer to him, and they fell into a quieter conversation between sips of their wine. I watched them from the corner of my eye, wishing I could step close enough to listen in without Ezra taking me for a spy.

A hand squeezed my shoulder—gently, still careful of the gunshot wound that now barely twinged even during my push-ups. I looked up to see Kaige beaming down at me. "What are you thinking?" he asked. "You shouldn't look so serious right now."

I tucked a strand of hair behind my ear. "Oh, it's nothing much," I said, and then decided to just be honest. Kaige would understand. "I can't shake the feeling that I'm missing something."

"Maybe you're missing six-foot three inches of pure muscle," he said, pointing a thumb at himself.

I laughed and swatted at him with my hand. When his eyes heated, I immediately found myself thinking back to the last time his cock had been inside me.

On the other side of the room, Wylder was watching us. When I swallowed, I could still feel *his* cock filling my mouth. We'd definitely have to do that again sometime.

"But really, what is it?" Kaige prodded.

"What is what?" Gideon asked. He'd ambled over to us, nibbling on a crab cake.

"Nothing specific," I said. "You still haven't turned up anything about where Colt was getting the drugs, have you?"

Gideon shook his head. "Unfortunately, no. And there's no sign of his mysterious associates either. They seem to have disappeared off the face of the Earth."

"That's good, right?" Kaige said.

I frowned. "I'd like to think it is, but nothing about this has been that simple before."

"It's possible they wanted something from him and he was unable to deliver," Gideon said. "I wouldn't let it worry you."

He was right. We were supposed to be celebrating. I shook off my uneasiness as well as I could. It was second nature after all those years under Dad's thumb, but he was gone too. I could make a fresh start for real now.

Anthea walked up to us carrying a plate full of pastries, and we each took one. As the sweetness exploded in my mouth, my worries seemed even farther away.

"So how's everybody feeling?" Anthea asked.

"Good as new," Rowan said, walking up to us. He gave me a small smile before taking a bite of a pastry. Only Wylder remained at a distance, almost as if he was unwilling to join our group. I wondered if it was because of Ezra's presence, and he didn't want to accidentally tip him off to how close the two of us had become.

"What do you think—" I started to ask, and one of the Noble initiates burst in from the hall.

"Mr. Noble, there's something you need to see."

Ezra gave the young guy a look that could have seared through steel, obviously pissed off about the interruption. "Not now," he said flatly. "We're occupied."

"I'm sorry—it's just there's someone outside. He says he has to see you, that it's a matter of life and death."

Ezra frowned but put his glass down.

A matter of life and death? What the hell was going on now?

When Ezra left the room, the rest of us followed without any discussion. Nervous tension wound around my gut again.

Ezra marched out the front door, Axel and his other men right behind him, their guns now in their hands. The guys and I slipped out behind them, staying on the landing while they went partway down the front steps.

A college-aged guy I'd never seen before was standing in the middle of the front walk, surrounded by four Noble men who all had their guns aimed at him. His clothes and hair were rumpled, and his forehead shone with droplets of sweat. He held a large tablet in his shaking hands.

"Here I am," Ezra said in a darkly cool voice. "What do you want?"

"You're Ezra Noble?" the man asked. His eyes darted from side to side before coming back to focus on the Noble boss.

Ezra nodded. "Who are you?"

A tremor ran through the guy's body. "I've been sent with a message for you." He tapped the tablet's screen.

An image appeared there: a man wearing a dark dress shirt posed in front of a white background. His wiry salt-and-pepper hair was pulled back in a short ponytail at the base of his neck, but several strands had sprung free around his square-jawed face. Even standing still, his wide-shouldered, barrel-chested body radiated strength.

But that wasn't what really caught my attention. Twin scars, identical Xs, marked his cheeks. And his fierce eyes, fixed on us through the recording, gave me a sense of chaotic energy powerful enough to make me shiver.

He spoke with a voice so deep it was chilling, as if it was echoing from a pit the sun never reached the bottom of. "Hello, Ezra Noble. My name is Xavier. I look forward to meeting you face to face in the near future, but for now we'll stick with this. I wanted to thank you personally for running the rats off the streets of the Bend. The mess you've cleaned up will make it easier for me and my people to sweep in and take what we've decided to make ours."

Ezra bristled, but he couldn't exactly talk back.

The man in the recording kept going, unaware of the reactions he was provoking. "I have to say, I like what I've seen of your style. You'll be entertaining opponents. I can't wait to tackle the challenge of removing all of Paradise from your grasp."

My heart sank. The war wasn't over after all.

But just when I thought I'd heard the worst I could have, Xavier raised his voice again. "Is my lost pussy cat still with you? She's made a lot of trouble for all of us since she came running your way, hasn't she." His gaze crept across the screen as if he was looking for someone.

For me, I realized, restraining a flinch. A lost cat that came running to the Nobles? Who else could he mean?

The guys were looking at me now, their stances tensing as if they could defend me from an image on a tablet.

A cruel grin stretched across the man's face. "I hope she liked the presents I left her. I put much thought and effort into each one. And don't worry, there's more to come."

Presents? My stomach flipped over. The drawing, the dead cat, the unearthed corpse—that had all been *him*.

But why? I'd never seen him before in my life.

"Until next time, Nobles," Xavier said, still grinning, and vanished into a hiss of static before the screen went black again.

Ezra was just opening his mouth to speak when the guy clutching the tablet exploded with an audible *boom*, splattering blood and flesh in every direction.

NEXT IN THE CROOKED PARADISE SERIES

Ruthless Queen (Crooked Paradise #3)

Heavy is the crown...

I thought getting my revenge would give me some kind of peace. Instead it seems to have brought an even worse villain to my doorstep.

Or rather, to the Nobles' doorstep, which the big

boss of Paradise Bend's most powerful gang is not at all happy about. I may have won over Wylder Noble and his men, but his father is another story entirely.

A brutally murderous story.

Stuck between a vicious gang king and a psychotic stalker set on total domination, I'm not sure yet whether I'm going to win this war or go down fighting. If I fall, will these men who've set my body on fire—and somehow worked their way into my heart—fall with me?

Not if Mercy Katz has anything to say about it.

I'm the heir to *my* father's throne, and I'm going to wear the hell out of that crown as long as I'm still breathing.

Get it at https://smarturl.it/RuthlessQueen

ABOUT THE AUTHORS

Eva Chance is a pen name for contemporary romance written by Amazon top 100 bestselling author Eva Chase. If you love gritty romance, dominant men, and fierce women who never have to choose, look no further.

Eva lives in Canada with her family. She loves stories both swoony and supernatural, and strong women and the men who appreciate them.

Connect with Eva online:
www.evachase.com
eva@evachase.com

Harlow King is a long-time fan of all things dark, edgy, and steamy. She can't wait to share her contemporary reverse harem stories.

Printed in Great Britain
by Amazon